RYDER

RYDER

A Delta Squad Novel

DIANA GARDIN

FOREVER
YOURS

New York   Boston

Forever Yours
Hachette Book Group
1290 Avenue of the Americas, New York, NY 10104
forever-romance.com
twitter.com/foreverromance

First published as an ebook and as a print on demand: February 2019

Forever Yours is an imprint of Grand Central Publishing. The Forever Yours name and logo are trademarks of Hachette Book Group, Inc.

The publisher is not responsible for websites (or their content) that are not owned by the publisher.

The Hachette Speakers Bureau provides a wide range of authors for speaking events. To find out more, go to www.hachettespeakersbureau.com or call (866) 376-6591.

ISBN: 978-1-5387-6260-8 (ebook), 978-1-5387-6258-5 (trade paperback POD)

ACKNOWLEDGMENTS

First of all, I'd like to thank God, who gave me the desire and skill to write.

Thank you to my family, who are always there for me when I put down my computer and unplug from all things writing. I'm so thankful they're along for this ride with me. Superman, Carrington, and Raleigh, everything I do is for you.

Thank you to my agent, Stacey Donaghy. You are more than an agent: You are my friend, and I'm so very thankful to have found you. I am even more thankful that you're always on my side.

To my fabulous editor, Lexi Smail: I adore working with you! You have such an understanding of where I want each character to go, and sometimes it's scary because I'm worried you might actually be reading my mind. You're the best.

To the team at Forever Romance: You are all such a well-oiled machine. From editing, to copyediting, to cover design and all the other inner workings I don't even get to see, you are all fabulous and I'm lucky to be a part of it all. Thank you for your efforts on my behalf!

To my favorite sounding board and the girl who's become one of my very best friends, Sybil Bartel: I don't know how it happened, but you're like the other half of my writing brain. You're there at all hours of the day and night, whether I need to get an idea out or I'm completely out of them. I only hope I help you as much as you help me! Love you, girl.

To the very best group of writers a girl could ever ask for, the NAC: Ara, Meredith, Kate, Bindu, Sophia, Laura, Missy, Jessica, Amanda, Jamie, Marie, and Marnee—you are my favorite source of sanity. Without you, this business would have ended me long ago! Love y'all!

To the authors I admire so very much and who are always willing to help me in any way they can, through promo, visibility for my books in their groups, or just an ear to listen when I need it: You'll never know how much you mean to me! Thank you so much to Rachel Van Dyken, Heidi McLaughlin, Susan Stoker, Willow Winters, K.A. Tucker, Jay Crownover, Jennifer L. Berg, J.B. Salsbury, Jo Raven, Lia Riley, Megan Erickson, and Brighton Walsh.

To an assistant I've learned I cannot live without, Jessica Shapnaka: You are willing to do so much for me, and all because you love my books. Thank you not only for being a fabulous assistant, but for being an amazing friend! I love you!

To my lovely review team: You are all so dedicated and I am awed by you! Thank you for reading my books ahead of time, and more than that, thank you for loving them! Your reviews drive my career, and without them I wouldn't be able to continue doing what I love. Thank you so much!

To the Dolls—the best fan group a girl could ask for: Talking to you guys every day, sharing my fictional world with you, receiving your feedback, it all keeps me going! You all recharge me and refuel me when I need it, and your support and positivity make this job so much more fun! Thank you all for being you!

To the bloggers who have supported me throughout this journey: There are too many of you to name, but you know who you are. You have read every single book, given me great reviews, and shared my work with as many people as you can. I couldn't do any of this without your help and your enthusiasm. A thousand thank-yous.

And last but never least, to the readers who find their way to Wilmington, North Carolina, to hang out with the sexy men of Night Eagle Security and the women who are strong enough to love them. I hope you fall in love with this world as much as I have, because without you, I'd be nothing. <3

Prologue

FRANCESCA

One Year Ago

I hurry out of the double front doors, leaving them wide open behind me as I hop down the massive stone front steps in my bare feet. The deliveryman grins as he views what must look like crazed excitement on my face, my arms spread wide for my little package.

"It's here!" My voice rises in a squeal. "Thank you so much!"

My house is a frequent stop on the driver's route, thanks to Eli's strange desire for me to shop online rather than in stores. The deliveryman touches the side of his hat in an exaggerated gentleman's gesture. No more than a year or two older than I am, he's never seemed daunted by the enormous mansion standing behind me when I open the door for a delivery.

"I'm just dropping off, Mrs. Ward. You doin' all right today?"

Knowing what's inside my brown parcel makes my smile extra sunny. "Just fine, Dex. Thanks for asking! I hope you don't have too many deliveries to make today."

Dex's smile widens until his dimple shows. He's a handsome guy, but I've never had eyes for anyone but Eli. No matter that his jealous streak might say otherwise. In the past six months, Eli's been watching me extra closely, and every time I even make eye contact with a man, he nearly loses his mind. It's such a drastic change from the sweet, loving way he treated me when we first met.

The first time he hit me, I didn't see it coming. It was after a party last New Year's Eve, the first since we'd been married. I'd had two glasses of champagne, and my best friend's husband and I had jovially made a go of it on the dance floor to celebrate the New Year rolling in. Eli had cut our night short afterward, and we'd just made it to the car when he'd thrown me up against it and grabbed me by the throat. Hitting me full across the face, he'd accused me of wanting to sleep with my best friend's husband.

I'd been in shock, unable to think straight, while he'd shoved me into the bushes and begun to choke me. It was only the sound of the front door opening at the house beside us that made him drag me into the car. His rage had been so great, so out of control, I'm not sure I would have survived that first attack had that person not opened their door.

Afterward, he'd cried. It was the first time I'd seen him shed a tear, and he'd been so ashamed, so devastated by his behavior that he'd sworn he'd never hurt me that way again.

I'd sworn to him I'd be more careful, that I'd never give him a reason to doubt me.

But now? Now I'm sure everything will change. I place a hand over my belly and stare with love down at the cardboard box clutched in my hands.

"I'll finish in no time." Dex's glance moves away from me to settle on the long driveway, where the sound of a car pulling in draws both of our attention.

Eli's Range Rover disappears into one of the four garages, and Dex gives me a wave. "Looks like your husband is home early today."

I nod, distracted. I wasn't expecting Eli until this evening. Dex climbs into his truck, which is sitting in the circular portion of the driveway in front of the house, and I turn to go inside.

Closing the front doors behind me, I hurry into the kitchen, opening the package in my hands as I walk. Pulling out a white onesie, I finger the soft cotton as I hold it up and read the golden lettering:

our precious gift

I purchased the onesie and had it monogrammed to use in baby announcement photos. It's how Eli and I are going to tell our family and friends that we're three months pregnant with our first child.

The door between the kitchen and the garage closes, and I glance up to see Eli standing there.

Holding up the onesie, I feel joy bubble up in my chest. "Look, babe! Look what just came! Now that I'm out of the first trimester, we can finally share our news with everyone we love."

Over the past year of marriage, I've shoved aside every warning bell that's been screaming at me to rethink my relationship with Eli. Our courtship was a whirlwind. His money and his power in our little Oklahoma city aren't what swept me off my feet. He was a businessman eight years older than my twenty-two years when we met, and I was amazed that he was showing me so much attention. He lavished me with gifts and trips, but that's not what blew me away. What got to me was how much he zeroed in on the fact that all I wanted was a family. Someone to come home to at night and cherish. Someone to love and call my own. My parents have always been self-absorbed, wrapped up in their own wants and materialistic desires. I've never felt like I'm the center of the world, and Eli understood that. When he came into my life, I finally had a partner, someone to share everything with. We were married within a year.

Even when he put his hands on me, I refused to give up that feeling of belonging.

But now that I'm carrying his baby? I know all that will be over. We're starting fresh. I'll finally see the man I fell in love with at his best, and his jealous streak will be over. He'll know that he and our child are the center of my life, and we'll be a happy, loving family.

We have to be.

Eli, still standing just inside the kitchen door, doesn't move. He stares at me, his eyes not even dropping to glance at the precious bundle of cotton in my hands. My stomach clenches at the stony expression on his face. My husband is handsome, his dark hair slicked back in a smooth style. But when he looks like this…all I feel is icy fear.

"I saw you flirting with him." Eli's voice is quiet, laced with a razor edge.

The first time I heard him talk like this, we were walking out of that New Year's Eve party. I hadn't recognized it as a sign of what was to come. But now, I know.

I take a step backward, my hand immediately going to my stomach. My other fist clutches the onesie a little bit tighter, holding it out as a peace offering. My voice pleads with my husband, and even as I beg, I hate myself for it.

This is wrong, Francesca. You should never have to beg someone not to hurt you.

I clear my throat. "I wasn't flirting with him, Eli. I was being polite." Despite the flurry of my heartbeat, my words are firm.

It's something I've never been able to be with Eli in the past, not when his face has looked like a thundercloud rolling across a prairie. But I have to be strong now, and not just for me.

For my baby.

Eli launches himself forward, advancing on me so quickly I don't have time to move out of the way. He pins me against the wall behind me with a hand to my sternum, knocking the wind out of me. My head slams against the wall so hard stars dance before my eyes. He doesn't remove his gaze from mine as he reaches down and yanks the onesie from my grip.

Holding it up, he finally looks at it. "You're carrying *my* baby, Francesca." Spit gathers at the corners of his mouth as his rage builds. "But you were looking at him like you wanted to fuck him on my front lawn!"

My eyes wide, I shake my head. My voice goes hoarse. "That's crazy, Eli—"

His fist lands against my jaw, sending a white-hot lance of pain screaming through my face. He releases me, and I crumple to the floor.

"You're a goddamned slut!" Eli screams.

When he screams, I know he's lost every ounce of control he has. Tears cloud my vision.

"The baby," I sob. "Eli, *please*."

Please, no. No.

Help me.

I turn my head just in time to see the toe of Eli's boot pull back, and I try to turn onto my other side. I only make it onto my back, and he kicks me in the soft flesh between my ribs and hip.

I scream. Hoping it'll save my baby's life, even though I know our house is located on five acres of property and the neighbors won't hear me, I let out a bloodcurdling scream loud enough to wake the dead.

Eli squats down beside me and yanks my waist-length blond ponytail so hard I feel some pieces separate from my head by the roots.

His face looms over mine. "I don't know why I bother with you. But you're my wife, and you're going to learn how to present yourself. You're going to regret making me angry enough to hurt you this way."

His face blurs as my eyes begin to close, and I know I'm losing consciousness. I just want to know if the baby I'm carrying is okay, and I think about my cell phone sitting on top of the kitchen island just a few feet away. I bite the inside of my cheek until I taste blood.

"I'm leaving now. When you're feeling better, get yourself cleaned up. I don't ever want to come home and see my wife making eyes at the fucking UPS man again."

Without looking at me again, he releases my hair and lets my head crack against the marble floor.

I listen to the sound of his footsteps walking away, and it seems like it takes forever for them to cross the kitchen and disappear out the garage door. As soon as the noise of his big SUV engine is gone, I raise my voice to trigger the voice-activated dialing on my phone.

"Nine-One-One, what's your emergency?"

A strangled sob escapes me. *Am I really about to do this?*

A sharp pain in my belly causes me to double over, and the woman on the line repeats her question.

"Help me," I scream. "My husband beat me. I'm lying on my kitchen floor, and I'm three months pregnant. Send an ambulance!"

1

THORN

"I want to help her. I really do, Boss Man. But I don't want to be a babysitter." When I glance toward the door, the heat from the warm, sexy little body on the other side floats toward me.

You're losing your shit already, Ryder. Body heat can't travel through solid wood doors.

"Wolf." Jacob Owen, my boss at Night Eagle Security, leans forward on the table and holds me in one of his notoriously scrutinizing stares. The other guys, my Delta Squad team, remain silent as they watch the exchange. Jacob continues, "How many times have I asked you to run point on a mission?"

My shoulders sink under the weight of his question. Jacob Owen has been everything to me since I left the SEALs. Father figure, superior, confidant. Along with the men I call my brothers, this company and Jacob have been my entire life since I left the Navy behind. Giving me purpose. Giving me a place to breathe and call my own.

"This is the first, sir."

Jacob stares, gray eyes not giving away a damn thing. "Are you really going to turn that down?"

I open my mouth to tell him of course I'm not, but he lifts a hand, not done with me yet. "And since when has NES been in the business of 'babysitting'? The company that I built from the ground up, the one that started with personal security and has now grown into a company that the government calls for private black-ops contracts, isn't good enough for you to run point on a mission I deem necessary?"

It's worse than being screamed at by your commanding officer during SEAL training. It's worse than being told how much you've disappointed your dad. This is Jacob, the Boss Man. And I'll be damned if I'll be the one to let him down.

"I'm sorry, sir. That's not what I mean. I just—"

Jacob isn't ready for me to talk. Out of the corner of my eye, I see one of my best friends and teammates wince as Boss Man's voice lifts. "And do you realize how important this assignment is? It's partly our fault that Ms. Phillips is in this predicament to begin with."

I glance up at that one, fire lighting inside my gut. "Actually—"

Jacob cuts me off with a glance that could slice a block of ice. "She didn't know we were investigating her husband, because they were estranged. Because he *beat the shit out of her.*"

I swallow, my insides going numb at the thought of Frannie, the woman in question, being beaten to a pulp by that piece of shit.

I don't know Frannie very well, or at all, really. But the second I met her a couple of weeks ago—while Lawson Snyder and his now-fiancée, Indigo Stone, were undercover in a case that involved Frannie's estranged husband—there was something about her I couldn't shake.

And apparently, now I'm going to be forced to face it head-on.

"I understand, Boss Man. I'll run point on her protection, and I'll make sure nothing happens to her while the feds continue to hunt Eli Ward."

Jacob nods, finally looking satisfied. "You're damn right you will. I expect nothing less, Wolf."

The use of my nickname for the second time doesn't escape me. In NES, we all have them, depending on what special skills we bring to the table. Some of our nicknames have to do with our Special Ops pasts. Mine, White Wolf, has to do with my predatory skills. I can hunt down an enemy in any situation, and I'm ruthless when I've got a scent.

The conference room door opens and Indigo walks in, followed closely by the woman in question, Frannie Phillips.

The two women couldn't be any more different upon first glance. Indigo's long black hair swishes across her back, her tank top showing off miles and miles of inked skin. Studs pierce up both earlobes, and her face—gorgeous and exotic-looking with her dark olive complexion and Latina features—is accentuated by heavy, dramatic makeup.

Frannie, on the other hand, is take-a-second-look beautiful. And it isn't because of any extra ink or metal she's added to her body, although the ends of her shoulder-length blond hair are tinged pink. She's got these big blue eyes that make me imagine what they'd look like hooded with lust, and a curvy little body that calls out for my hands to touch her, make her feel good, and mess up her Southern-belle perfection just a little bit.

There's nothing clean about me. The only thing that Frannie and I have in common is the blond hair and blue eyes. The likenesses stop right there. I glance down at the ink swirling up and down my arms, tattoos I had done during my years in the Navy, and then back at her flawless golden-tan skin. The pink hair is new on her, probably something she's trying, but I can't stop staring at her because the woman is the very definition of distraction.

She's not like anyone I've ever dated—not that I've really dated. She's not like anyone I've ever *fucked*. Too done up and doll-faced pretty. But right now, I can imagine those perky little lips wrapped right around my cock, and that's a major fucking problem if my focus is supposed to be on keeping her safe.

"I found Frannie sitting on the bench downstairs." Indigo's casual tone belies her curiosity, and I note that she can't keep her eyes from flitting to Lawson the second she walks into the room. He, in turn, sits up straighter in response to her presence.

"We were just about to call you in, Frannie." Jacob's eyes soften when he speaks, something we've all noticed. He used to be a lot tougher, but in the past couple of years he's rekindled a fire with his ex-wife and mother to his three daughters, and something about him is different. Less edge, unless he's in the field.

Frannie blows out a breath. "Whew. That's good, because I was getting tired of sitting out there swinging my legs while you big strong men decided what was going to happen with my life from here on out."

Sweetness mixed with Southern sass: This woman is going to fucking kill me.

Jacob's eyebrows lift, and he gestures toward one of the empty seats at the table. This meeting involves only the Delta Squad, and Indigo is here purely as a consultant, since she no longer works for the Wilmington Police Department as a detective. After she and

Lawson worked on the task force assigned to take down Eli Ward's luxury car theft ring, Indigo left the police force and became a consultant for NES. She likes the flexibility the position offers, and the ability to continue working closely with her fiancé.

"We're not deciding anything about your future. That's up to you. Right now, we're just trying to figure out the best way to keep you safe."

"Keep you alive." Bain Foxx speaks up, something he doesn't often do unless he's spoken to directly. Out of the four of us on the team, Bain's the quietest, least predictable, and probably the deadliest. He also carries more secrets than the rest of us can even imagine. He hasn't said as much, but working with a man day in and day out, sometimes overnight and in dangerous places, makes you get to know him.

His eyes, a lighter shade of blue than mine, carry an intensity that makes most people flinch.

But Frannie stares right back at him.

"Yeah. I get that. I'd just like to be a part of the conversation is all."

Jacob leans back in his chair, fingers pressed together, assessing her. "The moment we decided to protect you, you became our client. Now, as it stands, the FBI is conducting a manhunt for Eli Ward. The feds are trusting us instead of sending you into witness protection like they wanted to. But that could change at any time. We don't want it to, and I'm guessing you don't either. Am I correct?"

Frannie nods, her hair brushing against bare shoulders. The turquoise top she wears wraps around her neck in a classy style, and I don't miss the way her white jeans accentuate shapely legs and rounded hips before she sits down. Ben McBride, the fourth member of our team, sits on her other side.

"I won't go into Witness Protection." There's an underlying ferociousness in her tone that I've never heard before. I've known her only a few weeks, but apparently this woman is half "honey" and "y'all" drawl, and half pure grit.

I've been staring at her since she came into the room, and when her gaze finally meets mine, I swallow hard and fight not to look away.

"We have a plan of action formed. Thorn Ryder here will take point on your assignment."

Her eyes flicker with something—recognition, maybe—and then she turns her gaze back on Jacob.

"You'll move into a secure condominium building owned by NES, a place that I've recently acquired for situations like this one, that can be surveilled twenty-four/seven. Thorn will be moving in with you, serving as your guard. He'll be charged with keeping you safe for the duration of your time as our client. From here, you'll go home to pack some bags, and you won't be needing your car. We'll park it in a secure location. To any outsider looking in, it'll look like you've left town."

Frannie smooths her hands over her lap. "I work three twelve-hour shifts at the hospital every week. Mr. Ryder here will accompany me and do what, exactly…chill?"

I clear my throat. "Um, no. You'll have to take a leave of absence from work until Ward is brought in. Don't know how long it'll be, but we can make the hospital understand."

Frannie turns to face me full-on, not even bothering to hide the fact that she's seething. "I. Will. Not. Quit. My. Job."

I lean forward, elbows digging into the table, jaw clenched tight. "No one said anything about quitting—"

Her words barrel forward as if I hadn't even spoken. This woman is all force and bluster when she's worked up—a tornado just getting started. "But you're telling me I can't go to work. I'm sorry, that's just not an option. I need my paycheck, and more than that I need my sanity. Work is my sanity. Can you understand that, Mr. Ryder?"

I'm silent. Because, yeah, without NES I'd be a fucking shell of myself. I was able to put all the turmoil inside me, the emotions churning me up for the past ten years, away in a box because I had a mission in life.

Always a mission.

First I kicked my way through boot camp. Then I rose through the naval ranks as quickly as anyone possibly could in my position. Then I went out for SEALs and became one of the elite. There was no looking back for me. The more intense the job, the better it was for my sanity. And I know a lot of guys who felt the same.

Maybe it's like that for Frannie. Maybe, in order to overcome whatever she went through in her past, she needs to nurse others back to health.

Who are we to take that shit away from her?

"If you work…" My voice is grudging, gruffer than I intend it to be. "I'm there with you. For every shift. Tailing you. Shadowing you. Get used to it, Frannie, because I'm not going anywhere. It's my job to keep you safe, and the rest of the team will be weighing in as needed."

She meets my gaze, her baby blues steady and wide and full of determination. In them, I see her agreement before she gives it to me like a gift.

"Fine. If that's how it has to be, I'm in."

2

FRANNIE

Hell has come to live right here on earth with me. And not in the form of Eli Ward, but in the form of Thorn freaking Ryder.

"Your face is saying a lot of things right now, Frannie, but I don't know exactly what's going through that head of yours. Talk to me."

Concern flashes in Indigo's cinnamon-colored eyes. She's pulled me into the staff lounge following the meeting, the two of us the only people in the cushy break room.

Pressing both hands against the counter, I drop my chin against my chest as I take a shaking breath. "I can't do this, Indigo. Not after what I went through with Eli."

Her voice is gentle behind me. "You're scared."

I whirl to face her. "You're damn right I'm scared. I promised myself I'd never be at risk again. And I know he's supposed to be protecting me, but living with a man one-on-one like that, especially someone I don't know…" My voice trails away as I picture it. A shudder rolls through me.

Indigo closes the gap between us and cups my shoulders with her hands. "Listen to me, Frannie. Thorn Ryder is someone you can trust. I promise you that. You can count on my word, okay? He will keep you safe, and he's nothing like your ex. You have nothing to fear from Thorn."

You have two choices here, Frannie. Put your trust in Night Eagle Security and Thorn Ryder, or disappear completely into Witness Protection.

It's not even an option. I *can't* leave North Carolina. Looking into my friend's eyes, I give her a shaky nod. "Okay, I'll take your word for it."

Indigo's lips tilt in one of her signature smirks, her hand letting the ends of my pink-tinged hair flutter through her fingers. "I like the pink. It suits you."

I return her smile. "Thanks. After Eli resurfaced, it felt like time for a change."

Indy's eyes carry a knowing glint. "Stay strong, girl. We'll catch the bastard. Until then, stay safe. Stay with Thorn."

A couple of hours later, I've said goodbye to my apartment and am riding shotgun in Thorn's car. It's like the dang heavens above sent him down to mess with me. My head needs to be clear right now, more than ever. I'm hiding in plain sight from the devil himself, the devil I happened to marry. But there's so much more to my story than Eli Ward.

So much more.

Earlier, I kept Thorn's profile in my peripheral vision as we walked out of the NES offices, located in the gorgeous and luxurious Wrightsville Beach area of Wilmington, North Carolina. The man is built like a Greek god, like every woman's fantasy come to life. At least, if that woman's got a lick of sense in her head, which I'd like to think I do. He's all brawny, golden muscle. Literally rippling with it, his broad chest accentuated by the blue Dri-FIT T-shirt with the Night Eagle Security logo on the front. The guys all wear them in different colors, but this pacific blue is my favorite on Thorn. His eyes are almost the exact same shade, and a woman could fall straight into those suckers and drown if she isn't careful. I allowed my eyes to scan down his arms, packed with lean muscle just like the rest of him.

My mouth actually watered.

When he stopped in front of a shining black BMW sedan, a gleaming beast of a vehicle, my steps stuttered to a halt. "This is your car?"

He paused, hand on the passenger-side door handle as his gaze raked over me. "Yeah. Why?"

I shook my head, feeling stupid. "I don't know…Just thought…Shoot. I just thought you'd be driving a truck or something."

Thorn's lips curved into a smirk. "Love trucks. Just love fast cars more." The door unlocked with the touch of his hand and I climbed inside, settling into the buttery-soft leather.

I watched him walk around the front of the car to his side, his steps unhurried, calculated, like a predator's. He tossed his keys into the air and caught them twice before reaching the driver's side. He seemed carefree, but I didn't miss the stealthy gaze he aimed at our surroundings just before he got into the car.

And now I can see why he's my protector until Eli is put behind bars.

A shudder goes through me just thinking about Eli. Moving to the Carolinas from Oklahoma was a calculated move. Lobelia, an old childhood friend, lives only an hour away, and Eli doesn't know about her. I cut all ties with everyone I knew from Oklahoma, especially my parents. It didn't matter to them that I ended up in the hospital after Eli beat me...even when I was pregnant. Eli paid the mortgage on their lavish home, kept them living in a luxury they never would have been able to afford otherwise.

Thorn's voice interrupts my thoughts, the tenderness and intuitiveness there sending my heart pounding against my ribs. "He won't get to you. Our team would never allow that to happen. You don't need to be afraid, but you have to be cautious. Life is going to change for a while."

My throat clogs with emotion that I can barely hide in time. Glancing toward the window, I make a decision right then and there. Thorn Ryder *will not* get under my skin. The man might be sexy and strong and who knows what else, but kindness is where I draw the line. I can't do kind.

Kindness in a man right now just might break me, or draw me in. And I can't afford either one.

My life is complicated, and Eli is just one of the reasons why.

I blink a few times to clear the wetness gathering in my eyes, swallow hard around the lump in my throat, and look at Thorn. "So, *Ryder*, why don't you tell me about yourself?"

Calling him Ryder is safer. Gives me a little bit of distance from the man sitting beside me.

Ryder stares at the road straight ahead, his expression unchanging and his body unflinching. Strong shoulders, steady hands, granite features that can apparently soften at just the right moment.

Lordy.

"Not much to tell. Been working at NES now for a year and a half. Used to be a SEAL. I'm no stranger to protecting people; keeping the bad guys away from the good ones. You're safe with me."

At his last words, his deep blue eyes meet mine, like he's checking to make sure I know he's serious. And I do. There's not a shred of humor in his tone, and I know he means what he says.

But Eli isn't just any bad guy. He's not a terrorist with an agenda or an insurgent with a kamikaze complex. And I'm guessing from Ryder's military background that those are the types of criminals he's used to dealing with.

Eli is certifiably insane. And that insanity mostly pertains to me. As his wife, I was his trophy. I had no idea that he was laundering money through the businesses I thought were legitimate until after I left.

Instead of saying this to Ryder, I just nod. "Thank you. For doing this."

He makes the turn to take us out of the ritzy Wrightsville Beach area and into the main part of Wilmington, which is pretty suburban. Although no matter where you are in the city, the smell of the ocean and a view of palm trees are never far away. It's so different from Oklahoma; it's one of the reasons I fell in love with it when I fled.

We ride in silence through the city. It's late summer, and the evening hour is doing nothing to dampen the brightness outside.

After a few minutes, we pull into a gated community on the Masonboro Sound. Inside the gates are upscale condominium high-rises, and I crane my neck to look up.

"Holy crap." The exclamation is out of my mouth before I can stop it. "This place is swanky."

Ryder chuckles. "Lots of amenities too, so we shouldn't get too bored. There's activities we can do on the sound. Are you good on the water? Paddleboarding, kayaking?"

He pauses at the gate and keys in a code. The black iron rails before us slide open without a sound and he drives through them, heading to the left.

He catches me staring at him. "What?"

"You do know I grew up in Oklahoma, right? So I'm water challenged. Unless it's a swimming pool, I can't do it, buddy."

The deep rumble of his chuckle is a sound I could get used to, dammit. "Oh, yeah? Well, we'll have to get you in the sound, then. It's easier than learning to do that stuff on the ocean, because the sound is calm. There's a pool here too, though. And tennis and a ton of other stuff to do."

I raise my eyebrows. "So being under the protection of NES is like being on vacation?"

He laughs and pulls the BMW smoothly into a parking garage under one of the condominium buildings. I notice how secure it is when a large door slides shut behind us. It seems like the garage is only for the condos in this particular building.

Shutting off the car, he looks at me. "Sit tight while I grab our suitcases. Then I'll open your door for you."

"Is that an order, Ryder?"

An exasperated look crosses his handsome face. "Is everything going to be a question with you?"

Tucking my hair behind my ear, I widen my eyes. "What are you talking about?"

With a sigh, he exits the car and opens the trunk. When he's got the suitcases sitting outside the car, he opens my door and I step out. I make to grab my suitcase, but Ryder shakes his head.

"I've got it."

There's no room for argument in his voice, not that I'd want to argue with a man who's gentleman enough to carry my suitcases, and so together we walk toward the elevator at the end of the garage.

Inside the elevator, Ryder keys in a code on a pad beside a button labeled with a letter *P*. My stomach drops and he turns toward me, scrutinizing the wide-eyed look on my face.

"Remember that Jacob owns this building. We get the penthouse. Only the Delta Squad team and Jacob have the penthouse code. It changes each time someone needs to use the place."

He ends this sentence with a grin, and the elevator doors open into the foyer of the most gorgeous space I've ever seen.

I mean, if I had all the money in the world and could choose where I'd live, it'd be this condo. This one. *Right here.*

Just inside the foyer is a contemporary-styled two-story great room with windows from floor to ceiling. As I stare, openmouthed, at the gorgeous view of the sound and horizon beyond, Ryder steps up beside me.

"Don't worry about exposure," he murmurs, his voice a deep rumble that settles inside my bones. "Those windows are so darkly tinted that no one can see anything happening in here."

I nod, turning slowly to take in the room, the white walls with modern art, brushed steel finishes on all the hanging light fixtures and appliances.

"There's a balcony," he continues.

My attention focuses in that direction, and I catch sight of a metal porch encircling the entire first floor, loungers with teal cushions sitting in the sun and a table with four chairs under an umbrella.

"But I'd rather you not go out there alone." Ryder's words imply that it's a request, but his tone tells me that it's no such thing. "Remember, no matter how amazing this place is, you're here for a reason. And it's my job to make sure you stay safe."

I salute him and continue into the incredible kitchen. Commercial-grade appliances with a huge concrete counter island. Navy blue cabinets with white stone countertops. I can't keep my eyes from bouncing from one luxurious, beautiful finish to the next.

"I'm gonna cook my ever-loving *pants* off in this kitchen." It's an announcement more for Ryder's benefit than my own, but it's true all the same.

When I look at him, he's leaning against one of the pillars separating the living space from the dining area and kitchen. There's a crooked grin on his face as he stares at me, the expression in his eyes dark and unreadable. "That right? There's going to be cooking without pants?"

My cheeks flame. "You're not from the South, are you, Ryder?"

His eyes flare. "What's with the 'Ryder' business?"

Instead of answering, I step around him and wander down the hallway toward the…master suite? The bedroom is large and airy, featuring a vaulted ceiling with white beams and decorated in ocean-themed colors with a king-sized bed right in the middle. The bathroom is equally beautiful, with finishes similar to the kitchen. My gaze lands eagerly on the Jacuzzi tub before slipping over the glass-enclosed shower. And all of a sudden, I realize that this is my home for the foreseeable future, but I won't be living here alone. My conversation with Indigo back at NES headquarters drifts through my head, and I swallow the doubt creeping back in. If my friend told me that I could trust Ryder, then I can. As difficult as it is for me to do that, I have to try. My heartbeat thuds in my chest and my breathing takes off as I whirl and race back down the hallway.

I find Ryder exactly where I left him. He comes off the pillar immediately when he sees the look on my face, eating the distance between us in two strides and placing strong hands on my shoulders. The heat of his palms warms me instantly.

"What is it?" His gaze searches my face before he moves me behind him and scans the hallway from which I just came.

"No, no." My voice is breathless. "It's just...where's the other bedroom?" I swallow, my whole body becoming flushed with slowly spreading heat.

Ryder turns around slowly, hands still on my shoulders, assessing my expression. "There's two more bedrooms upstairs. I don't feel comfortable sleeping a floor away from you when I'm supposed to be protecting you, though. So you'll take the master, and I'll take the couch."

He doesn't ask me if I'm okay with those arrangements, he just says it like that's how it'll be. I frown. "That doesn't seem fair. Why don't we just both sleep upstairs?"

He shakes his head. "Negative. I want to be close to the front door and the windows on the first floor. But don't worry, we're on the highest floor of this building, so we're safe, Frannie."

Frannie. It's the first time I've heard him say my name. I changed my last name when I moved to North Carolina, but I've kept my first name. I always went by my full first name, Francesca, in Oklahoma, but my nickname suits me so much better. And hearing it roll off Ryder's tongue is…*whoa.*

"Yeah. Okay."

Ryder rubs his hands together. "We have a fully stocked kitchen here. How about we get settled and then either you get those pants off and start cooking, or we find some takeout menus?"

3

RYDER

The following morning, I leave an NES man stationed outside the penthouse's elevator door. It isn't ideal, but staying in top physical shape is a part of my job and I won't let a day go by without working out. Although I didn't originally want this job, there's something about Frannie Phillips that makes her case seem even more important than a normal assignment. I can't put my finger on why, though.

After I finish up at the building's gym, I wrap a white towel around my neck and head back to the penthouse. I pause outside the private elevator doors, where Bain stands. He's wide awake even though it's barely six a.m., his feet planted wide and his arms folded across his chest. His black T-shirt with the NES logo mirrors the one I'd probably wear later today if I weren't going to the hospital with Frannie. As it is, I want to fly under the radar as much as possible while I'm out in public with her.

"Everything okay in there?" I jerk a thumb toward the private elevator that leads up to the penthouse.

Bain lifts his chin once. "Haven't heard anything from up there.

Thought about going up, but didn't want to scare her. I know there's no other way into the condo than this elevator, so I waited right here."

Patting him on the shoulder, I punch in the code press the button that'll take me upstairs. "Good man. Thanks."

He doesn't answer, instead pressing the elevator button across the hall that'll take him down to the lobby. "No problem. Your team is here to support you in this. It's why we're here."

The doors close in front of him and I step into my elevator. Bain's probably the guy I'm closest to on my team, but you can get only so close to a dude like him. He's got skeletons, the deep and dark kind that no one can touch. We've all got them, but he's a special case, and none of us know the extent of what he's been through. At least my team knows that I lost my sister to a drug overdose and that my issues spark from that. None of us know exactly what Bain sees in his nightmares.

When the doors open I'm greeted by the sight of Frannie whipping around the kitchen like a little hurricane.

Damn sexy.

And it shouldn't be, because she's wearing navy blue scrubs, but damn if that cotton fabric doesn't fit to her curves in just the right places. Her black Nikes don't make a sound as she bounces around the kitchen, and the smell of frying bacon assaults my nose and makes my mouth water as my feet carry me forward.

Her back is to me, and I take a second and watch her. She's in her own little world, whirling from stove to sink to coffeepot. I was dead-on when I compared the woman to a storm.

I'm walking toward her when she turns. Seeing me, she drops a pan back onto the stove with an iron clatter before whipping her body to a drawer and pulling out a pistol. Turning to face me fully, she points the gun at my chest. Her features are rigid in a tumultuous mask of fury and fear, but recognition dawns as I raise my hands into the air and bark her name.

"Frannie! It's me. Easy, now."

I stand completely still while she looks at me, and I allow myself to assess the way she's holding that pistol. It's a Ruger LCR, .22 caliber. It's the perfect size and weight for her to wield, and she knows exactly how to carry it. She has it aimed at my chest, eyes wide open, and there isn't a hint of doubt in her stare.

I'm staring at a woman who, despite her doe-eyed, innocent look, knows exactly how to use a firearm.

She lowers it to her side and there's a visible release of air leaving her body as she exhales. "Jesus Christ, Ryder! Don't sneak up on me like that! I almost shot you."

Fury lances through me, at the exact same moment my dick takes a very vested interest in the woman standing in front of me. Ignoring my misguided cock, I stalk toward her, enter her space, and pluck the pistol out of her hand. Placing it back in the drawer, I put my arms on either side of her and lean down until my face is inches from hers. Her pupils dilate as her eyes widen a fraction, her chest rising and falling against my own.

"What. The fuck. Are you doing with a gun?"

She takes a few deep breaths in and out before she answers. Finally, her sweet breath hits my face with her words. "I have a crazy-ass husband who's currently hunting me down. Do you think I'm not packing? What's wrong with you? It's registered, they both are. And I know how to use them."

I take a big step back, staring at her, electricity jolting through my body like I've been hit with shock paddles. "Did you say 'both'? You have *two* guns here? And you didn't bother to tell the guy who's protecting you?"

She shrugs. "I don't really know you that well, and it didn't exactly come up yesterday."

I blink. Once. Twice. And then I turn around and pace away from her, my hands smoothing over the short hair on top of my head. When I turn back to face her, I've taken a few deep breaths. "Let's try this again. Where is the other gun hidden, Frannie?"

Her face is calm. She eyes me just before turning around and flipping off the gas stove where the bacon is frying. "In the nightstand drawer. That's where I always keep one of my guns. And I always keep the other in the kitchen. Unless I leave the house, of course. And then it's in my purse."

I pinch the bridge of my nose. "Do you have a concealed weapons permit?"

She nods.

"Jesus fuck."

She rolls her eyes, and I have the strongest urge to pin her against that kitchen counter and press my lips and my body against hers until her eyes are rolling for a much different reason. Until my name is on her lips because she wants to feel every inch of me inside of her, pleasuring her, making her feel things she's never felt before.

She gestures toward the food. "My shift starts at seven. We'd better hurry up and eat, or I'll be late."

We sit at the kitchen island and eat the best breakfast I think I've ever had, and then she waits for me while I jump in the shower.

We're getting ready to head out the front door when she goes back to the kitchen. My voice is firm when I call her name. "Frannie."

She stops midstep, looking over her shoulder.

"You don't need it. You have me."

She hesitates, and her face doesn't convey a whole hell of a lot of confidence. She reaches out and snatches the firearm out of the drawer, sliding it into her purse before following me to the elevator. We ride down to the garage level and climb into the BMW.

She ignored me. How am I going to protect a woman who thinks she can do a better job looking out for herself?

Gritting my teeth against the frustration weighing me down, I start the car.

"How'd you learn?" I ask the question as we're pulling out of the condo's garage and into the main parking lot.

She's staring out the window into the steely light of early morning. "Learn what?"

"How to use a firearm."

She's still not looking at me, but she sounds like she's been anticipating the question. "It's not hard. It's just practice and routine. I took lessons when I moved here. I made a choice to get away from Eli, and part of that choice was learning how to protect myself. Eli Ward is ruthless. I knew a new location wasn't enough. So I went to a gun range and took lessons. Turns out I'm kind of good at it."

Recollecting her stance in the kitchen earlier, I tighten my grip on the wheel.

It's not that I don't want her to be good with a weapon. I've seen that crazy son-of-a-bitch husband of hers in action. Last month, NES was part of a task force that involved the FBI. The task force was investigating a luxury car theft ring and Eli Ward was the head of it. Apparently, the man had a home base in Oklahoma while he traveled to the East Coast to steal cars and sell them to international buyers. Lawson went undercover with Indigo, while she was still a detective with the Wilmington Police Department, to gather intelligence and find out when the auction was going down. During the course of the investigation, it came out that Frannie was Eli's wife from Oklahoma and that she was on the run from him. Unfortunately, Eli got away…but only after he had Frannie kidnapped and almost killed Lawson.

"Yeah. You seemed well-trained. But I want you to know that even though I'm glad you have those skills, you can also count on me to protect you. I'm here to keep you safe. Do you trust that?" There's more urgency to my tone than I intend. *Trust* is a sacred word to me…something I can't negotiate. I don't want it; I *need* it.

She turns to face me, and when I glance at her, those sky-blues are burning into mine. "I don't trust anyone but myself. Not anymore. Eli Ward was someone I trusted. Someone I loved. And he took that and turned it into something ugly. When I close my eyes, I still see his fists as they punch me. His boots as they kick me. I don't know if that'll ever go away. I'll never allow someone to hurt me that way again. And if it takes carrying a gun to make me feel safe, that's my business."

I see the cold, detached determination on her face, and it feels like I've been punched in the gut. The world around me goes dark, like all the light's been sucked into a vortex.

Fuck. Fuck. Fuck.

I'm sure in that moment that I'm looking at a woman who is but a fragment of who she used to be.

And it's all because of that bastard who forced her to retreat. Who taught her that people couldn't be trusted.

That when she gave her love, it would be returned with a fist instead of tender touches and loving words.

And for that? I want to kill him. I want to end his life.

I don't even know Frannie Phillips. But I know one thing for sure. She deserves a whole hell of a lot better.

We're only ten minutes from the hospital where she works, so I swallow the emotion attempting to geyser its way up my throat and try to make small talk. "So you like being a nurse?"

Frannie pulls a strand of her hair between two fingers and tugs. She's more animated now that we're no longer talking about Eli or weapons. Apparently, nursing is something she's comfortable discussing. "It's what I always knew I wanted to do with my life. A way I could help people by getting in there and *doing* something. I love it."

I've read her file, learned her backward and forward, so I already know the answer to my next question. But I ask it anyway, because I like the way she's lit up talking about her job. "What department do you work in?"

She grins. "I'm an ER nurse."

"Isn't that…a lot of blood and shit?"

Looking at her, you'd expect her laugh to be a light, tinkling sound. Like a fairy or an angel or something. But it's not. It's deep, sexy, and throaty, and it makes my body respond in ways I wish it wouldn't.

"Yep. All the blood and gore. I wouldn't trade it. There's a rush working in the ER you don't get working anywhere else. And yeah, some days it's nothing. A lot of mundane stuff. But on the crazy days…it's what I live for."

I nod. "I get it. Living for the crazy, I mean. I love my job, don't get me wrong. But the day-to-day isn't the best part. The best part is the stuff that most people wouldn't do for a million dollars. The dangerous stuff that puts lives at risk. The shit that *saves* lives."

We stop at the red light at the intersection right before the hospital, the big brick building looming before us, and she turns her head to face me. Our eyes lock, and a strong cord of understanding strengthens between us. A sense of familiarity rights itself right there, cementing, firming, becoming permanent.

We stare at each other, not knowing what to say, or not needing to say a damn thing.

Something in my soul calls out to something in hers, and it's a goddamn *moment*. Unlike anything I've ever experienced before.

A horn blares behind me, and I jolt, realizing the light has turned green. Frannie startles the same way I did, bouncing in her seat, and I ease through the intersection and into the hospital parking lot. Following her directions to where I should park, I try to control my breathing.

I'm not sure what the hell just happened, but this bodyguard gig isn't as easy as I thought.

In fact, it might just be the most difficult mission I've ever been assigned.

4

FRANNIE

When I walk Ryder past the ER waiting room, he arches one of his thick brows. I shrug one shoulder and keep my steady pace, scanning my badge to open the big double doors.

We bypass two of my nursing coworkers, who give Ryder curious looks before we reach one of the less conspicuous patient waiting rooms at the back of the floor. There's hardly ever anyone back here; it's mostly used as a place to take families of patients who are being triaged during overflow situations. We're a large hospital with plenty of room, and during a weekday we don't often get a huge crowd, so I figure Ryder will be fine here during the shift.

Bored as hell, but fine.

"I'd let you hang out in the staff lounge," I tell him with a tiny twinge of guilt, "but I'd rather not have everyone asking questions about you. I try to keep a low profile here, you know?"

Ryder looks me over carefully, peering into my face as if searching for weak spots in my armor that he can poke through. "Why? You don't make friends with your coworkers?"

I fold my arms across my chest. "You know my situation. If Eli ever showed up here, I want to be prepared to cut and run. And I don't want anyone around here to be able to tell him too much about me. I no longer have my married name, and in Oklahoma my hair was longer and darker. I changed a lot about myself when I moved here, started going by Frannie instead of Francesca. With the exception of meeting Indigo a couple of months ago, becoming close to people isn't a part of my life in Wilmington. It can't be. I think it only worked with Indy because she lived right next door, and I sensed the same kind of spirit in her I had inside myself...she was holding something back. We needed one another."

He holds on to my gaze for a moment too long, turning the inside of my chest to warm honey.

Finally, he nods. "I'm willing to stay here and let you do your thing at work, as long as you check in often. Once an hour at minimum. I gotta know that you're safe. That means on your twelve-hour shift, I see your pretty face peeking through that door twelve times. Otherwise, I'm coming to look for you."

His tone, dead serious and full of promise, makes a shiver tiptoe down my spine. I dip my chin in understanding just before scurrying out of the room like my scrubs are on fire.

So far, I've checked in with Ryder eight times, and I'm now sitting at the nurses' station, catching up on paperwork. We had an interstate pile-up come in around lunchtime, and I was bustling around the ER checking on patients and assisting doctors for a few hours. Coffee in hand, I scroll on the computer screen in front of me.

Light foot traffic flows around me as nurses and doctors and the occasional patient float by, but the burn of eyes penetrating my skin causes my fingers to pause in their typing.

Deep sienna eyes meet mine. A chin drops into a hand as a huff escapes impatient lips, and dreadlocks pulled into a ponytail practically tremble with unasked questions.

"Can I help you, Denver?" I bite my lip, trying hard to hide my smile.

Denver Hall, probably the only person other than Indigo I could actually call a friend here in Wilmington, is an X-ray technician here at the hospital. He works day shift too, and stops by to see me regularly when he knows I'm working.

"First of all…" Without moving his face from his chin, Denver gives me one long blink. That blink is so full of attitude I can feel his irritation from across the large nurses' station.

I swallow.

"…We haven't gone out for a drink in more than a minute. And second of all, word around the hallways today is that you came in this morning with some tall, delicious drink on your arm. And I haven't heard shit about it. Where have you been, and who is the man?"

My mouth goes dry. *How are people talking about Ryder? I didn't think more than one or two people even caught sight of him this morning!*

I sigh, frowning. "I'm sorry we haven't been able to grab a drink. I've had a lot going on…in my personal life lately."

Denver stands up straight again and arches a brow. His handsome face transforms, expression becoming curious. "For real? The personal life you like to keep tight-lipped about?"

I roll my eyes and wave a hand, my heartbeat picking up. "That's because it's always too boring to talk about. *Your* personal life is much more interesting."

Denver's eyes narrow at me as he takes a beat, and then he grins. "You're right. Okay, we'll come back to that. What about the man?"

He props a hip on the desk and folds his arms. Tattoos cover the dark chocolate skin of both biceps, partially visible beneath the short sleeves of the light green scrubs he wears. The silver hoop looping through one of his nostrils winks in the fluorescent hallway lighting. "Talk, girl. You know I'll find out."

Panic flares, flames of heat licking at my insides, forcing words to leave my mouth before I've really thought them through. "My brother's in town. Um. He's visiting from where he lives. Yeah, in…Florida?" My voice rises at the end like I'm asking Denver where my brother lives, instead of telling him.

Denver's dark eyebrows lift nearly to his hairline. "Oh, really? You never told me you had a brother. Well, great. I can't wait to meet him."

Panic bubbles faster. "Um, well…he's pretty shy. I brought him in so he could see the hospital and he's just sitting in the lounge working while I finish my shift."

His eyes pop, the whites showing around the dark brown irises. "He stayed? For your *entire* twelve-hour shift?"

Making a snap decision to get myself out of this situation, I wave my hand and stand from the desk. Grabbing a stack of files, I quirk my lips upward. "Bye, Denver. I have work to do. I'm gonna deliver these files to radiology, and I'll talk to *you* later."

Rushing away from him before he can stop me, I don't turn around until I'm inside the elevator at the end of the floor. When I glance back toward the nurses' station desk, Denver is staring at me with a knowing expression. I'm glancing at the smart watch on my wrist just as someone jams their finger into the button in the hallway so the doors remain open.

Ten minutes until I need to check in with Ryder.

A man steps onto the elevator and I scoot back, realizing I haven't pressed in the fourth floor, where radiology is located.

"Four, please," I murmur as I scan the names on the folders to make sure I have all the ones I need.

The man dressed in scrubs in front of me presses the button for four and the button for three for himself. The elevator begins to move, and I glance up to watch the glowing numbers change.

Only they don't change, because the man in front of me stabs his finger on the bright red emergency stop button.

Small details come into focus, strange details that I wouldn't have noticed otherwise. The bright green threads of his scrubs, individualized and separated as I focus on each fiber. The dark scruff dusting the man's jawline in stark contrast with the lighter complexion of his skin. The squeak of the rubber soles of his sneakers against the tiled elevator floor, grating against my inner eardrum as he turns to face me in what seems like slow motion.

My limbs seize; my fingers tighten around the files in my hands as the blood in my body turns icy and sluggish.

Before my mind forms words to force from my mouth, the man is upon me, shoving me against the elevator's back wall. His big hand presses against my mouth while his hot, sour breath washes over my face. I've never seen him before, not at the hospital or outside of it. His dark brown hair brushes the tops of his shoulders, and bushy eyebrows crawl like caterpillars toward the center of his sun-lined face. He's relaxed, like he has all the time in the world, but when he speaks there's nothing jovial in his tone. Nothing but cold, hard menace that sends a shiver running from my hair to my toes.

His voice is low, intimate. "There you are, Francesca." My breath escapes me all at once, in a whoosh of compressed air. "Eli sends his love. He'll be along to see you soon, you hear?"

I just stare at him with wide eyes, and when I don't answer him, there's a sharp metallic snap and a cold, sickening pressure against the soft skin of my neck.

Against my will, my knees start to tremble and my skin grows cold.

"Did you hear me, Francesca?"

His voice. Jesus, his voice.

Like Eli's, it holds a note of cruel finality. Like no matter what happens, he'll get his way. But where Eli's voice always carried familiarity and a strange sense of warmth—like he knew he was doing what was best for me, even if I didn't—this man's is just cold and vile.

I shiver, and I feel the blade slice my skin.

"Careful now, darlin'," the man chides. "Wouldn't want to hurt you. Eli loves that pretty face too much. Listen up, because I have a message for you. Are you listening?"

I say nothing, and he digs the blade in a little deeper.

"Yes," I gasp. "Yes, dammit! I'm listening."

"Good girl. Tell that man you're riding shotgun with not to touch a hair on your head. Because all those hairs belong to Eli. And he'll be along to pick you up soon. You got that?"

He moves the knife just enough for me to nod, and then he's gone. I feel the absence of him just as surely as I felt the heaviness of his bulk surrounding me, and the energy releases from my body all at once.

A noise escapes me, an ugly cry ripping from my throat—a quiet mixture of rage and fear and righteous indignation. But the man is there and gone again, pressing the red emergency button and slipping out of the elevator, the ghost of his weight heavy on my skin like moss clinging to a damp log.

My legs threaten to drop me to my knees right there on the elevator floor, but I force myself to walk. I learned a long time ago that staying in one place is never the answer. Taking shallow breaths, I walk down the hallway, completely forgetting about the files hanging limply in my hands.

It doesn't surprise me that Eli knows where I am. I already knew that he'd found me. And the fact that he's sending people after me isn't a shocker either. That's why NES is protecting me. That's why I have Ryder sitting in my hospital waiting room right now...

Oh, shit.

Ryder.

My wrist automatically lifts so I can check the time. I'm one minute late for my check-in. The last thing I want is for that Goliath to storm the halls of this ER, looking for me, causing a scene. Especially after what just happened.

But somehow, the thought of Ryder's face when I tell him about what just happened in the elevator scares me only slightly less than what actually happened with the man in scrubs. Thorn Ryder's fiercely protective nature has become perfectly clear in the short time that I've known him, and it would take only one incident like this for him to take away something I need in my life right now...the one thing that hasn't been stolen from me.

My job.

5

RYDER

When my watch buzzes against the skin of my wrist, I don't even have to check it to know that little Pistol Annie has missed her deadline. My gaze moves to the doorway, expectant. She hasn't missed the mark all day, and I don't expect any less now. I lean forward in my chair, resting my elbows on my thighs as I turn my phone over and over again in my hands. My laptop sits on the chair beside me. I finished the work I needed to catch up on an hour ago, and I've just been killing time reading on my Kindle app.

The seconds tick by, and as they turn into minutes, the anxiety swirling in my system twines tighter around my chest like a vine twisting around a tree trunk. As the day went on and Frannie continued to check in, the nerves I'd carried into the hospital with me had quieted, but now she's five minutes late and I'm right back to where I started. I never should have let her out of my sight.

Popping to my feet, I'm heading toward the doorway when she coasts around the corner and skids to a stop ten feet in front of me. He face is two shades paler than her usual tan complexion, her blue eyes full of something that makes me swallow around the emotion rising too quickly in my throat.

Fear.

It's scrawled across her face like a carefully scripted letter, and I'm quickly crossing the distance between us and placing my hands on her upper arms.

"Frannie? What the hell happened?"

She shakes her head and swallows, and my eyes track the movement to her throat. A trickle of blood snakes in a thin line there, daring to mark the otherwise perfect satin skin, and my thumb brushes the spot in a gentle caress. She lifts her hand, her fingers closing around my wrist.

"I'm fine, Ryder. But…" Her bottom lip disappears into her mouth, and a growl rumbles somewhere deep inside me.

"But what?"

"Eli got to me."

Faster than she can blink, I push her behind me, drawing my Glock. I face the doorway, edging forward, a liberal litany of curses flying from my mouth. "Where?"

She's whisper-shouting behind me, slapping her small hands against my back. "No, no! Put that away, Ryder! Jesus Christ. The guy is long gone now. It wasn't actually Eli. Just some man he sent to scare me."

I holster my gun but keep my hand on it. "We're leaving." My voice is clipped, tone angry. "Right now."

"My shift's not over—"

I whip my head around to look back at her, a warning in my eyes and in my tone. "Don't give a fuck about your shift."

She snaps her mouth closed and doesn't say another word, except to throw the excuse of being ill at her supervisor as we hurry out of the building. Her boss makes her promise to call her and let her know how she's doing, which Frannie swears she'll do, and then we're in the parking lot, striding to the car.

Every inch of me is in battle mode; scanning for danger, listening for the sound of approaching threats, making sure that Frannie is as protected as I can get her in a place as wide open as a hospital parking lot in broad daylight. I'm hustling her faster than her much-shorter legs should be able to go, and I practically throw her into the passenger side of the BMW before closing her door.

Once I'm inside, I use the car's Bluetooth system to call Jacob Owen.

"They found Frannie at the hospital today," I say by way of greeting when he answers. "She's not going back there."

"Like hell I'm not!"

Jacob's voice thunders through the speakers. "Was it Ward?"

My palm slams down on the steering wheel as I pull out of the parking lot and turn toward the condo. "No. It was someone he sent. Frannie got a look, but he was gone before she even told me about him."

Jacob's cool, methodical. "I'll send Snyder and Foxx to the hospital with someone from the PD and they can get a look at the security footage and talk to the staff. Gather some intel. If we can find him, maybe he'll lead us to Ward. Meantime, keep Frannie safe and we'll check in with you later to update you."

"Sounds good, Boss Man."

When I end the call, the waves of animosity rippling toward me from the passenger seat can't be ignored. I glance over at Frannie and throw both hands in the air when I see her expression. Dropping one hand back on the wheel, I explode.

"I'm sorry, Pistol Annie, but did you really think I was gonna let you just waltz back into that place after you were *attacked*? Do you have any idea what could have happened to you?" My voice is raised, and in the small confines of the car it sounds like yelling, but the emotion of what nearly happened today is rising too quickly to the surface.

"What do you think could have happened? Eli wants me alive, do you think I'm a moron? He wants *me*, not me in a body bag! And that guy wasn't going to drag me out of a hospital full of people kicking and screaming! I knew that."

Frannie's just as pissed, her chest rising and falling with her breaths, anger causing heat to pink her cheeks and strain her neck muscles. Her eyes are wild, her hands splayed out in front of her on the dashboard, fingers tapping an inconsistent rhythm on the leather.

A sign ahead of me reads BEACH ACCESS, and even though it leads away from the condo, I take the road. I don't think being confined in the enclosed space of our temporary home will be the best thing for either of us right now.

The beach access road isn't too crowded with cars for this time of year. Unfortunately, it's also not deserted, which is what I was counting on.

"Where are we going?" She glances out her window, watching as the beach comes into view and the shops become more tourist-oriented.

"Don't really feel like going home right now. Thought we'd take a walk."

I pull into a metered spot on the side of the road and tell Frannie to stay in the car while I use the mirrors to check the street and sidewalks around me. There are couples and families walking to and from the ocean, and there's an ice cream shop and a pizza parlor on the corner in front of us. Behind us, there are houses lining the block.

Knowing my gun is strapped to the holster at my side, I exit the car and walk around to the passenger side.

Still continuously scanning the street beyond.

When I've evaluated our surroundings enough to deem it safe for Frannie to get out of the car and walk with me, I open her door and she climbs out.

Leaving the sidewalk and entering a side street that leads to the beach, we shuck our shoes off at the entrance to the sand and continue without them. There are other people around, walking like we are or still stretched out on the sand as the last fading rays disappear into the horizon.

We walk, the sound of the ocean breaking against the shore setting a comforting rhythm to our silent steps melting into the sand. The anger that's been radiating within me since I first saw her hurt and scared back at the hospital has finally started to dissipate.

My voice is calm when I finally speak. "Tell me something, Frannie."

She glances over at me, those big blue eyes finding mine. There's so much hiding behind her gaze. Staring into those eyes sends a stab of fear piercing straight through me, because they remind me so much of another pair of eyes that hid secrets from me long ago.

Echo.

Internally, I jerk back like I've been punched. I think about my sister every single day, but it's been a long time since I've been reminded of her in this way. Her eyes were green, not blue like Frannie's, but they hid her secrets in the same shuttered way.

Frannie's tone is cautious. "What?"

I take a breath to steady myself, though inside, I'm reeling. "Tell me why you'd be willing to risk your life for a job. Nursing jobs are a dime a dozen, right? If you don't go back to this one, you can find another one. And that's worst-case scenario. Why would you risk him getting to you at work?"

I need to understand why she'd put herself in danger this way. It doesn't make sense to me, and I need things to make sense. If I'm going to protect her, she has to meet me halfway. She stops walking, as if her legs are no longer willing to move. When I catch sight of the tortured expression on her face, my chest constricts, my breath catching in my throat. Frannie's head drops as those slender hands rise to cover her face.

But before she can completely retreat into herself, I wrap my hands around her wrists and gently tug her hands away from her face. I hold them captive between us, taking a step into her space. "Talk to me, Frannie."

I keep my voice low, scared that she'll pull back and run from me. I want her to talk to me, tell me why she's pushing this issue so hard. There must be a reason.

"I have to work," she whispers.

She attempts to look away, but I don't let her gaze drop, following her eyes by moving my head down. "It's about the money?"

Frannie's face turns a pretty shade of pink. "I need to work," she repeats, with more force. "I have rent, other bills to pay. This is my life we're talking about here. I can't just stop working until Eli is put away. He took my job away from me once before. *I can't* let him do it again."

Understanding swells inside me. And something more than that fills me up. Pride in the way this woman takes care of herself. Compassion for the way she doesn't want some asshole with a vendetta to change the way she lives her life. Admiration for how damn tough she is threatens to swallow me up.

My hands squeeze hers. Her eyes drift shut in response. Her breath, warm and fresh, brushes against my face as I lean closer. "No, sweetheart. He can't. This isn't about him. But it *is* about making sure he can't hurt you ever again. It's my job to make sure you stay safe. The only way I can do that is if you take a leave of absence from nursing. Just for a little while. Just until we catch the son of a bitch. Can you do that for me? NES has got you financially until then. We have a fund with a stipend for our clients, and Witness Protection has an allowance for you too. You just have to allow us to help you."

My thumbs caress small circles against the backs of her hands. "Think you can do that?"

Her eyes flutter open, long eyelashes framing pools of ocean blue that strike a place deep in my chest. She's opening her mouth to respond when a scream ricochets down the beach.

"Help! Help, my son!"

Frannie's head whips around, but I'm already moving, placing my body between her and the sound of the woman screaming a little way down the beach from us. She's standing over a little boy lying prone on the sand, and there are a few people milling around like us. Two men are rushing over to help, but there's no threat that I can detect in our immediate vicinity.

Frannie peeks around me. "Move, Ryder. I need to go see if I can help."

Her small hands slap my back gently, and I move aside and allow her to move forward, keeping step beside her. We approach at a quick clip, and as we get closer I can see that the mother is frantically trying to hold her son still while he seizes on the sand.

Frannie drops to her knees beside the boy, who looks about six years old.

"I'm a nurse," she explains to the wide-eyed mother. "Does he have a history of seizures?"

The mother shakes her head.

Frannie glances at me. "Ryder, call 911."

I pull out my phone and make the call, keeping my eyes on Frannie. She makes all the onlookers move out of the way and asks the mother not to touch the little boy. Frannie rolls him onto his side and explains to the mother that she's making sure he can breathe in case he vomits while he's seizing. She says that while she doesn't have the medication she needs in order to stop the seizure, it should stop on its own, and that help is on its way. "I'll stay with you until they get here," Frannie continues.

The mother nods, her eyes glued to her little boy, tears streaming down her face.

Frannie takes the mother's hand, catching the woman's eye. "It's scary, watching your child when they're sick or hurting. When you know there's nothing you can do to help them and you have to put their safety in the hands of someone else. But your little boy is going to be just fine. Okay?"

There's depth to Frannie's tone, a sincerity that makes me stare at her, my heart picking up speed as I watch the fierce way she talks to the boy's mom. Something about it burrows down inside me, digging deep.

From Frannie's other side, I focus my attention on the woman. "What's your son's name?"

Her son, who's stopped shaking, lies still on his side. He appears to be sleeping, and Frannie leans over to check that he's still breathing. She nods as she sits up, and I continue to focus on the mother, trying to keep her talking to me until the ambulance arrives.

"His name is Diego," she murmurs, stroking the boy's black hair away from his face. "He's such a good boy."

"Yeah? What does he like to do?"

She glances up at me with a watery smile. "He loves to do tae kwon do. He has a lot of energy."

I nod, returning her smile. "I'm sure he's gonna be back at it soon."

Frannie's eyes meet mine, tenderness melting me like butter in a pan.

A few minutes later, paramedics are loading the little boy onto an ambulance.

"Thank you," the mother says to Frannie as she climbs up beside the stretcher. "Thank you so much for being here."

Frannie nods and smiles at the woman. "Your little boy will be okay."

The mother gives one last tearful smile before the paramedics close the ambulance doors and drive off the beach.

I look at Frannie. "Have you had enough excitement for one night?"

There's a teasing tone to my voice, but I can't hide the note of awe.

She shrugs. "No way. Let's go do something crazy." She grins. "Skydiving? Bungee jumping?"

I stare at her, hands on my hips, and then laughter bursts from my lips. Pointing us in the direction of the car, I guide us back down the beach.

"Nah, Pistol Annie. You've given me enough excitement for one day. I think we'd better just go on home."

She snorts. "Snooze."

Rolling my eyes toward a sky that's just becoming dotted with twinkling stars, I mutter a curse. She's a handful and she has me wanting to say yes to her.

When we reach the BMW, I open the passenger-side door for her and then walk around to my side. Once we're settled in the car, I glance over at her before starting the ignition.

"You were amazing tonight with that little boy. I get that you were made to help people. I'm not trying to take that away from you. I just want to keep you safe. You get that, right?"

She nods. "Yeah, Ryder. I get that."

And I believe her. She understands my reasons. But I remember the expression on her face when she spoke to the mother on the beach earlier.

"You seemed to have a real connection with that mother on the beach." I let the words hang between us, waiting for Frannie to reach out and grab them, explaining the strange feeling I got when I watched her speak to the woman.

Frannie shrugs. "Comes with being a nurse, I guess. Or a woman. We relate on another level sometimes."

Letting my eyes slide to hers, I nod. "Was that all?"

She nods. "Must have been."

Her explanation makes total sense, and it should clear everything up.

But I still see secrets in her eyes.

* * *

This is a call I've been dreading making, but I know it has to be done. As soon as I let Frannie into the condo, I excuse myself into my upstairs bedroom and close the door. Pacing the room, I hear the phone ring only twice before the quiet voice on the other end answers.

"Thorn?" Nevaeh's clear tone is breathless, like she's excited to hear from me.

Just hearing the anticipation in her little voice sends guilt coursing through me.

Nevaeh is the only kid at the Boy's and Girl's club who is on a first-name basis with me, and I'm about to disappoint her. Something I swore I'd never do.

"Hey there." A smile crosses my face despite the news I'm about to deliver, because I miss this kid. "How ya doin', kid?"

She sighs. "I'm good."

"Yeah? Got your summer reading done today?"

She barely swallows a groan. "Yes, Thorn. I always do my homework. You know that."

Chuckling, I shake my head, because she's such an eleven-year-old. "Yeah. You're a good kid. Listen, I gotta tell you something."

"Okay."

"I'm probably not going to see you for a little while. There's something important I have to take care of at work, but as soon as I can, I'm going to be right back at the club. You know I wouldn't stay away unless it was important, right?"

There's a moment of silence on the other end of the line. Something heavy presses down on my chest. I volunteer at the club because a long time ago, I gave up any hope I ever had of having a family. I lost my mother, and then I lost Echo, and my father took off.

Maybe having a family won't ever be an option for me, but being there for kids who need someone is something I *can* do. And right now, it feels like I'm letting down someone who's pretty damn important to me.

Nevaeh's voice is much quieter when she answers. "How long?"

I swallow. "Not long, sweetheart. You can still call me anytime you need me, and I'll be there for you. I promise you that."

"Okay."

There's a gruff voice that sounds like it's coming from somewhere on her end, and I strain my ears to try to listen. "Everything okay there?"

"Yeah. I have to go, Thorn."

My stomach tightens. "Anytime, sweetheart. Call me if you need me."

"Okay."

She ends the call, and I'm left worrying about a young girl, not for the first time in my life.

When I enter the living room a moment later, Frannie is in the kitchen. I stop at the island separating the two rooms and watch as she pulls ingredients from the cabinets and lines them up on the counter. Flour, sugar, butter, eggs. She's clearly about to throw down, and I pull out a barstool and sit, ready to watch the show.

"What are you doing?" My tone is amused.

"Baking." She pauses, reading my expression. "Everything okay with your phone call?"

Bobbing my head in acceptance, I drum the fingers of my right hand against the concrete surface of the counter. "Yeah. I had to take care of something, but I'm good. What are you about to make?"

Her lips curve into a soft smile. "You mean what are *we* about to make? I could use an assistant in here."

"Why are we baking at all?"

Her expression clouds. "It helps me when I'm stressed."

I push off of the stool immediately, coming around the island until I'm standing right beside her. "Then put me to work."

Her smile brightens the entire room, and I take note of the adorable pink blush in her cheeks. It matches the tint at the ends of her hair, which is thrown up on top of her head in a bun. She reaches into a drawer and pulls out a rubber spatula, handing it to me.

"You're going to mix the batter after I measure the ingredients in. We're making walnut and caramel blondies."

"Jesus. That sounds fucking delicious."

I've never considered myself a dessert guy, but my mouth actually waters.

She turns and starts adding butter to a big silver mixing bowl. "Oh, just wait, Ryder. Just wait."

We find a comfortable rhythm, Frannie giving me gentle orders as we move around the kitchen together.

"Is this something you and Eli did together?" I don't even know where the question came from or why I asked it.

But I find myself wanting to know more about her. About how she ended up falling for someone like him.

She freezes, the batter she's pouring into the pan slowly coming to a stop as her eyes skitter to mine. "No. Eli never would have helped me in the kitchen."

Her words are soft, but there's an edge to them that I've never heard before.

I nod, turning back to the sink, where I'm finishing up washing the bowls and utensils we've used. "Seems about right. A man like him would assume being in the kitchen was beneath him. You realize you're so much better than him, right?"

Frannie is quiet while she finishes pouring the batter that at first I think she's not going to answer. When she finally does, it's after she places the pan in the oven. She turns to face me, folding her arms across her chest.

"Yeah. I do now. There was a lot about his personality that he masked in the beginning of our relationship. Within a year of meeting, we were married, and I was only twenty-two years old. He's eight years older than me, and he had money and prestige in our town. I didn't know then that he had a criminal background. He hid it all so well."

Something inside me clenches tight, like a fist is balling up inside my stomach. "When did it turn?"

She takes a breath and holds it, looking up at the ceiling as she lets the air out slowly. Her jaw tenses for just a second before the words pour out.

"It was a New Year's Eve party. Our first, actually, as a married couple. One of my bridesmaids had us over with some other friends, and everyone was having a great time. They weren't Eli's friends, but everyone seemed to like him. I had gone to school with all of these people, and I was dancing with my best friend's husband, who I had known forever. I didn't even know Eli was pissed about it until he yanked me out of the party a few minutes later. He hit me, right there in the driveway. Then he choked me and threw me in the bushes."

Rage, boiling hot, almost overtakes me. My knees buckle when I think of a grown man hitting her.

"Fuck." I grip the edge of the counter to hold myself up. "I'm so sorry, Frannie."

Her voice is hollow when she replies. "I never should have gone home with him that night. I should have screamed my head off, called for my friends, and never looked back. But I was in shock, and I couldn't imagine that the man I'd fallen in love with could treat me that way. So when he threw me in the car, there was nothing I could do but go home. And he cried that night, Ryder. He was truly apologetic. He was sick about what he'd done. And so was I. He promised he'd never do it again."

My throat thick, I try to swallow around the block. "They always do. But an abuser always repeats."

She looks at me, and the pain in her eyes is so fresh, so acute, that it's like not a single day has passed since she experienced that night. "You're right. It happened again. And again. Until the woman I thought I was almost disappeared completely."

I turn away from her, because I can't stand it anymore. I'm not sorry I asked, but *damn*. I had to know, and I'm glad I do. It explains so much about who she is today, and the path she's taken to get here.

"But I'm stronger because of what I've been through and the choices I've made, Ryder. Do you get that? No matter what Eli wants from me now, he's not going to get it. Not this time."

I turn back around to face her, and the look of determination on her pretty face proves there's no doubting her.

6

FRANNIE

Three nights since the incident at the hospital, and everything has been quiet. We haven't heard from Eli, and there's been no sign of him from the investigators on the case. The NES guys have been doing their job as security detail perfectly, but as much as I'm grateful, there's a small part of me that wishes they weren't quite so good so I could sneak away.

Three days without work and I'm already going stir-crazy in the condo with Thorn, and his irritation with me grows by the minute.

"Jesus, Frannie," he says with a sigh. He glances at the kitchen counter, now lined with rows of three different types of cookies. "I promise I'm not complaining, but do we have a never-ending supply of butter and sugar?"

I spin around from my spot in front of the stove and point a spatula at him as he sits on the couch, flipping through programs on Netflix. "This is what I *do*. When I'm stressed, I bake. When I'm worried, I bake. When I'm excited, I bake. And I'm bored to freaking tears in this condo."

Thorn's mouth curves with amusement. "Want to watch a movie?"

I prop my hands on my hips, a frown hovering around my mouth. "No, I don't want to watch a movie. We watched one last night, and two the day before that. Didn't you say this community has amenities? Let's go check them out."

Thorn's expression brightens. "Yeah. Okay. Go get your swimsuit on. We'll hit the pool and clubhouse today."

I toss the spatula on the counter, biting my lip to hold in my squeal of excitement. Lying by a pool might as well be an Olympic sport for me. Disappearing into the bedroom, I rifle through the drawer where I placed my bathing suits.

Ten minutes later, I'm standing in front of the full-length mirror in the master bathroom, studying my reflection. I don't have the perfect bikini body. Too many curves in the hips, thighs, and boobs. But my skin is firm and supple, and my stomach is flat enough, even though I'm not boasting six-pack abs. The bikini I'm wearing is one of those high-waisted ones, with a ruffled off-the-shoulder top that shows just a hint of my ample cleavage. The perfect suit for lying by the pool with a drink in my hand.

If I can't be at work, at least I'm going to be lounging around in style.

Screw you, Eli.

Throwing a sheer cover-up over my shoulders, I shove a pair of sunglasses on top of my head and march myself into the living room. When I cross the threshold, Ryder jerks to his feet. The magazine holding the bullets he was loading into his gun clatters to the coffee table and his hands rise to his hips as his eyes rove over my body inch by painstaking inch.

"You look…" His voice trails away as his gaze lingers at the bare expanse of legs extending from my bikini bottoms. "Ready for the pool."

He's now wearing dark red swim trunks and a snug white T-shirt, with sunglasses pulled on top of his head, and little flutters dance in my belly. "You too. Can we go?"

He grabs a messenger bag from the floor beside the couch. Grinning a sheepish sort of smile, he gestures and lifts one shoulder. "Hard to stay armed when I'm in the water, so I'll bring this bag with my weapons."

My ears perk up. "Should I bring weapons?"

Ryder shakes his head slowly. "Nah, Pistol Annie." His voice is wry. "Why don't you leave the firearms to me for now? Let's head down."

We ride the elevator to the lobby level and Ryder exits before me. I'm used to his ever-cautious nature now, even though the casual passerby wouldn't think much of it. He acts like a protective boyfriend looking out for the girl he cares about. Another flutter floats through my stomach, and I place a hand over it, a firm reminder that isn't true. We aren't a couple, and he doesn't care about me.

This is a job for Thorn Ryder, nothing more. And for me, this is a matter of survival.

We pass the building's luxurious fitness center and sauna before pushing through the double glass doors leading to the pool area. A satisfied smile lifts my lips as I survey my surroundings. The pool, a long rectangular sea of blue, is surrounded by coral-cushioned lounge chairs and white accent tables. The pristine white building is the backdrop, with majestic palmettos leaning and swaying in the breeze surrounding the entire area.

"Wow," I murmur. "This looks like a place celebrities would hang out."

There are a few residents lounging on chairs and some swimming laps or sitting in the pool, but the area isn't crowded. Probably because it's a weekday at eleven a.m.

Ryder leads us to a couple of lounge chairs and sets down his bag. He lifts a brow under his sunglasses as I lose my cover-up. I feel his gaze burning into my skin, hot like fire singeing into my flesh, but I don't turn to look at him as I reach into my bag and grab my sunscreen.

Parking myself on the chair, I apply the cream to my legs and do my best to ignore the man sitting beside me. But it's not more than a minute before my eyes wander toward him, my gaze drawn to his body as he grabs his T-shirt from behind his neck and pulls it off over his head. Rivulets of hard, corded muscle on display, miles of tanned skin highlighting vines of beautiful ink that decorate his arms.

I've never been attracted to men with tattoos. It's never been my thing. Before Eli, I always dated men who were buttoned up in polos and khakis. The student-council types in high school, and then the frat boys in college. Eli was different, but I didn't know it at first. He put on a front that fooled everyone.

But there's something about Thorn Ryder that speaks to my soul, way deep down inside me. In a place I keep hidden. Especially now, when I'm trying to build a life on my own, without Eli, or any man for that matter. I have other priorities in my life now.

"You haven't been around a lot of guys with ink, have you?"

Ryder's voice makes me jump about a mile in the air, because my covert spying apparently wasn't that covert at all.

Finished applying my sun block, I settle in my chair and close my eyes. "I haven't, actually. How'd you know?"

A low chuckle makes its way to my ears. "It's written all over your face when you check me out."

My eyes pop right back open again. "*Excuse me.* I wasn't checking you out. I was merely curious about the art on your body, that's all. Did you get them randomly, or do they have meaning?"

Ryder's quiet for a few minutes, and my eyes drift closed again. He doesn't speak for so long, I think he's not going to answer me at all.

But finally, he says, "They all mean something. I don't have anything on my body I didn't think long and hard about."

I nod. Because when it comes to Ryder, that doesn't surprise me. He doesn't strike me as an impulsive type of guy.

"Well, they're beautiful. Really. I'd like to know more about them one day." Propping one foot up beside the opposite knee, I squirm until I'm settled into the soft cloth of my chair.

Ryder leans back also, but he doesn't close his eyes. I can see them, behind his sunglasses, darting around periodically from one direction to the other, all around the pool area. Keeping watch.

"One day," he murmurs, "maybe I'll tell you."

"What do you usually do when you're at the pool?" I flip a hand toward the water.

He glances toward the ocean-blue topaz liquid and then back at me, eyebrow lifted in question.

"I mean," I continue, "I feel like I'm holding you back. I know you're my protection detail. But you're an ex-SEAL, right? Don't you, like, live in the water or something? Don't let me stop you. I'm safe here, right? Take a swim."

Ryder sits up, his motions deliberate as he plants both bare feet onto the patio between his chair and mine. Leaning forward, he flicks his sunglasses onto the top of his head, and I'm suddenly met with the intense pressure of his blue eyes bearing into mine.

"First of all," he begins, "my priority is you. I'm not on vacation right now. If you're lounging, I'm lounging. And my eyes are wide open for any threats that could occur while you're sitting in that chair."

My mouth opens, but when I can't think of a reply, it closes again.

He reaches forward and pulls my sunglasses off my face so that he can see my eyes. "Second," he continues, "I do want to get in the pool today. So don't plan on lounging in that chair forever. If you don't get up on your own, I might be throwing you in."

A yelp makes its way free from my throat. "You wouldn't."

Ryder, a satisfied smirk plastered on his lips, leans back in his chair and props both knees up. "I would. I don't make idle threats, Pistol Annie."

An hour and a half later, the sandwiches Ryder ordered on his phone app arrive. I sink my teeth gratefully into my turkey and cheese on rye and moan in delight. Sunning yourself takes a lot out of you.

Sitting cross-legged on my lounge chair, I lean over my foam container and take another large bite of my sandwich. After swallowing I glance over at Ryder. "How's yours?"

Ryder ordered a club sandwich on white bread. It's the biggest sandwich I've ever seen, and he's torn into it like he hasn't eaten in weeks. With every second I spend with this guy, the little things about him continue to prove how much of a *man* he is. Which is ridiculous. I mean, seriously. The food he eats?

Who the hell cares?

But for some reason, I do.

He glances over at me, grinning as he chews, giving me the thumbs-up signal.

I want to throw my hands up in the air, but then I'd lose my sandwich and that's not an option.

Inside my bag, my phone dings with a text message. Placing my sandwich back in its container, I dig through my bag until I find the burner phone.

Scanning the screen, I take note of the sender. When I open the text, my stomach turns to Jell-O as a photo appears. A breath escapes my lungs and I lose myself in the image on the screen. The photo that I asked Lo to send me this morning is exactly what I needed today, even though we normally don't send them. Reading the text that comes along with it, I don't notice that Ryder is watching me.

"Everything okay?"

I jump at the sound of his voice.

"Uh, yeah. Everything is fine."

I glance at Ryder, who's watching me with careful scrutiny. "Who's texting you?"

Because of the job he's doing right now, the question isn't unusual. But the skin on my arms prickles in irritation just the same. "It's no one, Ryder. None of your concern."

He doesn't answer, but the disapproval he can't hide hits me full force from his lounge chair.

We finish our sandwiches in silence. When I crumple up my napkin and toss it in my container, Ryder reaches over and grabs my empty box and carries it over to the trash can.

When he returns, he bypasses his lounger and parks himself on mine, facing me with one leg on either side of the chair. The intensity in his eyes doesn't allow me to avoid his stare.

"If there's something you need to tell me, Frannie, now's the time. I'm here for you, but I can't do this job unless I'm clued all the way in. You understand that?"

I nod automatically. "I get it. I have nothing to hide."

He doesn't move, studying my face with some deep emotion I can't read until he gets whatever answer he was looking for. With a slight shake of his head, he pushes himself off my chair and into a standing position. Holding out a hand, he gestures toward me. "Let's go."

I suck in a breath. "Go where?"

"Your lounging time is up. I'm about to toss you into this pool. Let's see if you can swim, Pistol Annie."

With a startled yelp, I try to exit my lounger in the opposite direction of Ryder. But he grabs me around the middle, pulls me against his warm, solid chest, and lifts me off my feet. Instead of throwing me into the pool, he cradles me to his chest and jumps in with me tucked against him.

Water covers my face as I hold my breath, and when I come up I gasp in a deep lungful of air. The first thing I notice is Ryder's deep chuckle. The second thing is that he's still holding me tight to his chest.

The third is that every ounce of my body is heated and turned on, and it's all because of the man in entirely too close proximity to me.

Alarm bells begin to ring inside my head. Attraction from a distance is one thing. Looking at Ryder across the room and knowing he looks good is all fine, but flirting up close and personal is a different story.

There was a time, not so long ago, when I was attracted to Eli. I actually thought he was a good man. How bad was my judgment?

I haven't been attracted to a man since then, and I'm not ready to start now.

I can't allow this to happen.

"Hey." Ryder's voice in my ear brings me out of the silent panic I've slipped into. "What's going on, Frannie? You just went all tense on me."

He moves in the water, towing me to the side of the pool and then coming around to my front so he can look in my eyes.

I shake my head, words failing me. "I...you're going to think I'm insane."

He nods seriously. "Maybe."

Laughter bubbles up inside me, and I shove a small wall of water at him. "Ryder!"

He grins. "I'm kidding. Tell me what you're thinking."

The tension broken, I take a deep breath. "I just...haven't been up close to a man like that since Eli. And it brings back all kinds of unpleasant memories with me that are hard to beat back in the moment sometimes."

Ryder goes still. "I scared you?"

Slowly, I nod. "Not in the way you're thinking, and I know you didn't do it on purpose. But being close to you in general scares me. I'm messy, Ryder."

He holds my gaze, the intensity in his full of nothing but truth. "I can handle messy. I never want to scare you, Frannie. If it ever happens again, I want you to tell me so I can adjust. Let's open the lines of communication here, okay?"

A smile curls my lips upward as my heart squeezes inside my

chest. Those words never would have come out of Eli's mouth. "Okay."

He slowly reaches out, his hand hovering beside my cheekbone with his thumb. "Can I touch you at all?"

His voice, low and rough, reaches inside me to a place no one's been for a very long time.

My skin heats as a blush flames in my cheeks. "I-I think so. How about I let you know if it's ever too much?"

Ryder nods, the backs of his knuckles barely grazing against my flushed skin. "I can handle that."

7

RYDER

I'm not the serious-relationship guy. I've had my share of women in my life, but when I'm done spending a few nights with them, a few weeks max, I'm done. I'm ready to move on. Commitment isn't my thing. I'm not so far out of touch with my own fucked-up emotional state that I don't realize it's because I haven't dealt with everything that happened with my sister all those years ago. The last thing I want to do is get involved with someone, really involved, and have them yanked from my life the way Echo was.

Just the thought of it makes me want to puke. And if I really allow myself to think about letting a woman into my life and her not trusting me the same way Echo failed to trust me...well, I just can't deal with it. The entire reason I lost Echo was because she didn't trust me with her secrets. If she had told me about her drug addiction, she might be alive today.

But I also can't deny how good it felt, jumping into the pool with Frannie in my arms. Something happens to me when I think about the way Eli treated her. When I think about how emotionally scarred she still is, a year later, because of it. I don't want him to have a hold on her. And as I spend time with her, I have to wonder if that has anything to do with *me* wanting a chance to prove to her that all men aren't like him.

But that's not what I want, is it?

Shit. My head is fucked when it comes to her. This assignment has me spinning.

Frannie's sweet drawl catches my attention, and I focus all of my attention on her.

"You're like a fish." She pulls herself up onto the side of the pool, allowing her legs to dangle in the water.

She smiles down at me, those blue eyes sparkling.

Flipping onto my back, I stroke past her, letting my fingertips brush her legs slightly. "Not a fish, a SEAL."

"That's kind of badass, Ryder."

My arms cut through the water, carrying me to her side. Spreading my arms out against the side of the pool, I lean my head back and look at her. "It was hard work to get there. But once I was a SEAL, I loved every second of it. Kind of like how I think you feel about being a nurse."

The corner of her pretty mouth tips up and she bumps my shoulder with her knee. The contact sends sparks of electricity tingling down my arm. "You get me, Ryder."

Bumping her back, I savor the sound of her light laughter.

"It seems like you've let loose today. Is that a normal thing for you, Frannie?"

She sucks in a breath, chest rising and falling, and I allow myself to be distracted by the movement as her breasts push against the top of her bikini.

Her lower lip pulls between her teeth. "I guess not. Not really. There's a lot on my plate right now, you know? And fun isn't a part of that equation."

"Because of Ward?"

She nods, and her pretty blue eyes shutter momentarily. "Among other things."

"What other things?"

Her shoulders stiffen at the same time her expression shuts down. "Just work and trying to keep myself afloat as a single woman in a new town without a support system around me. It's been a hard year for me."

Sliding closer, I use my stare to force those clear eyes to focus on mine. "What aren't you telling me, sweetheart?"

Her tongue darts out, swiping across her full bottom lip. My eyes follow the route it takes, and I lean a little closer because damn if I don't want to follow that path with my own tongue. But I can't, and I need to remember that.

"Nothing," she whispers. Her voice is hoarse, like she's reacting to my closeness. And I hope to hell she is, because being this close to her is causing all kinds of reactions in me that I shouldn't be having.

This is supposed to be a job, not a playdate. And yet…

"Nah. There's something. And if I'm going to do my job to the best of my ability"—I lean in until my lips are only a breath from hers—"I need to know what you're keeping from me. You can trust me, Frannie."

She glances down and I follow her gaze; water glistens on her skin. Her voice is quiet. "Trust isn't something I have a lot of to give, Ryder."

Something inside me deflates. Of course she doesn't offer her trust easily, and after what she's been through, can I blame her?

"Maybe not. But we'll get there."

She looks up, a question burning in her eyes. "Why do you want to?"

It's a question I'm asking myself too. Frannie sparks something in me that's been quiet for a long, long time. She makes me want something for myself that I never thought was possible.

Slowly, so I don't scare her, I reach up to stroke my knuckles across her cheek. Just the lightest touch. Her eyes latch onto mine.

"Because," I answer, "your trust matters to me."

The urge to pull myself up toward her, to claim her mouth as mine is too strong. And if she were any other woman, I'd steal this moment and do exactly that.

Instead, I let my hand drop and pull away. Then I grab her hand and tug her down into the pool, enjoying the sound of her squeal as the water covers her.

This afternoon will be about fun for Frannie, and building the trust between us.

Everything else can wait.

"Can I pick the movie?" Frannie's tone is hopeful, her forehead puckered as her brows lift.

Frannie and I had a repeat performance of yesterday, lounging this morning and afternoon by the pool. When I suggested we choose a movie and spend the rest of the day on the couch with a few snacks, she didn't object.

I round the kitchen island with a bowl of popcorn in one hand. Frannie's set out a plate of brownies on the coffee table already. I put the bowl down as I join her on the couch.

"You pick, and I get one veto."

She sighs. "I guess that's fair."

She scrolls through the options, and I take in her profile. We both showered after the pool, and her hair's pulled up into one of those messy buns on top of her head. Her legs are bare in a pair of gray shorts, and one shoulder peeks out of her oversized T-shirt. She's not even making a little bit of an effort right now with her appearance, and she looks fucking beautiful.

Goddamn.

I'm wondering how the hell I'm going to sit on the couch and focus on a movie with this woman.

"Found one!" Frannie turns triumphant eyes my way, and I already know I'm not going to exercise my veto.

I'm going to agree to whatever fucking movie she picks because those big blue eyes are damn hard to say no to.

"I've been wanting to watch this one about this couple who're stuck in space on board a ship where they're the only two people awake."

Sci-fi. Awesome.

Not my thing. At all.

"Start it."

With a giddy smile, she hits play.

"You're into science fiction?" My eyes flick to her legs as she pulls them underneath her and leans back against the cushions.

Frannie looks over at me, grasping a lock of hair between her fingers and pulling. "I wouldn't say I'm really into it. But for some reason, this movie looked good. You?"

I shake my head. "Not really. But if this one doesn't have aliens shooting at each other, we might be okay."

A giggle escapes her, and I like the sound. A lot.

We both focus on the movie, but I can't help being hyperfocused on Frannie. It's my job. I'm aware of her position on the couch beside me; I'm focused on how I'm positioned related to the door in case of an intruder. But it's more than that. The scent of her fruity shampoo as it wafts toward my nose when she leans toward me, the intake of air when she gasps at something happening onscreen. The slide of skin against skin when she crosses and uncrosses her legs.

I'm aware of all of it.

And it's damn near driving me insane.

8

FRANNIE

I can barely focus on the movie.

Everything about Ryder is a distraction.

Yesterday, I told him that I needed him to be careful with me. And he's followed that direction to the letter. But now, all I want is more. More of his gentle touches. More of his strong arms wrapped around me. More of his attention, focused solely on me.

What the hell is wrong with me?

As he sits beside me on the couch, watching the movie, the smell of the body wash he uses in the shower surrounds me. It's spicy and fresh at the same time, mixed with a scent that's so wholly Ryder. It's taking over my senses, driving me crazy.

Glancing at him out of the corner of my eye, I watch the muscles ripple in the arm stretching across the back of the couch. And I want to know what those corded muscles would feel like folded around my body. An instinct deep down inside me knows that those muscles, those hands, those arms, would never be used to hurt me. It's a direct contrast to the way I felt when I was with Eli last. That safety, that security wasn't there.

With Ryder? It is.

He looks over at me, catching my eyes locked on him. I'm stuck there, staring, instead of glancing away. He freezes, reading the expression in my gaze.

We both sit, watching each other, neither of us saying a word. The tension between us stretches tight, a rope in danger of breaking if either of us pulls too hard.

"Frannie?" His voice is low. "Talk to me, sweetheart."

I swallow. "What do you want me to say?"

He shifts, his body turning toward mine. Slowly, like he's afraid he'll scare me away, he uses the same gesture he did at the pool yesterday. The back of his hand grazes my cheek, and his touch sends sparks shooting along my skin. He's so gentle, taking such care with me that my heart squeezes. The last thing I want is to think about Eli right now, but I can't help but compare them. Ryder touches me like I'm something precious to him. Eli always touched me like I was a possession he was careless with.

I close my eyes, lost in the sensation of this one small caress.

The rasp of his voice has them flying open again. "Tell me what you want, Frannie."

"I want…"

Will he give me what I ask for? I'm not even sure if he wants the same thing I do in this moment. What if he refuses? There are a million reasons he could.

"I want you to kiss me, Ryder."

His eyes widen for just a second before he closes the last bit of distance between us. His lips brush against mine once, twice, like he's giving me the chance to feel him before finally fitting his mouth more firmly against mine.

Ryder kisses me, and *oh God*, he does it exactly like he does everything else: with precision and expert control. His mouth fits over mine like he was made to kiss me, and his tongue licks at the seam of my lips until I moan, opening for him. He sweeps inside and explores me with hunger, our tongues tangling gently at first, and then with more intensity.

His hand slides to the back of my neck, angling my head so he can deepen the kiss, groaning as I take his bottom lip into my mouth and suck.

My senses are working on overdrive, threatening to explode as everything becomes Thorn Ryder. His scent, the hum of approval he makes deep in his throat as he kisses me, the feel of his hands and his mouth and the nearness of his body to mine. It's all almost too much.

But it's also not nearly enough.

I need more.

He pulls away slowly, only far enough to let my forehead rest against his. "Jesus fuck, woman. Trying to kill me?"

I smile. "Maybe. Can…can you take me to the bedroom?"

He goes still, and then pulls back so he can really look at me. "You sure?"

There are a lot of reasons why this is a bad idea. But I don't want to listen to a single one of them right now.

"I'm more than sure, Ryder."

We stand and Ryder pulls me against him. A groan escapes his throat as my body presses flush against his.

It feels like this is where I'm supposed to be.

The thought flashes into my head right before he erases it by catching my bottom lip between his teeth. We fuse together, legs, hips, and mouth, and heat surges, crackles, fizzles between us like the air just before a lightning storm. His hands cup my ass as he lifts me into his arms. I wrap my legs around his waist and he turns and carries me into the master bedroom.

Laying me down on the center of the bed, Ryder takes a step back and just looks at me lying there. Self-consciousness hovers, threatening to cover me up and make me shy, but he speaks before it can take over.

"Do you know how fucking gorgeous you are? Been waiting for this since I met you outside Snyder and Indy's apartment. I tried so hard to forget about this attraction." As the words pour from his mouth, he pulls his T-shirt off over his head and loosens the tie on his athletic shorts. When they fall off his hips, his hard, erect cock springs free.

My gaze falls there before skimming over his legs and torso and then finally making it back to his face. "I never thought..." I sit up on the bed and reach for the hem of my shirt, slowly lifting it over my stomach and chest before dragging it off my head and dropping it on the floor. I don't break eye contact with Ryder, pulling my bottom lip between my teeth as I reach around behind me, undoing the clasp on my bra. It falls to the bed beside me and I toss it to the floor. Then I shimmy out of my shorts, sliding them off my legs and tossing them down to join my top. Ryder's eyes follow my every move, darkening as my black lace bikini briefs follow my shorts.

Kneeling on the bed before him, completely naked, I bare my soul. "I never thought a guy like you would give me the time of day. I mean, I'm messed up inside, Ryder. You know that. I've got the kind of baggage no man wants. And you're the kind of man who has it all together. Great career, sexy as sin, all this badass swagger. I can't figure out why you want to be with me."

With every word I utter, he moves closer to the bed. Placing one knee down on the mattress, he gently grips the back of my neck with one hand and stares into my eyes.

"Listen to me. We all come with our own set of fucked-up shit. Yours is no worse than mine. All I want is for you to trust me with it. The mess is less messy if we wade through it together. SEALs taught me that. You're beautiful, you're strong as hell, and you're exactly who I want. You hear me?"

I nods, eyes wide, my hands pressing to either side of his face.

"And if there's ever a time that you're feeling like this is too much, or I'm hurting you, or scaring you…all you have to say is the word 'stop.' You say that word, and I'll listen. No matter what. I'll never hurt you, sweetheart."

I nod again, and after that, words are no longer necessary. My mouth becomes his.

Pressing me back onto the bed, he nudges my knees with one of his until my legs are spread wide open. One hand cups my breast, his thumb circling my pebbled, tender peak, and I whimper and writhe underneath him.

I gasp. "Please, Ryder."

Dipping his head, he takes my nipple and sucks, like I'm a piece of candy. Weighing me in both hands, he switches his attention to the other nipple and licks me until my hips are bucking restlessly against his stomach.

I knew I needed this man to keep me safe. But I never expected to need him to make me feel alive again.

He dips his head to my ear, and his words cause a shiver to roll down my spine. "Baby…I need to be inside you right now."

His tone's apologetic, but I nod my head emphatically. "Yes…God, yes."

Kissing my lips again, he pushes back. "Don't move. I have condoms in my bag in the other room."

He leaves me lying there and jogs out of the room. When he returns, he's ripping open a foil wrapper and rolling the condom onto his cock.

Positioning himself above me again, he nudges at my entrance and I sigh, gripping his shoulders.

He stills, watching me. Serious eyes scan my face, concern etched in his gaze. One of his hands strokes my hair as he glances down to where we're about to be joined.

He's so beautiful.

Resistance was futile. This was always going to happen, wasn't it?

I run my fingernails gently up and down his bare back.

"I want this," I remind him. "I want you."

Relief settles in his eyes, and he nods as he pushes into me slowly, so achingly slowly. I moan, lifting my hips forward to meet him. When he's sunk to the hilt, a feeling of peace that I've never felt before overtakes me. Ryder goes completely still, staring into my eyes.

I'm staring into his.

I don't know how many moments go by before he starts to rock; when his body rocks into mine I answer every move he makes. Each thrust sends a spark of fire fissuring through my nerve endings, and it doesn't take long before my walls are vibrating around him.

"You're killing me, sweetheart," he says, panting. Reaching between us, he grasps my clit between his fingers and pinches with gentle pressure. "Come for me. Come *with* me."

My voice pitches higher. "Ryder! Yes!"

I start to quiver around him harder, and he doesn't hold back. Cradling me in his arms, he pounds into me over and over again until I can feel his release pouring into me. He roars, his body going tense right before he collapses onto the bed beside me.

For the next few minutes, all we do is breathe.

"Holy shit," I finally say. "We just had sex."

Chuckling, he climbs out of bed and heads for the bathroom to take care of the condom. When he slides back in between the sheets beside me, he pulls me in next to him. "Yeah, we did, Pistol Annie. And we're gonna talk all about that when we wake up. But right now, I'm thinking a nap sounds perfect."

And a nap does sound perfect. But the idea of Ryder's muscled body pressed against me while he lies in the bed beside me sounds even better.

9

FRANNIE

Ryder's breathing is heavy and even beside me, and nothing I can remember has ever felt as good as his arms around me. I feel safe. Relaxed. For the first time in years.

I don't think he'll ever understand the gift he's given me.

And I'm about to betray him. Hopefully he'll never find out.

I haven't closed my eyes for the past half hour, since Ryder fell asleep. My mind is reeling. I'm not sure what I was thinking on the couch when I first asked him to kiss me.

Well, that isn't exactly true. I was thinking that he was close and my attraction to him was overpowering, and I wasn't above using it as a distraction from all the other thoughts running around inside my head. The lurking fear of Eli catching up to me is enough to deal with, and I now have a bodyguard and am in danger of going into Witness Protection. That can't happen. Just the thought has my skin breaking out into a cold sweat lying next to Ryder's hard, warm body.

The sex—oh my *word*. It was hands-down the best sex I've ever had. Every time I glance over at Ryder all I want to do is leap on top of him and start all over again.

The feeling of him being inside me rushed through my entire body, and it wasn't just physical. The wave swept from my sex to my brain to my heart and straight through to my soul. I was shaken to the core, and when I looked into Ryder's eyes, I saw my feelings reflected there.

Testing his grip, I lift his arm off me with some difficulty and slide out from under it. Silently placing it back down on top of the pillow, I tiptoe to the closet and grab some clothes. Dressing in the living room without a sound, I take one last look toward the bedroom before pressing the elevator button and thanking my lucky stars that it doesn't make the loud *ding* that most elevators do.

Pulling out one of the burner phones I have stashed away, I call a car to meet me outside the condo building in five minutes. While I wait, I pace. And I text.

When the car arrives, I climb into the backseat and settle in for the hourlong ride to Jacksonville. It'll be a steep fare, one that I can't really afford, but I don't care.

It'll be worth every penny.

The little yellow house is in a clean, modest neighborhood fifteen minutes off the interstate in Jacksonville. I've driven the route so many times in the last year it's second nature, and I don't even bother to give the driver an address to put in her GPS. I just give her turn-by-turn directions to the house.

When she pulls her Toyota Corolla up at the curb, I hop out and walk up the driveway in the approaching dusk. The front door opens as I approach, and a woman just a year older than I am comes out onto the front porch and leans against a white post. She's tall and willowy, with dark brown hair styled in a chin-length bob and angular facial features unblemished by makeup. Dressed in short overalls, she appears to be just like any other young mom on her block, but I know better.

"Hey, you," she greets me as I bound up the steps two at a time. "Are you okay?"

I nod and walk into her arms. She wraps them around me, and we hug for several moments before pulling away and holding each other at arm's length.

"I'm so sorry I haven't been here. You've gotten my texts?"

Her face pulls into a grim expression. "Yes. Come inside, Frannie."

Once we're standing in her front hallway, she shuts the door behind me.

"I'm sorry, Lo," I blurt. "I'm going to explain everything, but I can't go another second without seeing her."

Lobelia squeezes my upper arm, offering me the sympathetic smile that only a friend can give, and directs me into the living room. "She's right in here. Having some dinner in her high chair."

The air I've been holding in my lungs for what seems like days suddenly whooshes out as I walk into the small apple-green kitchen and lay eyes on the eight-month-old baby girl busily scooping mashed-up pasta from a tray and shoveling it into her mouth. She looks up when we enter, big blue eyes landing on mine.

"Ash," she says.

It doesn't matter that she can't actually talk yet. She might as well have just said *Mama*. My chest swells and my throat constricts and when she lifts her arms toward me with an expectant look on her face, I reach her in less than two strides. Raising the tray, I wipe her hands and unbuckle her harness. Then I lift my baby girl into my arms and cuddle her to my chest, her cheek resting against mine.

She smells like baby powder and milk, and something completely familiar and all mine.

"Ba," she coos, one chubby hand patting my cheek as she snuggles into me.

"Yes, baby girl," I whisper. "Mama is right here."

My heart, which was previously beating so rapidly in my chest it was in danger of taking flight, is now slowing down. Everything in my body is regulating as nature takes its course. I'm with my baby again, exactly where I should be.

I pull back, staring into her round little face, and she gazes right back. An aura of calm surrounds her, the way it always has. It's amazing, considering the circumstances of my pregnancy and her birth.

It's where she gets her name: the symbol for peace.

"Your little Dove misses you when you aren't here." Lo's remark reminds me that Dove and I aren't alone in the kitchen, and I turn with my little girl in my arms to face Lo.

"How has she been doing?" I brush a ringlet of blond hair—a shade lighter than mine—back from Dove's face and she hums and leans into my hand. "She seems so much bigger than the last time I saw her, a few weeks ago."

Lo smiles. "She's probably gained a pound or two since then."

I sigh, a heaviness settling on my chest. Because I want to witness every single pound my daughter gains, every single milestone she hits, every smile she's generous enough to dole out.

"I'm missing it." The desperate sadness in my voice is so evident that Lobelia approaches and wraps her arms around Dove and me.

My childhood friend and I have been close ever since we reconnected on Facebook a few years ago. She was the only person I could trust when the time came for me to run. And since my move to Wilmington, just an hour away from her home in Jacksonville, we've been as close as sisters.

Which is why, when a whisper from back home gave me a clue that Eli was working an angle on the East Coast, I called on Lo to take my little girl until I knew it was safe to bring her home again. Although nothing indicated that Eli knew where I was or that Dove existed, I felt it was safer. I thought I could just lie low and hide Dove for a little while.

The day I met Indigo and Lawson, I was baking a kitchen full of brownies because I'd just taken my baby girl to live with my best friend.

And then everything went down with Eli and the luxury car theft ring, and I didn't have time to grab Dove and run, the way I'd planned to do if Eli ever found me again. So for now, Dove is safer with Lo.

For now, as long as no one knows that she even exists.

"Let's go into the living room and talk." Lo rubs a tiny circle on my back. "I want to hear about what's been going on since I've seen you last."

We move into the cozy little living space with a couch and a love seat, the television anchored over the fireplace, and I pull Dove onto my lap and settle her there with a few of her teething toys and a soft Velcro book with textured pages.

"Do you remember the new neighbors I told you about? They moved in the day I brought you Dove. I became friendly with the woman, Indy. I didn't know it at the time, but she was an undercover police officer who just happened to be investigating Eli…and the car theft ring he was operating."

Lo shakes her head, her expression dumbfounded. "What? Seriously? I still can't believe the man you married is *that* man…" Her eyes dart down to Dove. "Sorry. Talking about him gets me all worked up. So what happened? I know Eli found you, but how?"

I rub the side of my neck, where a band of tension is forming. "Eli found me because he broke into Lilliana Snyder's headquarters. Well, Eli found my records."

When I arrived in North Carolina with Lo, Lilliana was a huge part of my new life. Her nonprofit organization, the Underground, is a program for women who are escaping abusive situations. She helps relocate them, find housing and jobs for them, and acts as a general lifeline for those who feel like they've lost a piece of themselves to their abusers.

Lo's shoulders hunch. "Jesus, I'm sorry, Frannie. I know you told me not to worry, but I am concerned. Does he know about Dove?"

"No, he didn't find information about Dove because Lilliana and I decided when I registered not to include her information in my file. Thank God we made that decision."

Lo slaps a hand over her mouth. Her eyes well. "I can't believe…I'm so sorry, Frannie. You've been through enough."

I reach out a hand and squeeze my friend's knee. "Stop. It's fine. Talking about him gets me all worked up too. Listen, I brought you a check, but money might be tight for a bit."

With a frown, I explain the rest of the story. How Eli got away from the police and is now on the run and most likely coming after me instead of doing the smart thing and getting out of the country. I tell her about Night Eagle Security and how they've placed me under their protection. And I tell her about Ryder, leaving out the part where we slept together this afternoon.

"So I'm not going to be able to work for a while. They say that they'll provide for me, but I'm not quite sure how I'll be able to send enough money for Dove. I promise I'll figure it out, though." A pit forms in the bottom of my stomach as I consider not being able to provide for my baby girl.

All I've ever wanted since the second I found out I was pregnant was to keep her safe. From the father who'd hurt me even after knowing she was growing inside me. From the grandparents who didn't care about anything except cashing in on a son-in-law who made millions in dirty money. From anyone or anything in this big, bad world that would ever want to hurt her.

Lo chews on her bottom lip. "I'm not worried about the money. You and Dove are my family...don't worry about that for a second. But I have been wondering something. I hate to ask this...but should you be here right now, Frannie? I mean, if Eli hasn't been caught and you have an around-the-clock bodyguard who you had to sneak away from, is it safe?"

I considered the possibility that I could be putting myself in danger, not to mention Lo and Dove. But if Eli was going to make a move, if he knew where I was when I was at the condo, he would have done it while I was waiting for the car. The sooner he has me, the sooner he can get out of town.

He doesn't know about Dove. And I intend to keep it that way.

I squeeze my baby girl a little tighter to my chest and she leans her head back against my sternum. "It's safe. Thorn Ryder's going to be in a state when he finds out I gave him the slip, but as far as Eli is concerned, he doesn't know I'm here. I'm sure of that."

Lo nods. "And they don't know about Dove—the people who are protecting you? You don't want to tell them?"

I hesitate for just a second before I shake my head. "It's better if they don't know. They're not a law enforcement agency, but they're connected to the authorities. What if they tell them? And what if the information about Dove gets back to Eli? I can't take that risk. I don't want Eli to know about her, I don't want his family to know and try to make a claim on her. I don't even want my own parents to know about her. I'm not ready to share her with any of them. Not yet, Lo."

Lo's eyes go soft at the corners. "I understand. I have the pistol you bought me, just in case. And I've been practicing at the range. I promised you that I'd keep Dove safe until you were able to do it yourself. And I'm not going back on that promise."

My hand finds Lo's, and I grasp her fingers tightly in mine. "Thank you. I don't know what I'd do without you."

She holds on just as tight, but the expression in her eyes is the only response she offers. And it's all I need. It's full of friendship and warmth.

Family without blood. That's what Lo is to me.

I allow myself to stay at Lobelia's house for another hour, playing with Dove and talking to my best friend. My heart plummets when I look at the clock mounted on the wall beside the kitchen entrance.

"I've been here too long. They're going to think something bad happened to me. I have to go." Pulling out the same burner phone, I schedule a car to take me back to Wilmington. Before I go, I'll leave the phone with Lo to have her toss for me.

With a heart so heavy it feels like it's been weighted down by stones, I pick up my baby and carry her to the crib Lo has set up in her second bedroom. I flash back to my two-bedroom apartment in Wilmington, where I made a nursery for Dove. I had to erase every memory of her there, pretend she never existed when I found out that Eli was close enough to reach me. Walking by her empty bedroom every night nearly broke me. There were some nights when I'd just sit in the hallway outside her door and sob, crying until there wasn't a drop of moisture left inside me because it felt like a piece of me had been ripped out.

And all because of Eli.

But at least I hadn't actually lost her the way I'd pretended I had.

I hadn't miscarried, the way I'd made my parents—and everyone else in my Oklahoma town—believe before I'd fled to Wilmington to start a new life.

Dove was alive, despite the beating I'd taken from that bastard. She is the epitome of strength, and she made it to full term despite the fact that she was nearly taken from me because of that man.

Never again. I settle her down into the soft blankets inside her crib, kissing her forehead as her eyelids are already fluttering closed. She lets out a soft sigh as she drifts off, most likely about to sleep through the night. Because she's an angel baby sent from heaven for me because I've already been put through hell.

Never again will I allow him to hurt us like that. I'll die before I let him get to my little Dove.

10

RYDER

The smell of her surrounds me before I open my eyes. It's funny how accustomed I am to her scent now—lavender and honey—like I've been swimming in it for years instead of only hours. Sleeping beside her was like taking a pill; it was only a nap but it was the soundest, most restful sleep I've gotten in as long as I can remember.

It takes me a second, but my eyes suddenly snap open at the absence of her. My arms reach for the spot beside me to pull her in close, but I already know the truth before they hit the empty sheet.

Frannie is gone.

I bolt upright in the bed and grab my cell phone from the nightstand. Checking the time, I realize that I've been asleep for a couple of hours.

Swinging my legs over the side of the bed, I hold completely still and just listen.

The only sounds I hear in the condo are the ones symbiotic to the building itself. The humming of the air-conditioning unit as it cools the penthouse. The ticking and clicking of the icemaker traveling from the refrigerator in the kitchen down the hallway. A drip coming from one of the faucets in the master bathroom.

But there's no sound to indicate that Frannie is here.

Nausea rolls in the crater forming in my stomach at the same time that my body kicks into gear. Silently, I pull on my shorts. Clearing the bedroom doorframe and heading out into the hallway, I keep my ears trained for every potential sound and my senses available to react to every potential threat as I head for the living room to retrieve my gun.

But as I travel through the condo, opening doors and clearing rooms, I realize that there's no danger here. In fact, there's nothing here but me.

I'm completely alone.

The nausea in my stomach gets stronger, and a feeling of panic rises until it almost overwhelms me. Springing for my phone, I dial Jacob Owen's number.

He answers on the first ring. "Owen."

"Boss Man. I've lost the client."

There's silence on the other end of the line, and then, "What the hell did you just say?"

Thirty minutes later, the Delta Squad sits or stands in the penthouse living room, all staring at me as I explain the events leading up to Frannie's disappearance. Just the fact that they're calling it her "disappearance" makes me want to simultaneously throw up and slam my fist into something solid. She's my responsibility, and I failed.

Again.

Shutting down my mind against the rampage of thoughts about

the last time I failed to protect someone I cared about, I finish my story and aim my gaze down at the floor, solidly refusing to meet the eyes of my teammates.

Jacob begins barking out orders. "I don't give a shit that Wolf's already done it. Bull's-Eye, check the condo for any signs of struggle or foul play. If she was taken out of this place against her will, I want us to find out about it right now. Sleuth, get Sayward on the phone and see if she can track Frannie's cell phone."

The cotton filling my mouth makes it difficult for me to speak. "Actually, she left her phone here. I tried calling it already, but it started ringing on the kitchen counter where she left it."

Jacob's icy stare has my own gaze hitting the floor again. Shame consumes me, and fear. Fear for Frannie. Because of what happened between us this afternoon, my feelings toward her are amplified. Knowing she's out there alone? It's killing me.

What if she's scared? What if she's hurt? What if she's—

Everyone's voices die away as I fall into the spiral of my dark thoughts. Worry gnaws at my insides, and I get up from the couch and pace away from the rest of my team. Standing in front of the windows, I settle my hands on top of my head, my fingers interlocking.

I'm not sure how long I remain like that before Ben approaches, standing silently beside me for a moment while we both stare out into the dark night.

"She's going to be all right." His voice is quiet, subdued. "No one got into this building, bro. And no one got into this unit, not with you guarding it. She was lying in bed right next to you; there's no way he stole her out from under you. You know that."

And deep down inside, I do know that. All that keeps flashing in my mind is the way her face shut down earlier when I asked her to tell me what she was hiding.

"She's keeping something from me." The words fall out of my mouth before I can stop them, sullen stones that land between Ben and me with heavy thuds.

"And that upsets you because it makes it harder to keep her safe? Or for other reasons you aren't ready to admit yet?"

And Ben McBride, for all his joking demeanor and lightheartedness, has gotten to the heart of the matter before anyone else managed to.

"Doesn't matter. She's keeping secrets, and now she's gone. I need to get her back before he finds her, Cowboy." The urgency in my voice scares me.

"We will." There's no doubt in his voice, no room for negotiation.

Jacob's gruff voice calls us back to attention. "We're going to have to call in our friends at the WPD. Put out an APB on her so that cruisers can be on the lookout."

With a heavy exhale, I nod. "Yeah. Okay."

Jacob is putting his cell phone to his ear when the elevator slides open. Five pairs of eyes focus on the pair of silver doors.

Frannie walks into the condo. Breath enters my lungs again at the sight of her.

She stops short as her big blue eyes land on all of us and go wide. "Oh, crap."

Stalking toward her, I grab hold of her wrist and pull her into my body, crushing her against my chest. I don't give a flying fuck that my boss and all the members of my team are standing behind me.

She's home.

Frannie sighs against me. "I'm okay." Her voice is muffled.

Pulling back, I place one hand behind her neck and examine her face before allowing my eyes to scan her body. There's not a single cut or bruise on her, and my breathing comes just a little bit easier. My anger, however, starts to boil somewhere deep in my chest.

"Where the hell have you been?" The words explode out of me, the eruption louder and more violent than I expected it to be.

A throat clears behind me, but I don't turn to face the guys. Frannie's eyes flick toward them. I can feel them all standing, and when they file past us on their way toward the elevator, they each have their own way of saying goodbye.

Lawson uses his words: "Catch you later, Wolf," whereas Bain just grunts his irritation. Cowboy chuckles like he knows something the rest of them don't, and Jacob instructs me to fill him in in the morning on what's gone down in Frannie's absence.

When the elevator doors slide shut behind them, Frannie walks away from me. I watch, my jaw clenched tight, as she sidles through the living room without a word, down the hallway, and into the master bedroom.

Where she closes and locks the door.

All the air inside of me rushes out, and I sink onto the couch. My head falls into my hands, and when I hear the shower turn on, I let out a groan loud enough to wake the dead.

When she returns, she's showered and dressed in tight black leggings and an oversized long-sleeved T-shirt. The scent of lavender and honey almost knocks me on my ass as she settles into a corner of the couch.

"I needed some space." She doesn't look at me when she speaks, instead playing with the hem of her dark purple shirt.

"Excuse me?" Because I can't have heard her right. "Because of what happened between us this afternoon?"

She doesn't answer, but her fingers continue to fiddle with her shirt.

"I asked you, Frannie. Before we slept together, I asked you if you were sure it was what you wanted. You said yes. Are you suddenly having amnesia?" The words are hurtling from me like bullets, because I'm pissed and confused and more than a little hurt.

She ran. From me.

It becomes painfully clear to me that I had a vision this afternoon, for a fleeting moment, of that lonely future I've always seen for myself shifting. Of that picture of myself alone, no family, changing into something completely different. And Frannie being gone without a trace disrupted that completely.

It scared the shit out of me.

"It's not just that…it's everything. I'm cooped up here like a caged animal. I was feeling claustrophobic. I needed a break from all of it. From the babysitting, from everything." She folds her arms across her chest and seems to sink further into the couch.

I throw my hands up. "What the fuck do you expect me to do here, Frannie? You're basically in Witness Protection. I'm all you've got. I'm trying to make this experience as enjoyable for you as possible, but you've got to meet me halfway. Why don't you just try telling me what you need instead of just running away next time?"

Her bottom lip disappears into her mouth. "I can try. But I can't make any promises. Sometimes I need my space."

Flying off the couch, I pace across the room. "Yeah? Well, dying men in the desert need water. But they don't always get it. My job is to keep you safe. You can't run off like that, or I can't do my fucking job. You get that? Dammit, Frannie, don't do it again."

She just stares at me with defiant eyes.

I eat up the distance between us in two strides and place both of my hands on her thighs. "Do you know how it felt for me tonight? To wake up and expect to have you in my arms and instead to feel nothing but an empty bed? And then the panic that I felt when I realized you weren't even in this condo? I thought something bad happened to you, Frannie. On my watch. And that? That would have damn near killed me. Do you understand that?"

Her eyes fill with tears. "I'm sorry."

As one streak of wetness slides down her cheek, my thumb automatically glides across her cheekbone to wipe it away. "Don't do that. Don't cry, sweetheart. Just don't put me through that again. Please."

She closes her eyes, agony scrawled across her expression. I watch her face, waiting. When she opens them again, she locks gazes with me.

"I'll try, Ryder. I'll try really hard. That's all I can promise."

And for tonight, that'll have to be good enough.

11

FRANNIE

I don't know how long I lie awake in bed that night. Thoughts about Dove and the fear that Eli will find out about her swirl and mix with my confusion and attraction for Ryder until my brain is such a jumbled mess that my limbs are twisted in the covers and my body breaks out in a cold sweat.

Sleeping in the bed alone again feels wrong. I only had an hour in it this afternoon with Ryder, and I didn't even sleep, but there was a sense of belonging there with us that couldn't be faked and now can't be erased.

After finally drifting into a restless sleep, I wake in the morning with a throbbing tension headache behind my eyes and a feeling of foreboding that my life is spiraling out of control. The smell of coffee guides me, still in my leggings and oversized T-shirt, toward the kitchen.

"Morning." Ryder leans against the kitchen counter, and I fully appreciate the view.

Thorn Ryder, dressed in nothing but black sweatpants, barefoot, ripped torso on display. Two days' growth of blond stubble dusts his jaw, and his intense blue eyes are focused exactly where I don't need them to be—on me.

I clear my throat and head for the coffeepot, which happens to be right beside the hulk of man oozing nothing but sex appeal. "Good morning."

"How'd you sleep?"

Lie. "Good."

Ryder eyes me over the top of his mug as he takes a sip. "Glad you did. I sure as hell didn't."

My hand shaking slightly, I pour creamer in my mug first, then douse it with steaming black liquid. "Oh? Why's that?"

Ryder doesn't move, and his gaze doesn't lose any of its intensity. "Likely because I wasn't in that bed with you where I wanted to be."

I take enough steps to take me across the kitchen and away from Ryder, giving me a healthy distance. Both of my hands wrap around my warm mug, and I shake my head, causing some of the hair from my high ponytail to come sliding down around my face.

"Ryder…yesterday was amazing. It was exactly what I needed. But right now what I need is a clear head. And I can't have that if we're…you know. I want space."

More lies. Space is not what I want. In fact, what I want is to toss my mug on the counter and throw myself into his arms. I want to climb up his body and ravage him, force him to make me feel the exact same way he made me feel yesterday. Safe. Secure.

Loved.

Even if it's false, and temporary.

I don't *want* space from Thorn Ryder. But if I'm going to keep my wits about me, and keep my baby girl's best interests at the forefront of my thoughts, then I *need* that space. Getting closer to Ryder might make me spill my secret. Eventually, the truth about Dove will have to come out. But I'm not ready for that day to be today. I've carried the secret around with me for so long, I don't know how to let it out. Keeping her a secret has meant keeping her safe. Divulging her to the NES team might mean telling the authorities about her, and I just can't take the chance that Eli might find those records.

"Space." Ryder turns the word over in his mouth like it leaves a bad taste, a frown trailing lines in the middle of his forehead. "You sure that's what you want?"

He lifts a brow and scans my body, and I know that every second of what we did yesterday is running through his mind. Every place on my body he touched with his magical fingers, every place he tasted with his very capable tongue. I almost burst into flames from that heated glance alone.

My voice tremulous, I nod. "Yes. That's what I want."

He swallows, and my eyes watch his throat work.

Jesus. Literally every inch of this man is sexy. Every. Single. Inch.

"I'll do that, then. I'll give you space. Until the exact moment you beg me not to."

He tosses those words back over his shoulder as he strides into the living room, his long legs making the journey a short trip, and my toes curl on the hardwood.

Placing my mug down, I press my hands on the counter and take five deep breaths to steady my hammering heart and calm the heat now throbbing between my thighs.

I find some yogurt in the fridge and cut a banana into a bowl, scooping the yogurt on top. Adding some granola from the pantry, I bring my bowl to the dining table outside the kitchen and sit, watching Ryder out of the corner of my eye where he stands in what seems to be his favorite spot: at the window overlooking the ocean crashing against the shore below.

"Since you seem to be having trouble staying in the condo…" Ryder doesn't turn when he begins talking, but my spoon pauses midway to my mouth.

He continues. "I'm taking you out today."

I drop my spoon. It clatters against the white ceramic of my bowl. "Out where?"

Still not turning, Ryder shifts his weight from foot to foot, like he's stretching those long leg muscles. "We have a meeting to attend with our contact at the WPD. You remember Sergeant Russ Walker? He was Indigo Stone's supervising officer when she was a detective, and a part of the task force that was originally put together to bring down Eli's car theft ring."

My head bobs as I recover my wits. "Yeah. Why are we meeting with him?"

"We're meeting with him and my team, along with Indigo—who you know consults for us now—because we want to know what the hell is going on in the manhunt for Eli and how close they are to finding him. They're staying pretty tight-lipped about the whole thing, because there's still a jurisdictional battle going on as to who's going to get to collar him when he's finally brought in."

I roll my eyes and bring my spoon back to my mouth. "So everyone is pulling out their measuring sticks to see who has the biggest one, and whoever wins will get to arrest the bad guy?"

The thought of it pisses me off, and it doesn't bode well for the fact that my daughter is out there, waiting for me to come and deliver her from this whole mess. They quicker they catch Eli, the better off Dove and I will be. It isn't a game for me, and it shouldn't be one for them, either.

I haven't planned what I'll do once Eli is in prison. I know that I can't keep Dove a secret forever. If he's caught, I'll be able to bring her out of hiding, but then I also run the risk of him finding out about her through the grapevine. He could file a request to see her and ask for proof of paternity. It could become a big mess, and it's the last thing I want for my daughter.

She's my best-kept secret, and she's worth it.

"Russ thought it'd be safer for you if we all just met here." Finally turning to face me, Ryder keeps his expression shuttered. Unreadable. "But I told them we'd come to them. So we're going to meet at Lawson and Indigo's house, which is halfway between here and NES."

I continue eating, and when I've swallowed the last bite of my yogurt, I stand and rinse my bowl. Entering the living room again, I avert my eyes from the bare chest and rippled ab muscles on display and head for the hallway. "I guess I'd better go get ready, then."

An hour later, Ryder and I are headed down one of Wilmington's main roads in his BMW. Ryder looks delicious in worn, washed-out jeans and a sky-blue V-neck that brings out the color of his eyes. One hand rests on the gearshift while the other maneuvers the steering wheel.

"So." He easily moves the sleek car around a slower-moving vehicle in front of us. "Tell me what you miss most while you're in protection, other than nursing."

My baby girl. "My boxing class at my gym."

He glances at me, his gaze invisible beneath mirrored aviators. "Your what?"

Twirling a piece of blond-and-pink hair around my finger, I

smirk. "That's surprising? Why, because I'm small? I have two guns, Ryder. If I'm in a situation where I can't get one out fast enough, what am I going to do then? Or what if my gun jams? I need to be able to defend myself. So I take classes to make sure I can."

Ryder shakes his head. "I don't know why I'm surprised. I'm sorry; I shouldn't be. You keep throwing me these curveballs. I should expect them by now."

I stay quiet, watching the road in front of us.

"It's really smart, though." The deep rumble of his voice travels along my skin, raising the hairs along my arms.

"What is?"

"Making sure you can keep yourself safe." He glances at me again, this time with a small quirk of his full lips.

Not just me. "I told you I never wanted to be in a position again where a man has that kind of physical power over me. I meant it."

He grunts his acknowledgment. "Noted."

Twenty minutes later, we're pulling up in front of the curb at Lawson and Indigo's Kure Beach home. Excitement at seeing my friend again fills me. Indigo and I hit it off the moment we met, back when I had no clue she was an undercover police officer and she and Lawson lived in the apartment next to mine.

Ryder opens the gate on their little white picket fence, and as we're walking up the sidewalk the front door swings open.

"GoGo!" Running the last few steps, I wrap my arms around my taller friend's tattooed shoulders. Pulling back, I smile up at her. "Engaged life agrees with you. You look gorgeous."

Her long, dark hair hangs loose around her shoulders, her makeup is flawless, and the camouflage-print swing dress she's wearing is paired perfectly with black peep-toe ankle booties.

"I missed you." She scans me from head to toe. "Are you hanging in there?"

Pulling me inside the house, she smiles when I offer her a nod. Ryder follows us in, and the three of us turn into the open-concept family room where Russ Walker and the rest of the NES team already wait.

The room is big enough that everyone is able to find comfortable seating on the sectional leather couch and oversized chairs. Indigo offers everyone fresh sweet tea to drink, and I settle onto one of the chairs closest to the window.

Instead of finding his own seat, Ryder takes up a spot standing just beside my chair, his arms folded across his chest, tattoos visible.

Ben McBride tosses me a wink from his spot on the couch, and I offer him a smile in return. He's such a nice guy, definitely the most lighthearted of the crew. Lawson and Ryder both bring high levels of intensity to their team, in different ways. While Lawson seems to be like a dog with a bone who won't stop until he gets to the bottom of whatever he's trying to figure out, Ryder is more of the lying-in-wait type. He processes everything at once, it seems like, taking snapshots and holding them in his memory until he formulates a plan—and then he attacks.

Sitting on the other end of the couch from Ben, Bain wears his usual stony, indecipherable expression. Even though I've been around him more than a few times now, he still scares the shit out of me. If he's the team's sniper, I feel sorry for whoever is set in his scope.

"We called this meeting today," Jacob begins, leaning back in his chair and looking at Russ, "because we need more information on the Ward case. We want to know what progress has been made, whether or not he's been spotted, how close you all are to finding him."

Indigo, sitting beside Russ on the couch, stiffens. Russ has been her mentor since she was a teenager, and I can almost see her hackles rising.

"Russ is doing the best he can," she interjects. "He's caught in the middle here, between several agencies. Everyone wants a piece of this case."

Lawson places his hand over hers, a gesture of comfort rather than restraint.

Jacob nods. "And we understand that. But we only have one job here. And that's to keep Frannie safe. We can't do that if we're missing pieces of information. You understand that, don't you, Sergeant Walker?"

Russ leans forward, lacing his fingers together as he rests his elbows on his knees. "I do understand that. And Ms. Phillips's safety is a priority for us as well." He glances at me before looking back at Jacob. "But there are certain items in our investigation that we can't share. That's for Frannie's safety just as much as it is for the sanctity of our investigation."

"Bullshit," mutters Ryder. He steps forward. "You can say more than you're telling us. You're just choosing not to. Why?"

Russ throws his hands in the air. "Because this is a high-priority investigation that we're being pushed to solve immediately! If anyone understood the kind of pressure we're under, I thought it'd be you guys. My back's against a wall here."

Silence cloaks the room, so heavy I can feel the tension coating the back of my neck.

"Listen." Russ rubs the side of his nose with an index finger. "I'll tell you this. We're getting all kinds of calls about potential Ward sightings, but no leads are coming through from any of them. He's like a ghost. So he's either found a way to get out of the country, or he's damn good at hiding."

Every instinct in my body tells me it's the latter.

"He hasn't left."

Every pair of eyes in the room swivels to look at me. "I'm what he wants. He won't leave until he has me. And he's smart, cunning, and pure evil. So yes, he's damn good at hiding. You're probably looking in all the wrong places."

There's sympathy in Russ's voice. "Ms. Phillips, I understand that you're scared. But I promise you we have our best on this. And the feds are all over it, too. Which, in my opinion, slows us down rather than helps, but whatever. It's going to get done. He'll be found. And when he is, he'll be brought to justice."

"Did you hear what she said?" Ryder's tone carries a razor-sharp edge. "She said you might be looking in the wrong places. Don't you want to know where she thinks you should be looking?"

"No." Russ's answer is flat.

Indigo turns to face him, her shock evident. "Russ—"

He shakes his head. "No, Indigo. She's not like you. She's not a cop. I want this investigation to be left to the professionals. Ms. Phillips can stay safe and secure under NES's protection as long as we feel like she's actually being protected there."

Ryder steps forward. "What's that supposed to mean?"

I think I hear an actual growl come from Bain.

"It means you've been doing your own withholding. We have no idea where you're keeping Ms. Phillips, or the conditions she's living in. We don't know for sure if you're doing your jobs."

I'll give it to Russ. He came to this meeting with some big brass balls. Because at his words, four huge men stand from their seats. Only Jacob, Indigo, and I remain sitting.

"What the fuck are you trying to imply? That we're not good at our jobs?" Ben's face is growing red, and I realize now that I was wrong to think that he's always lighthearted. His breathing is coming fast, and his hands are clenched into fists.

"She's my first priority right now. My *only* priority. She'll be safe as long as PD can manage to get that asshole off the streets." Ryder's jaw is clenched, his words shot like arrows toward Russ.

Lawson's expression is just as angry as his teammates', but he glances back and forth between a confused and upset-looking Indigo and the men who are like his brothers.

Jacob's usually rough voice has gone deadly quiet and calm. "We haven't informed you of her safe house location because we don't have to. Our assignment is to keep her safe, and that's what we will do. Your job is to apprehend the man hunting her, and you've failed at that, haven't you? It's been nearly a month. Where is Eli Ward? How much closer are you to finding him?"

Russ holds up his hands, placating. "Calm down, boys. I didn't mean to insult you. I was jus trying to point out the fact that exchanging information isn't always as easy as it seems. Case in point: We're following a trail to Eli based on the testimony of his cousin, the mechanic, and we're digging into some of the leads we've found through his old contacts. We'll get to him. He's underground, lying in wait somewhere dirty and seedy, and we just have to dig deep enough to pull him out."

Wrong. Wrong. Wrong.

"You know what?" I lean forward, suddenly intent on making

myself heard in this conversation. "I know Eli, and if there's something he doesn't do, it's *underground*. It's just not his style. He's the kind of man who would hide in plain sight, and laugh at you for not realizing it."

The room is silent as everyone's attention shifts toward me. Russ just nods at me before glancing away. "I hear what you're saying, and we're covering all our bases where Eli is concerned. I promise you that."

Russ rises to his feet. "And another thing. The WPD and the feds agree on one thing. This isn't an NES job. Finding Ward isn't your assignment here. Protect Ms. Phillips. Leave Ward to us."

Bain growls again, and Indigo leads Russ quickly to the door.

After it's closed behind him, the men of the Delta Squad explode.

12

FRANNIE

"Are you shittin' me?" Cowboy paces back and forth through the living room, hands clenching and unclenching by his side. "He has the balls to question whether or not we can do the job of keeping Frannie safe? When he damn well knows that if given the chance we could have found Eli by now?"

Jacob steeples his index fingers together. "Not our job right now. I'll use my connections in the WPD to find out exactly what's going on in that manhunt, because Russ clearly isn't sharing. I get the impression he doesn't want us stepping on any of the investigators' toes."

Lawson nods, looking toward Indigo, who stands just inside the front door. Her arms are folded across her chest, a small frown wrinkling her nose. "He's not telling us everything. You see that, right, Indy?"

With a deep sigh, she slouches into the room and falls onto the couch. "Yeah. I just don't get it. Russ is one of the most genuine, sincere guys I know. So he must be getting pinched from the top, or by the feds. It's not his fault, you guys."

Bain speaks up. "He's an ass. Ain't got time for bureaucratic bullshit. I want to find that bastard and bring him in myself. Just say the word, Boss Man."

Jacob stands, placing the throw pillow he'd dropped on the floor back onto his chair. "The time might come for that, boys. But for now, we stay the course. Let me get as much intel as I can on my end." He aims a stern look in Ryder's direction. "Wolf's got Frannie, and nothing will happen to her on his watch."

Ryder lowers his chin in acknowledgment, his expression serious.

"And for now, that's all that matters."

After that, Indigo grabs hold of my arm and steers me firmly into the kitchen. She pours us two more glasses of sweet tea, and then we escape onto the back porch.

The last time I was in Indigo and Lawson's backyard, I was a witness to the two of them getting engaged. It was a beautiful moment in their lives, and the memories come flooding back now. The wayward thought strikes me before I can stop it. *I wonder if I'll ever have that kind of happiness in my life.*

Seeing as how I just pushed away the only man I've had a true connection with maybe ever, that doesn't seem likely to happen anytime soon.

If ever.

But my baby girl is all I need, and if we ever get out of this Eli mess I'll be thankful to have a life with her without looking over our shoulders all the time.

"Tell me what's going on." Indigo points toward one of the cushioned seats on the outdoor sectional she has on the covered patio. I plop down, kicking off my sandals, tucking my legs underneath me, and taking a sip of my ice-cold tea. "How are you doing?"

I settle back into my chair and stare up at the blue sky: white fluffy clouds moving at their own Southern pace along toward the horizon. "Things are…complicated."

Indigo takes a seat beside me, resting one leg under the opposite knee. Producing a bottle of rum from Lord knows where, she spikes both our glasses of tea with it.

"This isn't a sober kind of conversation." She tops off our glasses and then puts the liquor down on a glass-topped side table with a smile.

I groan, placing a hand on my forehead. "How'd you know?"

She tilts her head to one side, taking a sip. "A girlfriend knows this shit. Tell me. And does it have anything to do with the hot piece of man who is doubling as your bodyguard these days?"

My mouth falls open. "Why would you assume that?"

She smirks. "Do you forget so soon? I was undercover with Lawson for weeks. Confined to an apartment for the most part, just the two of us. It didn't take long before I couldn't resist his fine ass any longer. And from the look on"—she indicates my entire body—"every single bit of you? The same thing has already happened to you."

I gasp, ogling her before taking a large gulp of my spiked tea.

"And you could do worse, you know," GoGo continues. "Thorn is fucking hot."

Rolling my eyes skyward, I let my head drop against the back cushions of the outdoor sofa. "This is not what I want to talk about. There is nothing going on between me and Ryder."

She lifts a brow. "You call him Ryder?"

I flip a hand toward her. "It's a long story and it kind of just stuck. Anyway, there's nothing going on. I mean, there might have been something. Like, for a few hours yesterday. A really amazing something. But I cut it off and now it's done."

Indigo's eyes are triumphant. "See! I knew it." And then her gaze narrows. "And why would you cut it off?"

I explode. "Because I have enough on my plate with Eli and…and everything else! I can't go to work, I can barely leave that damn safe house for a second! The last thing I need is to be playing house with a man with a superhero complex. I don't need to be saved, Indigo. I can save myself."

Indigo's smile is knowing. If there's anyone who understands standing up for yourself, it's this woman. Her background is as wild as they come, and the result is a woman who's a little rough around the edges but who can take care of herself and those around her. I admired her before I knew she was a badass cop, and now I'm proud to be able to call her my friend.

"Just trust me, GoGo. This isn't the right time for me to have a man in my life. Maybe one day. But not right now."

She gives me the side eye, sipping her tea. "Uh-huh. Keep telling yourself that, sweetie. And in the meantime, Thorn is just gonna keep right on lookin' the way he does. And all those sparks I sense between the two of you are just gonna keep on flamin' and growing stronger. There are just some things you can't fight. No matter how hard you try."

"Well, that didn't exactly go the way I expected it to." Ryder's voice is still strained as he drives us back from Kure Beach.

"No…I guess not. We're not close to finding out where Eli is, are we?"

Or how close he is to finding out about Dove.

There's a tremor in my voice, and Ryder must have heard it, because he pulls the BMW over to the side of the road and turns, giving me his full attention.

"I don't want Eli Ward to take up any more residence in that gorgeous head of yours. Do you hear me?" He lifts my chin so that I'm looking at him. "He can't get to you. Not while I'm standing between him and you. Okay?"

I nod, taking a deep breath. "It's not that I'm scared of Eli hurting me, exactly. I've spent the last year of my life preparing for him. If he comes for me, I feel like I'll be ready."

Ryder's eyes flash. "But you won't have to be. Trust me. Let me protect you, Frannie. Let me *help* you. It doesn't have to be just you against him anymore."

It doesn't have to be just you against him anymore. His words play in my head over and over again. I allow my mind to wrap itself around them, let myself believe them.

What if he's right? What if I *can* trust him, and he can help me with everything I'm trying to take on alone?

All I want to do is tell him. Talk it through with the one man I feel understands me, despite the short time we've known each other. Something about Thorn Ryder makes me want to spill my secrets to him, and makes me feel so sure that I'll be safe if I do.

"Ryder—"

The back windshield on Ryder's BMW explodes. I don't register any sound except for that of shattering glass, but my brain works in slow motion as I try to focus on what just happened.

Did our car just get hit?

But then another blast breaks out the back passenger-side window, and I know what that sound is. Everything inside me grows cold and still.

Gunshots. Oh, shit…someone is shooting at us.

When the driver's side window explodes, leaving a ringing in my ears, Ryder is already in motion, flinging himself across the console and unbuckling my seat belt as his body covers mine. His left hand maneuvers the automatic seat control so that my seat flattens. He's talking, his words fast and hard, and it takes me a moment to realize that he isn't speaking to me.

His car's Bluetooth speakers have activated.

"Gunshots fired on Route Forty-Two. We're under fire. Unknown assailant could be approaching the vehicle."

Lawson's voice emits from the speakers. "I'm already in the car and on my way to you, man, hang in there."

Bain's voice joins in. "Cowboy and I are a mile out. Closing in fast. Be there in a minute, maybe less. How's Frannie?"

I register the movement of Ryder as he shifts above me. I understand that he's trying to redistribute his weight so that he isn't crushing me, but that information seems to be coming to me from very far away.

I've been beaten, I've been pushed, I've been broken.

But I've never been shot at.

"Hey, sweetheart." It's the tender voice that I've noticed Ryder reserves just for me. "Talk to me. Are you hit?"

His words register, but wrongly. Like they've traveled a long way to get to me and they've arrived through the thickest fog imaginable. I blink, the weight of his body against me making it difficult to speak. I try as hard as I can, but the shock that's quickly overtaking my body is making it hard for me to register my limbs. "I…I think I'm fine."

"That's good, baby. Stay with me, okay? I'm going to get us out of here."

No more gunshots have hit the car in the span it's taken for him to speak to his team and ask me how I'm doing.

"I'm going to get back in the driver's seat and try to assess the situation outside. You stay down, out of sight. You got me?"

All I can do is nod; my words don't seem to be working correctly.

"Good girl."

I feel it when Ryder moves, the absence of him feeling like my own personal security blanket has been lifted.

"Thorn." My voice is nothing but a gasp.

A sharp intake of breath. A strong hand engulfs mine where I lie in the front seat. "I've got you, baby. I promise, I've got you."

Air escapes my lungs, a breath I didn't even know I was holding.

Comfort. Solace. Assurance.

I'm scared. I don't want to admit it or say it out loud, but someone is *shooting* at us. And I have a daughter out there, waiting for me to come back to her. Dove needs me.

I can't die today.

Ryder moves, smoothly transitioning from his position above me to the driver's seat. I turn my head, craning my head to watch him. His neck swivels as he searches through the side window. The front windshield is blown out, so he doesn't have a clear vantage point, and he can't use his rearview because of the shattered glass behind him.

The only clue I have that something bad is about to happen is the curse Ryder lets slip from his lips just before the driver's-side window shatters in a shotgun blast.

13

RYDER

The driver's-side window shatters, but not before I have a chance to duck beneath the opening and pull my rifle from beneath the driver's seat. The assailant shot from a short distance, so I hold my ground, barely breathing, waiting until I actually hear the crunch of his boots approaching our vehicle. I know my team is mere seconds away from me, so I have nothing to lose when it comes to protecting the woman beside me.

She's my priority. I know that whoever has come for us has actually come for her. And there's no fucking way I'll let them get to her.

The intruder approaches, and when I sense he's close enough to the driver's-side door to make an impact, I make my move. Planting both feet against the door, I engage the handle with one free hand and kick out as hard as I can. Hurtling through the opening as nimbly as possible, I land on the asphalt outside the BMW, just feet away from the gunman I managed to knock flat onto his back. His grunt, discombobulated and pained, is all I need to push myself off the ground and keep moving.

Launching myself on top of him, I straddle his hips and whip his shotgun from his grip, pressing my gun against his throat.

It's been a long time since I've felt like this. Like I can kill without question. There's an enemy in my territory, and if it comes down to him or us, it's most definitely not going to be me or Frannie.

He's a dead man.

His windpipe is millimeters away from being crushed. Dark hair falls from a ski cap, black clothes give away the fact that he's up to no good.

The words that escape from my mouth are deadly. Calm. Precise. "Talk. You have *one* chance. Where is the man who sent you after her? Where is Eli Ward?"

He hesitates, staring into my eyes with bloodshot ones of his own. My entire body is working on overdrive, and half of me is still with Frannie in that car.

I didn't get to properly assess her health situation; I have no idea if she's hurt or just in shock. One thing's for certain: She's not herself. She's not responding in the way that she normally would, and that's not good.

The man beneath me shudders, and then musters enough courage and strength to spit in my face.

Motherfucking bastard.

"You think I'm fucking with you, you son of a bitch?" My voice rises to a roar, and I raise the butt of my rifle to beat the bastard in the side of the face.

But before I bring it down, a sick grin spreads across his lips. "I wasn't sent after *her*."

As I stare down at him, realization breaks through and I let the rifle continue its trajectory, slamming it against his temple.

His neck snaps to the right, and he moans.

Behind me, Lawson and Ben are here, pulling me away.

"Easy, man. We got you."

I yank my arms, straining to escape their grip. "Don't. I need to get me out of him. He shot at us... That motherfucker Eli wants me out of the way so he has a clear road to *Frannie*." My pulling and twisting is futile. My brothers won't let go.

Lawson's voice is low in my ear. "Give him over to Bain. He can get out of him what we want to know. You know he can."

My thought process is slower than usual, mostly because all I want to do is get to Frannie. She's definitely in shock, but she could be hurt as well.

I nod. "Yeah, okay. But the second you have anything worthwhile, you send me the information."

Lawson's look is solemn. "You have my word. I'll deliver it myself. Go check on Frannie."

With one last look at the sorry asshole lying in the gravel, now occupied by Bain, I turn back to the shot-up BMW. Climbing inside, I find Frannie lying in the same position where I left her.

"Hey, sweetheart. It's me. You're safe...we got him. Can you move?"

I don't want to touch her, too afraid I might touch an unseen wound or hurt some bruise that I can't yet see.

Her breath is coming fast, too fast, and she blinks at me repeatedly. When I grab for her hand, it's cold and clammy.

Shock.

"Fuck," I mutter. Climbing out of the car again, I jog around to the passenger side and open her door. With one click to release her seat belt, I pull her into my arms and yank her from the car. "We're going home, sweetheart. I'll have you checked out there. Sound good?"

She nods, almost frantically, twining her arms around my neck and pulling herself close to my chest.

For the first time since I've known her, Frannie is showing me her vulnerable side. And it's a side I didn't expect, but that I can't resist. I almost melt into her, the way she's cradled to my chest like she belongs there. Her scent envelops me, mixed with the smell of sweat and fear.

"Take me home, Thorn…please."

It doesn't escape my notice that it's the second time she's called me Thorn today. And all I want to do is get her somewhere safe. Give her the safety and security that she deserves more than anyone I've ever met.

"I've got you." It's the only thing I know to say, so that she knows that no matter what, I'm here for her.

No matter what.

It takes me less than ten minutes to make it the remainder of the way home, because I'm weaving in and out of traffic in Bain's car and breaking at least fifty laws to get her back sooner rather than later. When I pull into the parking garage and swing into a spot, I take one look at Frannie and realize she's still not doing well.

"Hey, sweetheart." Getting out of the car, I toss the words over my shoulder before closing my door. "Stay with me."

When I yank her door open and pull her into my arms, she's shaking. She also winces, and icy fear slips and slides around inside my chest.

"You're in shock, Frannie. Something hurts?" Swallowing hard, I kick the door closed with a foot and begin walking us at a clip toward the elevator.

"I'm f-f-fine."

I grit my teeth. "This is one time I need you not to be the toughest woman on the planet, Pistol Annie. You're not fucking fine. As soon as we get inside, I'm going to look you over."

We ride the elevator in silence, my heart hammering and the adrenaline still surging through my veins. As soon as the doors open onto our penthouse, I stride inside and order the wired smart speaker to call Jacob.

Jacob's voice comes through the condo's surround wiring. "I'm already at the scene. Did you get Frannie home safely?"

I pause in my trajectory toward the bathroom. "Yes. But I need you to send Dr. Hughes to check her out. She might be shot, and she's in shock."

Jacob's voice barks out, "Did you just say she might be shot?"

"I gotta go, Boss Man. I'm going to assess the damage. She's responding and she says she's fine. I need to see exactly what's going on. Send the doc."

"Done. And I'll call you as soon as I've minimized the damage here."

The call disconnects and I continue with Frannie in my arms down the hallway into the master bedroom. Bypassing the bed, I enter the enormous master bathroom and stand Frannie on the floor in front of the enormous double vanity. Noting that she's still shaking, probably worse than she was a few moments ago, I swivel and grab a thick, fluffy towel from the rack hanging behind us.

"I need you to undress, Frannie. At least down to your underwear. So I can see if you were hit with a bullet."

Her eyes widen. "I…I d-don't th-think…"

"Please. Do this for me."

She nods, and her shaking hands move to the button on the white denim shorts she's wearing. After she makes a few passes at the button, I fold my fingers around hers.

Gentling my voice, I wait until her eyes connect with mine. "Let me."

She answers with a jerky nod. Thumbing the button free, I slide the zipper down and then move the shorts over her hips and down her thighs. As they drop to the floor, I dip with them and allow her to step out one foot at a time.

Returning to standing, I place her shorts on the counter beside her. Once I remove her denim jacket, my eyes go to her torso, and I immediately find the blooming red stain marring her shirt near her rib cage.

Fuck. Fuck. Fuck.

Trying not to scare her, I keep my voice steady and even. "Frannie…you're bleeding. We're going to see how bad the wound is under here, okay? What's your pain level?"

She glances down, looking like she's surprised at the sight of the blood. "I-I don't know. It doesn't hurt that bad."

Shock. It's masking her pain. That could be good, or really, really bad. Jesus…how much blood has she lost?

The fear in my chest wraps itself around my heart and squeezes its iron fist.

Taking the knotted hem of the gray-and-white striped tank top she's wearing, I hold her gaze, making sure she knows that this isn't about anything other than checking her out, making sure she's okay. She stares right back, taking a shaking breath.

"It's…it's okay," she whispers.

I pull her shirt over her head. My eyes find the wound. It's bleeding profusely, but as I lean down to look closely, I can see that it's not a bullet hole.

Breath whooshes from my lungs in a relieved sigh. "It's a graze. Flesh wound. It's going to be okay. I probably could clean this up and bandage it for you."

"G-g-good. Then let's cancel the doctor."

I offer her a wry smile. "The doctor is coming. He can give you something for the shock and the pain."

Walking over to the shower, I turn it on hot. "I'm going to let you take a quick shower while we wait for him. When you come out, he'll probably be here. All right?"

She nods, wrapping the towel I placed in her hands around her shoulders. "Ryder?"

I stare at her, thanking anyone up there in the sky who will listen that she's okay. I can't remember the last time I was that scared…it felt like the way I feel when I'm on a mission and one of my brothers isn't responding.

It felt like it did when I got that last phone call from Echo and I knew something was really wrong.

Staring at Frannie, drinking her in, I fold my arms across my chest. "Yeah?"

"Thank you. F-for taking c-care of m-me."

Space be damned, I reach out a hand and cup the back of her neck. "You don't have to thank me for that. We're in this together."

Dropping a kiss on her forehead, I reach around her and tug on the shower door handle. "And I'm not done taking care of you yet. Is it okay if I come in with you to make sure you're all right?"

At her nod, I push her ahead of me. I pull the shirt over my own head and then shove my pants and boxer briefs down over my hips. Toeing off my shoes, I step out of my bottoms and get in the shower right behind her. Right now, I can't seem to let her out of my sight.

I'm thankful that not only is she still standing here with me after the harrowing day we've had, but she's allowing me to be the person who supports her now. Her tears mix with the hot water, and I pull her against me and hold her while she cries.

After her shoulders stop their shaking, I take a step away from her. The huge shower provides the room for me to lather up a sponge. As I run the bubbles along her shoulders, collarbone, and chest, she keeps my gaze trapped in hers. There's a story there. Pain. Suffering. Fear.

"No more," I promise, my words lifting over the sound of water against stone tile. "He won't hurt you anymore, Frannie. You're so much stronger than he knows. He thinks he can intimidate you into coming back to him. He's wrong."

Her shoulders lift as she stares up at me. "Am I? God, Ryder…I was so scared today. I still am. What if he comes back? What if…what if you had been hit by one of those bullets today? I know your job is to protect me, but if you were hurt as a result of it…"

Grasping her chin in my fingers to silence her, I shake my head. "Don't. We don't give in to his tactics, you hear me? Not today. Not ever."

She nods, her lower lips disappearing between her teeth. Setting down the sponge, I take the bar of soap in my hand and rub until my palms are soapy. Then I kneel in front of Frannie. So gently my touch is nothing but a whisper, I brush my fingertips around her wound, cleaning it with soap and water. She hisses between her teeth but stays still.

"That's my girl," I murmur, lifting my gaze to watch her. "So tough."

When I'm finished cleaning the graze, I stand in front of her again and pull her toward me.

Her words are almost lost in the roar of the water, but I catch them.

"I'm tough on my own, Ryder…but I think I'm even stronger with you."

God help me, I feel the exact same way.

14

FRANNIE

"You thought you could keep her from me? My own daughter? I don't need you, Francesca. We don't need you. I'm taking her and going someplace you'll never find us. Someplace you'll never see her again."

I hold Dove closer to my chest, cradling her in my arms. She whimpers, sensing the wrongness going on around her and the tension of my body. "No. Eli, you're going to prison for a long time. Leave us alone!"

Eli's ugly sneer curls his lips. It's the same ugly smile he used to wear right before he was going to hurt me. Right before he was going to hold all the power he had over me, knowing I was unable to fight back. Knowing I had nowhere to go.

But not Dove. I'll never let him hurt Dove.

But I seem to be losing my grip, no matter how hard I try to hang on.

"No!" I scream. "Don't take her! You can't have her!"

"Frannie! Easy, sweetheart! You're safe, you're with me. No one is trying to take you. Wake up, baby."

My eyes fly open, and I'm shaking all over. I sit up in bed like I've been electrocuted.

And that's when I notice that I'm in the bedroom at the condo, with Ryder kneeling beside the bed. My legs are twisted in the sheets from thrashing during what must have been one hell of a nightmare, the horrific pieces of it still clinging to my awareness like old filth.

"Oh God." I gasp for each breath, my eyes flying wildly around the room. Trying to find a focus, a shelter in the raging storm inside my heart.

"Hey. I'm here, baby. I'm right here."

Ryder climbs into bed next to me, lifting the sheet and untangling my legs, molding his big, hard body to mine and spooning me from behind. Slowly, but without hesitation, I relax against him. The tension in my body releases, one muscle relaxing at a time because of Ryder's proximity and the safety his body provides.

The gray light of early dawn disturbs the darkness in the room, creeping in through the wooden shutters. But I'm not ready to start this day. After all the wrestling I was doing against Eli in my dreams, my side hurts. Now that the shock has worn off from the previous night, I'm feeling the pain in my side like a bad burn that hasn't yet healed. Fire licks my skin and a moan escapes me.

Ryder pulls back. "Let me see."

Turning on the bedside lamp, he sits up and peels up the T-shirt I wore to bed. Hissing through his teeth, he climbs out of bed.

"You ripped the stitches the doc put in last night. He left some butterfly bandages in case we need them. Let me go get them and some gauze to re-dress it."

He's gone for less than a minute in the bathroom, returning with the supplies he needs.

"I can't believe I got shot last night." My voice is hoarse, like when

I used to be a high school cheerleader and strained my voice cheering on my team for hours on a Friday night.

"Last night was scary as hell. You are so fucking strong, Frannie."

Shrugging, and wincing at the movement as it tweaks my side, I shake my head. "I'm not strong. I'm just surviving. Like every other woman in this world. We have good days and bad ones. But all we can do is live them as best we can, and try to end the day being proud of at least one thing we've done."

He stares down at my side, his fingers so gentle and careful as he adds the butterfly bandages and then replaces the gauze and wraps it in tape. When he's finished, he puts his little bag of supplies on the nightstand and returns to the bed, lying in the same position beside me.

We're quiet for a few minutes, just breathing and watching the dawn break.

"What was it about?"

I know exactly what he's talking about, but I feign ignorance. "Hmm?"

"The nightmare. It was intense. When I heard you screaming, I thought someone was in here with you. Came running. Saw you tangled up in the covers, and the way you looked..." His voice breaks.

My mind flips toward everything Ryder has done for me. He's been there, without hesitation or question, every step of the way. And yes, his job is to protect me. But it seems to go deeper than that. He cares about me in a way that he hasn't quite verbalized, but that I can feel with every fiber of my being.

I owe him honesty. At least a part of it. I can answer this.

"I was dreaming about Eli. Taking everything from me. I've fought so hard to escape him."

His arms wrap around me, but lightly. Not tightly enough to hurt the wound in my side. "We won't let that happen. Me and you…we can take him. You trust me?"

Do I? I trust him enough to protect me, yes. But do I trust him enough to tell him my biggest secret? Dove is just too important, too vital a part of my existence to place her safety and well-being in anyone's hands but my own.

The nagging voice in my head disagrees. *But Ryder isn't just anybody. He's proven himself. Let him in.*

"You said something…" Ryder's voice is soft, his breath tickling my ear, his tone thoughtful. "You said, 'Don't take her.' Any idea what that was about?"

I can't help it, my body tenses. Ryder senses it, his arms loosening around me for a moment in reaction to my stiffness.

"What is it, sweetheart? What are you so afraid of? What am I missing here?"

I inhale through my mouth and exhale through my nose, something I learned from a psych resident at the hospital to calm anxious nerves. But panic swarms my stomach, as hard as I try to fight it. "I'm tired. Can we try to catch a few more hours of sleep?"

Silence. Then, "Sleep, tough girl. I'll be here when you wake up."

When I open my eyes for the second time, it's in the full light of late morning. I'm not sure what time it is, but I become immediately aware of the fact that I'm not in bed alone. The previous day and the early-morning hours come rushing back, and a profound sense of gratitude lodges in my throat.

Swallowing back the tears, I realize that no matter how long I have him for, no matter how hard I've tried to push him away, the man sleeping behind me has been entirely too good to me. I've been difficult at best, and terrible at my worst. And he's hung in there and stayed with me, protecting me without being an asshole about it.

And last night...last night and this morning, things shifted. I've made love to the man, and then taken a step back. But the tenderness he showed with me last night was on a different level, and now that I'm healthy enough to look clearly back on the way he undressed me, the way he looked at me and took care of me...I can't believe I missed it before.

Thorn Ryder cares about me.

Like...he really cares about me.

And right now, his warm body is pressed against mine, and the evidence of a morning hard-on is pressed against my back. Desire pools hot and fast in my belly, and a million dirty pictures flash inside my head like a movie, detailing all the things I want to do to him.

Turning slowly, I see that his breathing is deep and even. Ryder is still asleep, lying on his side. One hand was slung over my hip, and I gently nudge him until he's lying on his back. Ducking beneath the covers, I find the waistband of his boxer briefs, the only thing he's wearing in bed with me right now.

With lightning quickness, Ryder's hand grabs my wrist.

"What..." His voice is gravelly, low. Murky and sexy with sleep. "...are you doing?"

My voice is breathless with anticipation. "I was just about to wake you up."

Shoving his briefs down in front to free his thick erection, I fist him in one hand. He hisses through his teeth, a muttered curse falling from his lips.

"Shit."

Gripping him tightly, I stroke him up and down and allow my head to pop out from under the sheet. "Good morning, Ryder."

"Jesus," he croaks, eyes burning down on me. "What happened to space?"

"I think…" I dip my head and allow my tongue to swirl around the fat head of his cock. He groans, his hips thrusting upward of their own accord. "…you blew that out of the water last night, Ryder."

And I take him fully into my mouth, sucking him deep. And *damn* he tastes good. He's smooth as silk wrapped around a stone hammer, with a vibrant pulsing just beneath the surface that lets me know he's fully alive and all man. I bob my head on top of him, taking him into my mouth over and over again, responding to each grunt and groan he gives me like it's a gift.

"You're fucking"—he gasps—"amazing. Jesus."

Pulling back, I lick him from root to tip, and his hands delve into my hair. His hips thrust wildly into my mouth now, finding a rhythm he can't seem to control.

"Keep that up, sweetheart"—he grunts—"and I'm gonna come in that pretty mouth."

Instead of letting up, I continue swirling my tongue around the full, long length of him, and my opposite hand finds his balls inside his boxers and cups them gently, rolling them in my fingers.

"Oh God." I glance up to see Ryder's eyes roll back in his head. "Oh, fuck. I'm gonna blow, baby."

With a loud groan, he thrusts forward and tenses, his seed streaming into my mouth as he empties himself completely. His fingers toy with my hair as his hips slow and relax, and I swallow every last drop of warmth that he shot into my mouth.

Sliding up his body, careful not to rub my sore side against his hard planes, I settle back against him. Placing a hand over his chest, I feel the quickness of his heartbeat.

With a finger under my chin, he pulls my face to his and kisses me, long and deep. Slow. Languid. Tongue dancing with mine. When he pulls back, there's a grin on his face that's lighter than I've ever seen on him before. It pulls a smile right out of me in return.

"That might have been the best wake-up call I've ever gotten."

Satisfaction fills me. "Well, good. 'Cause it's definitely the best I've ever given."

He chuckles, and I sling a leg over his. "And that's enough space, for now, by the way."

He glances down at me, eyes crinkling at the corners. "Yeah?"

I offer him a coy smile. "Yeah. If I'm going to be locked away with you, we might as well have some fun."

A slow smile quirks his lips. "That's what I'm talking about."

But, as happy as I am in his arms, in the back of my mind I'm already planning the next time I can sneak away to see my baby girl.

15

FRANNIE

"I want to take you somewhere today." Ryder watches as I finish my omelet, scooping the last bit of egg, onion, and cheese off my plate and popping it into my mouth.

"Holy shit, that was delicious." I let my fork clatter onto my plate. "I'm usually the one who cooks. I don't know when the last time was that someone made me a meal."

Ryder's lips twitch. "Maybe it's time to let someone take care of you for a change."

I think back to the shower we shared last night, when Ryder held me in his arms while I cried. He was strong for me then, and sweet. Exactly what I needed. "Maybe. Where do you want to take me today?"

He grabs my plate and puts it in the dishwasher, along with his own. I have a future flash of a possible life with this man. A future where he cooks me breakfast, or dinner, and then puts the dishes away. A life where I'm his soft place to land when he's had a rough day, and where Dove and I are able to make him laugh and smile after a long day at work. A life where Ryder is our center, our protector.

Our everything.

It's a life that's so far away, such a whimsical dream, that the premonition makes me gasp with shock.

"I'll tell you when we get there. Just go get ready."

I lift an eyebrow, not moving from my seat at the dining room table. "You've got a surprise up your sleeve now, Ryder?"

He smirks. "Maybe. Go get ready. We leave in half an hour."

A lightning bolt of panic strikes me. When we left the condo together yesterday, someone found us. Bullets flew. I have the stitches in my side to prove it.

Ryder must see the shadow that crosses my face, because he crowds my space and tips my chin up. "We got the guy who shot at us yesterday. And I have a plan to make sure we aren't followed today. This is a learning curve, because we haven't been given much intel on Eli and what he's up to. But I can protect you, Frannie. I just need you to trust in that."

Hesitantly, I nod. "I trust you, Ryder."

He studies my expression, searching for something. "Do you?"

In my own way, I definitely do. I might not be ready to spill all my secrets, for my own personal reasons, but if there's anyone I trust right now, it's him.

"I do."

He gives me a rare, full smile. His bright white teeth nearly blind me, the dimple in his left cheek endearing me to him even more than I already am. "Good.

As I turn to walk toward the bedroom to get changed, Ryder slaps my ass. I yelp, and turn to glare at him. A false glare, because secretly I'm immediately turned on.

He merely winks.

The way that wink makes me feel, all giddy inside, like a school-girl feels when the boy she likes gives her attention…that should be a red flag. But it isn't. Instead, I just scurry off to the bedroom to shower and find something to wear for the day.

Half an hour later, we're back in the parking garage, but Ryder unlocks the doors to a different car. The BMW sits right beside it, windows intact and good as new.

"Why aren't we driving the Beamer?"

His voice is mournful. "Eli and his team of asshats made my car, so we can't drive it anymore. This is a rental."

The rental is a luxury brand, though, true to Thorn Ryder form, so I sink into the plush leather seats and in seconds we're cruising down Wilmington streets.

"How did you get the windows fixed so fast?" My curiosity bleeds through into my tone.

"Pays to know Jacob Owen. He had a glass company out here overnight. He also called me last night while you were sleeping. He let me know that the team took the man who shot at us back to the office. We have an interrogation room there we call the Cage. It's exactly like it sounds, so I'm not going to say anything else about it. He gave us a lead on Ward."

My stomach flip-flops. "And?"

"And my job is to be with you today, as much as I want to be hunting him down with the rest of my team. Lawson's the lead investigator when it comes to stuff like this, so he's working with Indigo to follow the scent. They'll find him, probably before the cops do. And when they do…I've asked for five minutes alone with him."

There's so much loathing in his voice when he talks about Eli that it makes me shudder. "Why?"

He glances at me as he turns onto the highway that leads away from the beach, toward the outskirts of town. "Why what?"

"Why would you want to do that? Ryder, this is a job for you. Why do you give two hoots about Eli Ward?"

Ryder pulls to a stop at a red light, engine purring, and turns his big body to face me. He grabs my hand from across the console and laces our fingers together. "Do you really think that after spending time with you, having you in my bed, hearing you scream out my name when you're coming...Jesus, Frannie. I know it hasn't been more than a week, but we've been through some shit together. It intensifies things. Do you really think that this is just a job for me?"

Uncertainty weighs heavy in my gut at his words. *What am I to Ryder?*

There was a time, not very long ago, when I didn't want to know. All I wanted was to keep him at as far a distance as possible so that I could keep my little girl safe, but also keep myself out of Eli's hands so I could be her mom without that monster in her life. But now? I still want those things. But I might be ready to trust someone again. Ryder's right...the time we've spent together hasn't been long, but it's been intense. The feelings I've developed for him in a matter of weeks are real.

So damn real.

The light changes to green, and Ryder doesn't release my hand as his foot stomps on the accelerator. We're leaving the beachy, touristy part of Wilmington and entering the more urban side of town. Every city has two faces, and this is the one the Wilmington tourist brochures don't show the world.

"So, is it just because I'm the woman you're protecting right now? Would it be like this no matter who I was? How many have there been like me?" My voice rises as my own insecurities take hold, wrapping themselves around my throat. "How many of your clients have you taken to bed?"

"Fuck." Ryder drops my palm and brings his hand to the back of my neck, gripping tightly enough to show possession but not an ounce of pain. "Look at me, sweetheart."

I do, glancing at him through a haze of the tears that have suddenly, maddeningly sprung to my eyes. He curses again, and his tongue runs over his full bottom lip.

"*None.* You hear me? I've never slept with a client. I've never even wanted to. You and me...this is something different for me. I don't know what yet. But what I have to show you today just proves to me that you're something more. And to be honest, sweetheart, I don't know if I'm ready for more. All I know is that when I'm around you I want to try. There's grief inside me that's been there for a long time, so long it's a part of me. I've learned to live with it. But when you're pressed up against me, or when I'm looking into those big blue eyes of yours, it hurts less. You make me want to heal. You *are* healing me. All I want is for you to let me in."

My breath catches. Because I want to let him in too. I've just been terrified, because for me there's so much at stake. He keeps glancing at me between looks at the road. "You feel me?"

I nod slowly. "Will you tell me about your grief?"

He nods. "Today, I will. And I hope that if I open up to you, you'll feel safe enough to talk to me. Because we all have our secrets, baby. I just need you to trust me enough to let me be a part of yours."

It feels like my heart is being torn in half. Ryder is ripping me apart. Half of me wants to hand him everything. But I know I don't have everything to give. Not until I know Dove is completely safe.

"Where are we going?" I whisper.

I glance out the window as we cross a set of train tracks, the brick apartment buildings and storefronts on either side of the car broken up by empty fields and basketball courts. There are people walking, all kinds of people, but they all seem to have one thing in common.

The people who live in this neighborhood don't have a lot of money. Maybe they work hard and don't make more than minimum wage. Maybe they're down on their luck. Whatever the reason, the people here struggle, and it shows in the general run-down look of the buildings around me. It's evident in the way that children and teens run around the streets with no supervision.

My heart aches.

Ryder pulls to a stop at the curb in front of a large brick building with a big blue symbol stenciled on the glass front door.

"This is the Boys and Girls Club," Ryder explains as he opens my car door and I climb out. "I volunteer here once a week if I can swing it with my schedule. If I'm on a mission I come less, but when I have downtime I try to make up for it."

I remain quiet as I follow him up the front sidewalk and into the air-conditioned building. Inside, it's set up like an open gym with a large basketball court. There's an office at the front, and a dark-skinned man with dreadlocks pulled into a ponytail strides out with a big smile on his face.

I'm glancing around at the bright colors on the walls and taking note of the sounds of children laughing and playing all around me when the man grabs Ryder into a bear hug.

"Been a couple, man. Good to see you!"

"Yeah." They release each other and Ryder scratches his chin, looking chagrined. "Sorry about that, Drew. You know the work schedule gets crazy. Want you to meet someone. This is Frannie Phillips. Frannie, meet Drew Ryan. He runs this branch of the Boys and Girls Club."

Drew holds out a hand. He's not as tall as Ryder, but he's very broad and well-muscled. He's like a teddy bear with his warm, brown complexion and big smile. I like him instantly.

"Hi, Frannie. Thanks for coming in with this knucklehead today."

Grinning, I shake his hand. "No problem at all. It's nice to meet you."

Drew nods toward Ryder. "You want to take your usual group?"

Ryder nods. "Yeah. I've had some art supplies in my trunk for a while. Been waiting for my next visit. Okay if I use that blank space on the back exterior wall I was talking about last month?"

Drew nods and clasps his hands together. "Sure, sure. They've been excited, waiting for you to come back. Well, as excited as teens will show; you know how it is. They're in the arcade room."

Ryder chuckles. "Nice, nice. I'm gonna go get a few of them to help me grab the stuff, then."

Taking my hand, he leads me through the gym and into a back hallway. My emotions are all over the place, my brain firing on all cylinders. "Ryder...I had no idea."

He arches a brow. "No idea about what?"

I gesture around me wildly. "About any of this."

He lifts a shoulder. "This is the least I can do to give back after..." He trails away, not finishing his sentence.

I'm taken back to his statement in the car earlier about grief, and my heart clenches. *Oh, Ryder. What have you been through?*

It should a big ol' scary red flag, how much I want to know this man. But instead, he keeps drawing me in. Closer and closer, and I have no desire to step back.

When he opens the door to the arcade, a chorus of voices lift. Eight boys greet us, all seeming to be between the ages of eleven and sixteen, and one little girl who's smaller than the rest. She looks to be about eleven. Their clothes reflect the fact that they don't have much money, but the smiles on their faces indicate that they're very happy to see Ryder. They surround him, exclamations and questions flooding from their mouths.

"Hey, hey, okay, guys. I'm happy to see you too. Let me introduce you to someone, all right? This is Frannie. She's a friend of mine, so be nice to her today. She's gonna help us with an art project. That cool?"

All the kids stare at me with curiosity, but the little girl looks at me with animosity in her eyes.

Uh-oh. I have some competition for Ryder's heart, I think.

Ryder leans over to whisper in my ear. "Will you stay here with them while I take a few of the bigger guys out to my car to grab the paint and cloths?"

I nod. "Of course."

He looks at me like he's assessing my comfort level. When he doesn't see any kind of apprehension, he grins. Pulling me into him, he drops a kiss on my forehead.

He turns away from me. "Darius. Joey. Come to my car with me to grab a few things, okay?"

Two of the boys edge their way through the throng of kids, and six pairs of eyes turn expectantly onto me when they're gone. I gesture toward the games. "What were you guys playing?"

"*Pac-Man!*" the younger boys yell.

The older boys were playing some kind of racing game on motorcycles, and they are bored enough with me that they get back to it. I take a seat on the couch in the room, and some of the kids follow. The little girl hangs back, but I motion for her to join me. She does with reluctance, perching on the edge of the couch and not looking at me.

Her skin is olive-toned, her long hair textured and hanging down her back in curly waves. Green eyes glance in my direction only once before looking away again.

"What's your name?" I ask her softly.

She doesn't look at me when she answers. "Nevaeh."

"That's beautiful. Is it hard hanging out with all these boys all the time, Nevaeh?"

She shrugs. "Sometimes. That one lives next door to me, so he's like my brother." She points toward one of the boys on the motorcycles.

The boy sitting on the other side of me scoffs. "She doesn't hang out with us. She's all girly and shit."

My eyes snap to his. He immediately looks down. "I mean, stuff."

I can't help my crooked smile.

Ryder walks back in with the two older boys and claps his hands together. "You guys ready?"

All of the kids jump up. "Yeah! What we doin', Mr. Ryder?"

"Come outside and I'll show you."

Ryder leads a line of kids outside and I bring up the rear, just as curious as they are about what he's doing with tubs full of spray paint cans and canvas drop cloths.

I had no clue Ryder even had an artistic bone in his body. It seems

I'm learning a lot about him today, probably more than I have since I've known him.

When we arrive outside through a back door, Ryder leads us around toward the back of the building. A big, whitewashed brick wall stretches before us. He and the older boys place the tubs of spray paint, assorted colors, out in front of the wall.

"Gather 'round me for a minute, y'all." All the kids move in close, and I notice that Ryder wraps an arm around Nevaeh as she sidles up close to his side. My heart starts to warm.

"Today," he says to the group, making eye contact with each kid, "we're going to put some graffiti on this wall." When murmurs of shock go up among the children, Ryder holds up his hands. "It's okay, because we have permission from the owner of this building. When you have permission, it's called 'commissioned artwork.' And we're doing this in honor of someone very special to me."

Nevaeh speaks up, her voice shy and quiet. "Who, Thorn?"

He glances down at her, a tender expression on his face. "My little sister. Her name was Echo."

When he says the word *was*, a stab of pain slices through my heart, so profound my hand automatically goes to my chest. Ryder's eyes meet mine, and the grief there is stark and uncovered for the first time since I've met him. For the first time, I realize that he's always been mourning something, someone. I've never known who or what it was, but there's always been a sense of sadness to him, of a sense that he couldn't or wouldn't be content no matter what.

This is the explanation.

Echo. What a pretty name.

"She died when she was a teenager, and I loved her very much. I want to remember her today, by doing the thing she loved most in the whole world. Art by graffiti. She didn't always do it legally, but it was always beautiful. Echo was a free spirit, so let's try to channel that now."

A somber silence has fallen over the group of children, like they somehow understand the pain and grief their mentor is feeling today. Maybe they've been through some type of similar losses of their own, some of them. I'm not sure. All I know is that slowly, one by one, they move forward and pick up the cans of spray paint.

And inch by inch, the side of that brick building becomes covered in graffiti art so beautiful it makes my chest hurt. I've never painted anything in my entire life, but I pick up a can and just start spraying. I keep glancing at Ryder, who's right beside me, a pained look on his face as he paints, pouring all of the hurt and grief in his heart out onto that wall.

I've never seen anything as beautifully heartbreaking as he looks in that moment.

I'm not sure if I ever will again.

16

RYDER

Frannie with a can of spray paint in her hand, interacting with the kids who have been like a saving grace for me, is the most beautiful thing I've ever seen.

Where did this woman come from?

Even Nevaeh, whom I noticed giving her the side eye when we first came in, is now standing beside her, watching Frannie spray lavender angel wings on the side of the wall.

"See?" Frannie's saying. "After I finish with these, you're going to stand right in front of them. And I'm going to take your picture. And since you're so gorgeous, and your name is 'Heaven' spelled backward, you're going to look just like an angel in the photo. And you know what I'm going to do with that picture?"

Nevaeh shakes her head, a look of awe on her face. Frannie leans down and whispers in her ear. An expression of delighted pleasure spreads over Nevaeh's face like the first rays of dawn on a cold winter morning, and that's when it happens.

That's the moment I lose my heart to this woman.

I thought shit like that only happened in the movies, this real de-
fined moment when one person falls for another. But I just *know*.
Nevaeh is my gauge, because she reminds me so much of Echo. After
we lost our mom, Echo was always trying to escape the world she
was forced to endure. She ended up turning to drugs to do that. And
Nevaeh is still so young, but her home life is forcing her hand, making her look for routes of escape I want to help her avoid. And I
know without a doubt that if Echo were here, she'd approve of Frannie. She'd be happy that I've found someone who makes me happy.
And she'd want me to do everything in my power to make sure that
woman stays safe by my side, no matter what it takes.

"Hey, Mr. Ryder." Joey, one of the older, Latino boys who helped
me carry the tubs of paint from the car, nudges me. "Is Ms. Phillips
your girl?"

Chuckling softly, I black out the edges of the big block letters
I've painted on the wall. We've all decided to paint a group mural
based on our own individual artistic thoughts and ideas. Standing
back and admiring my work, I read the large orange and red letters
rimmed in black: **WHAT WE DO NOW ECHOES IN ETERNITY.**

Smiling, I aim my gaze at Frannie, who's finishing up her angel
wings. "Maybe she will be. Why? You like her?"

"She's cool." Joey's tone is all serious. He flings his head to one
side, trying to get his long brown hair to flop out of his eyes. "You
seem different today."

Nodding, I put the cap on my paint and sling an arm around his
shoulder. "The right woman can do that for you, Joey. Remember
that." I evaluate the mural as everyone is finishing up. "This looks
pretty dang good, everyone. Proud of you guys."

"Ryder!"

I turn toward Frannie when she calls my name.

She holds out her phone. "Look at this gorgeous angel model I just photographed."

Nevaeh's expression morphs into a shy smile at her words, and my heart transforms into something soft and mushy inside my chest. I grab the phone from Frannie and study the picture. Nevaeh is standing on her tiptoes, skinny arms stretched into the air. Her long hair tumbles around her shoulders as her green eyes aim skyward, and the angel wings Frannie painted in the background on either side of her are perfection.

"Beautiful," I murmur, handing the phone back to Frannie and glancing at Nevaeh.

She beams up at me, and I wrap an arm around her shoulder. "Did you have fun today?"

"Yeah," she says, her voice full of open honesty. "Will you bring Frannie back with you again?"

My lips tip upward in a half smile. "Well, that's up to her."

Frannie puffs up her chest, standing to her full height of five foot three. "Try and keep me away."

Nevaeh grins. "Cool."

Their bond is cemented, and for me it's just one more reason I can't let Frannie slip out of my life before telling her exactly how much I want her to stay there.

We decide to order in dinner. I took enough of a risk with Frannie today, bringing her to the Boys and Girls Club with me, but I took a precaution. Bain followed in his truck, kept an eye on the street the entire time we were inside. Backup in this situation was necessary, since it's clear whoever Eli has looking for Frannie isn't against shooting at a vehicle with her inside it. Even though I switched to a different car today, we aren't taking chances.

Spreading the plethora of takeout menus across the coffee table and plopping down on the couch, I pat the cushion beside me. "What do you feel like eating tonight?"

She doesn't even glance at the menus. "I want Indian food tonight."

I burst out laughing. "Decisive, are we?"

She pulls her legs up under her, kicking off her silver sandals. "It's a waste of time, being indecisive. I know what I want, Ryder."

Those big blue eyes meet mine, the color of the sky on a cloudless day, the deepest kind of turquoise and as clear as any I've ever seen. I'm close to falling into them, and I'm leaning forward without even knowing I'm doing it. I know it's dangerous territory; I know that I'm catering to a woman who's still keeping secrets from me. And that's a line I drew in the sand a long time ago. But I also know that trust is a big thing when it comes to relationships. And I haven't even given her those words yet. I haven't even told her that's what I want from her. I haven't gone all in with her. So what reason does she have to give me everything?

I haven't given her a reason to trust me that way.

Maybe I should.

"Indian it is," I answer. "When I was on a mission with my team in Sri Lanka, I had some of the best Indian food I've ever tasted. Since then, Indian food has been my favorite, even though it's hard to get it anywhere near as good in the States."

Curiosity plucks at the center of her forehead, giving her expression a cute Y in between her brows. "Were any of the NES guys on your SEAL team?"

I nod. "Bain was. Ben, Lawson, and Grisham Abbott from the Rescue Ops team all served together on the same SEAL team, but Bain and I were on a different one. The bond is that we were all SEALs. But not everyone who works at NES was. Once we join the team there, it doesn't really matter what our background was. You know?"

Frannie nods. "Like Sayward? She wasn't military, right?"

"Exactly. She's one of us, and she wasn't military at all. She proved herself on a mission a few months ago. Drug cartel in South America. She's been through some shit with her own family. We all have a story, and everyone has their own abilities and talents to offer. Jacob Owen realizes that, and he's willing to let people bring their own unique set of skills to the table."

Frannie's quiet for a minute. She peruses the Indian menu and points to what she wants, and I use my phone to order our food online. Then she asks me more of what's on her mind. "You must know Bain really well, then."

I chuckle. "I do. About as well as anyone can know Bain."

Her eyes narrow. "That's what I thought. He seems pretty closed off, and he's kinda scary. Where does that come from?"

For a minute, I'm taken back to a certain mission where Bain, the normally quiet, reserved SEAL, received a call from back home that changed him completely. He went on leave after that, and none of us expected him to return. He did, but he was never the same.

"Bain's been through more than any of us. He's a good guy, truly. But he's seen darker shit than most people should ever have to go through. I don't think he's ever recovered from it, and I'm not sure if he ever will."

Her eyes soften at the corners. "That's really sad. Grief and loss hit all of us at some point in our lives. I'm sorry that it had to happen to him."

"Yeah. He's a brother to me, so when it hits someone like that, someone who's that close to you, it's like it's hitting your heart too. And when you're already dealing with your own pain…"

I trail away, letting my words end with the ache suddenly taking hold in my chest.

Frannie's hand covers mine.

"What happened to Echo, Ryder?"

I expect the question to crush my heart, to turn it into dust inside my chest. Whenever I'm forced to think of Echo, to recall what happened to her that night in detail, it breaks me all over again. But I take a deep breath, and then another, and instead of reliving the pain associated with Echo's death, I remember the beauty that was associated with her life.

And that's how I know I can recount her story without breaking.

"I had a pretty normal childhood. Two parents, a sister three years younger than me. My mom was a teacher, Dad worked in insurance and worshipped the ground my mom walked on. My sister was what I'd call a free spirit, an artistic kid who did what she wanted when she felt like she needed to do it. I was the rule follower, made sure she was okay most of the time. Beat up kids who messed with her, that kind of thing."

Frannie smiles, like the thought of me kicking some kid's ass who messed with my little sister makes her happy. I smile too, because thinking about those days makes me happy. Echo was a precious part of my childhood; every good memory I've ever had has her in it.

"She fell in with the wrong crowd of kids when she got to high school. I knew it was happening, but there wasn't much I could do about it. I was three years ahead of her, and I had my own shit going on. Sports, and I always knew I'd join the military at some point. Then our mom got sick. Breast cancer. She got surgery. Thought she was getting better, then it came back. Went through chemo, and that shit came back aggressively. She went fast. My dad completely lost it. Checked out. Took the life insurance money and his life's savings and went on a bucket list trip. On his own. Went to see all the places my mom never got to see while she was alive. Echo was seventeen, still a senior in high school."

"Shit," Frannie murmurs.

"Right." My blood starts to boil when I think of my dad. I haven't spoken to him, contacted him, in so long. I don't know if I'll ever be able to forgive him for it. I never even contacted him when Echo died. Didn't think the bastard deserved to know. I'm sure he found out eventually, but it wasn't from me. And we aren't in contact now.

"I was left to pick up the pieces. Echo and my mom were so close; my sister went off the deep end. If I thought she was hanging out with the wrong crowd before, she went off the rails when Mom died. Moved in with a friend who was just as wild as she was. Started hanging out with dealers. It was bad, Frannie. And I was trying to check in with her, keep an eye on her. But at twenty years old, I was doing the best I could. I just couldn't keep my little sister in check. I should have done better. I should have kidnapped her, put her under lock and key."

I don't even realize how shallow my breaths are coming, how fast my heart is beating, until Frannie pulls me into her. My face presses against her chest, and her hand smooths over the back of my head as my tears wet the cotton of her dress.

"You had no way of knowing what would happen." Her voice is

firm. "Thorn, you were still a kid yourself. And God, you loved her. You loved her so fucking much. I can tell."

My body is shuddering, her arms wrapping around me as far as they'll go, and I'm caving in to her grasp like a little boy giving in to his own grief.

"I lost her one night, Frannie. I got a call from her, begging for my help. So I got in my car and drove to her apartment, and her roommate didn't even know where she was. And when I finally found her…"

I trail away, and the sobs rack my body. I can't breathe. *I can't fucking breathe.*

"Finish this, Thorn. You have to tell me what happened. So you can heal. What happened when you got there?"

My chest hurts. My whole body hurts. My mind takes me back there. Back to that fucking drug dealer's apartment. Back to my beautiful little sister, broken by her grief, lying on the floor in an apartment belonging to someone who didn't care about her. Crumpled in a ball on the floor. She called me. She called for help.

But I didn't make it in time.

"She was lying there, on the floor. She'd taken too many pills. She'd overdosed. I called 911. I did CPR. I tried everything I could until the ambulance got there. But she was already gone. My little sister, the light of my life, she was gone, Frannie. And I couldn't save her. Fuck, I couldn't save her."

The words break, and the sobs I can't control anymore break free.

Frannie grips me tight, and I let her.

Fuck me, I let her.

17

FRANNIE

This man is dismantling me. One tiny piece at a time. I don't know how to stop it. Or if I even want to.

Thorn Ryder is the strongest man I know. If given the chance, he'd take apart any man trying to hurt me and string him up by his balls. Then he'd interrogate him and find out why he was trying to hurt me, who sent him, and what it would take to get him to stop coming after me.

And yet he's showing me weakness.

And for this simple fact, I think I just fell for Thorn Ryder.

Never, in the years I spent with Eli Ward, had I seen him show me an ounce of weakness. He'd only been worried about showing me how tough he was, what a man he was. When he was controlling me, hurting me, dominating me, he was making sure he knew that he was in charge, in control.

But Thorn Ryder is completely different, and as I hold him and stroke his hair and whisper in his ear, I fall for him.

Recklessly. Involuntarily. And irrevocably.

And I think about Dove. How good he'll be for her. How wonderful she'll be for him. My little girl has healing powers. One look at her, one cuddle with her in his arms and it'll be like a balm for his heart. And suddenly, I *want that*. I want them to meet. I want to see if they're as compatible as Ryder and I seem to be. Because as much as I'm feeling for him right now, it's all for naught if he can't feel something for my Dove. And vice versa. The next step is for him to find out about her. And I don't want to keep her from him any longer.

I just have to get to her first. And make sure that she's okay. Make sure that she's prepared to meet him. Make sure that Lo knows that I'm going to be taking Dove back into my life, and that I have someone with me who can protect my baby. It'll be a transition for all of us, but hopefully one that everyone can handle.

A smooth transition. That's what we all need.

A chime sounds throughout the penthouse, announcing a visitor from the lobby, and Ryder sits up slowly, my hands reluctantly letting go of his hair one strand at a time.

"Food's here." He offers me a wry smile, hesitant and reluctant, and I beam at him in response.

"It is. And when we're finished eating, *I'll* still be here."

His eyes brighten. "Yeah?"

I reach out to touch his cheek. "Yeah."

His gaze takes hold of mine for a moment, reading it, capturing it, and he must understand what he sees there because he nods before he gets up and strolls to the elevator. He presses the intercom and lets up the deliveryman.

Five minutes later, he's spreading out the Indian food on the table, and we're digging in. I took some of his advice on new dishes he suggested we order, and it's all delicious.

"Mmm," I moan. "I think I have new favorites." I shove a piece of curried chicken into my mouth. "I promise to take your advice from here on out when it comes to ordering food."

One blond eyebrow arches as his fork pauses halfway to his mouth. "Just when it comes to ordering food?"

I nod solemnly. "Yes."

He laughs, drops his fork, and stands, advancing on me. I place my fork down on the table and scoot my chair back. When he's close, I turn and flee for the bedroom. I'm about to cross the threshold when Ryder catches me from behind. I squeal as he lifts me against his chest, wrapping me into strong, viselike arms. His lips graze my ear as he whispers. "Caught you."

My breath comes fast as a giggle bubbles up from my chest. "What are you going to do with me?"

"Oh, baby." His voice is low, dangerous, as he walks me forward until I'm pressed against the bedroom wall. "Everything."

"Oh," I breathe.

"Yeah," he whispers. "Oh."

He plants his palms against the wall on either side of my head, his breath hot and heavy against my neck. "Lift up that little dress you're wearing."

I do exactly as he says, pulling the dress up and over my head and allowing it to drop on the floor. There's a difference between the order Ryder gives me and the ones Eli used to give. With Ryder, there's no condescension in the commands. With every word he says, there's a choice. If I say no, or tell him that I don't want to, I have every confidence that he'll back off. That wasn't the case with Eli. He led me with fear, where Ryder leads me with pleasure and a kind of dominance that leads to excitement and pleasure that I can't wait to experience.

"That's my girl," Ryder growls close to my ear.

I shiver, his voice sending ripples of pleasure up and down my spine. "Damn, this thong is sexy as fuck." His hand flattens against my bare ass cheek, stroking my skin. "Do you know how fucking sexy you are?"

His nose rubs against my neck, caressing me as his lips create a trail against the soft skin of my neck. His left hand grips my hair, making a ponytail as he pulls it to one side, giving him easy access to one side of my neck. I didn't wear a bra with the sundress today, and the cool air catching my nipples makes them peak, as do the dirty words Ryder whispers in my ear.

"Been waiting all day to touch you," he murmurs against my ear. His right hand snakes around, two fingers reaching inside my underwear to trail through my center. They come away wet, and he groans.

"Wet for me. Fuck, baby…this is exactly what I needed." He switches to his left hand, using his fingers to dip inside me. I cry out, pushing back against him, feeling the rough ridge of his erection pushing back. With his right hand, he undoes the button of his jeans, flicking down his zipper and freeing himself from his pants. He runs his rock-hard cock down the seam of my ass, making me moan, and then dips his thick head into the wetness between my legs.

"Is this what you needed, Frannie?" His tone is serious, urgent. "Tell me you needed me as much as I needed you."

"Oh God…Ryder, yes."

I reach behind me, shoving so that his jeans fall down to his ankles. A low note of approval sounds in his throat. "That's my impatient girl. Let me get a condom on."

He bends, reaching for the pocket of his jeans. The next thing I know, he's spreading the cheeks of my ass so that he can reach my folds with his tongue. At the first lick, my legs start to tremble. At the second pass, I scream his name.

"Ryder!"

And as he takes the bud of my clit into his mouth and sucks, his hand squeezing my ass, my knees buckle. He stands, quickly sliding the condom on, and in one swift movement, fills me with a forceful shove. I brace my hands against the wall and stars dance against the backs of my eyes as my lids are forced shut.

Holy fuck, holy fuck, holy fuck. It's never been like this.

The size of him, the feel of him...everything Thorn Ryder surrounds me. The sound of his grunts filling my ears, the feel of his cock filling me to the brim, the scent of his sweat and cologne surrounding me and swirling inside my head...everything is him. It's almost too much. My walls start to clench almost immediately.

"That's it, baby...I want you to come for me. I want you to come so hard you remember it's me who made you scream my name and that's it. Just me. Only me." His words are a growl in my ear as his knees bend and he shoves upward, filling me again and again, until my body rocks and explodes.

"Thorn!" I scream, his name erupting from my lips in a way that I've never screamed before.

"Yes, fuck me, *yes*, Frannie..." Relentless, he rams into me again and again in a frenzy. He's lost control and I don't mind, because this is the Thorn Ryder who isn't holding back, who's showing me everything he's got.

And it's everything I want.

And when he's cresting over the edge, he pulls me close to his body, one hand over my breast, his mouth to my ear, and he chants my name over and over and over again as he peaks.

And God, it's everything.

It's everything.

After he's left me shaking against the wall to throw the condom away, he returns, scooping me into his arms and carrying me to our bed. He lays me down naked and pulls me in close beside him. As our breathing settles, he pushes my hair off my forehead and stares into my eyes.

"This isn't just sex for me. And I'm pretty sure you're not the kind of woman that it'd be just sex for you, either. So I'm going to lay it all out on the line. When I took you to see the kids today, that meant a lot for me."

I press my hands against either side of his face. "I could tell how much they mean to you. And God, that little Nevaeh. She was so sweet. And I can tell she's been through so much. She's missing a lot in life. She needs you, Ryder. It's so obvious. The fact that you let me into that fold…it meant a lot to me."

His hands wrap around my wrists. "It meant a lot to me too. Everything. Those kids picked up the pieces for me. They fill in the gaps where work can't. When I lost Echo I filled in the missing pieces, I healed with the military. And when I came back stateside, NES was waiting for me. It helped. But where it couldn't fix me, the kids did. And where the kids can't…God, Frannie. There's you. Where'd you come from? How'd you find me?"

I smile. "How'd you find me?" I pause. "After Eli…" I shudder. Ryder scowls. "After Eli, I never thought I'd be able to trust a man again. I thought there'd be guns, and there'd be…protecting myself and anyone else around me who needed protecting. I thought it was just me. From here on out. But then I met you. And the whole NES team. Everything changed. I don't know how it happened, but you made me fall for you. And I'm scared shitless, but I'm willing to try. Okay? I'm willing to try."

"I lost my whole world a long time ago," he admits. "And since then, I swore to myself that if I ever found it again, I wouldn't be afraid to admit it."

I hold my breath.

"So don't let this send you running, Pistol Annie, because I'd really like you to stay. I'm pretty sure I love you."

18

RYDER

During the following days, Frannie and I stay close to home. She seems more content with being inside the condo, getting used to ordering meals in and hanging out by the pool. And I can't complain about seeing her in her bikini most of the day, every day. The words that I offered her four nights ago hang between us, but they aren't awkward or heavy. Instead, every time Frannie looks at me, she tilts her head to the side and smiles this secret smile. But instead of making me uneasy, whatever it is she's thinking about fills me with elation for what might be coming in our future.

And just as often as she's wearing that bikini, she's *not* wearing it. Not gonna lie, I'm a big fan of naked Frannie. In the kitchen, on the couch, or in our bedroom, I knew damn well there was a reason I gave her the nickname Pistol Annie. She's a little pistol in and out of bed, and keeping up with her is becoming my sole reason for breathing.

I've just peeled her bathing suit off her and sat her on the bathroom counter, checking her stitches to make sure they've healed the way Dr. Hughes said they would. She no longer needs the bandage, and the puckered skin beneath her ribs looks healthier every day. The shower water runs behind me, making the bathroom fill with clouds of vapor that leaves slippery droplets on her naked skin.

Pulling back, I drink her in. She stares right back, blue eyes hooded with the lust I've learned to read on her expression like lines in a script. Reaching up, I pull the elastic band out of her hair, bringing the blond-and-pink strands cascading down around her shoulders. She doesn't move, leaning back against the mirror, her eyebrows lifting in a challenge.

A dark chuckle breaks free from my lips. "What do you want, sweetheart? You know you drive me insane." I glance down, the obvious erection tenting my swim trunks making itself known.

Her small hands push the waistband of my shorts until I'm exposed, my dick springing free and straining toward her, long and thick and hard.

"Just you," she whispers, staring at the drizzle of moisture dampening the tip. "I want you, Ryder. I trust you."

Her words do something to me, pulling a groan from deep inside me. Pulling the tangled vines of emotion inside my heart, the ones I buried a long time ago, right to the surface. Making me unafraid.

"I love you," I tell her, seriously.

A smile tugs on her lips. Genuine emotion swims in her gaze. "Be patient with me."

"Always."

Leaning my forehead against hers and gripping the back of her neck with one hand, I drag two fingers between her legs. Humming in my throat, I push inside her. "So fucking wet for me, baby. So goddamn hot."

Her voice is breathless. "Only for you, Ryder. You know that, right?"

Pulling my fingers out slowly, I press my thumb against her clit. She whimpers. "Say it again."

Frannie's lashes flutter as her eyes drop closed. "I'm yours, Thorn. Only yours."

Those words... *those fucking words*.

"Wrap your legs around me." The words are no more than a growl as I grip her tightly in my arms and walk toward the shower. Stepping inside the steaming sauna, I sit on the bench and set Frannie down on top of me.

The sound of the water mingles with our moans as it becomes the best shower of my entire fucking life.

Our bed has become our favorite place in the condo. I'm stroking her hair as her small fingers dance across my bare chest, silence settling around us as the room grows dark with the night.

"Not sure what we're gonna do when this is all over. All we do is fuck, chill by the pool, and lie in bed. Real life is coming soon, sweetheart." There's a smile in my voice, but Frannie's silent. Her fingers still.

"Hey." I glance down at her, trying to read her expression in the dark. "What's going on?"

"What's your place like? And where is it?"

I shrug. "Nothing fancy. I own a loft near NES. Studio. I bought it because it's close to work and the beach. It's a drive when I go volunteer with the kids, but that's okay. I like being close to the water."

Frannie's face falls. "My apartment is on the other side of town. And it's not very big, either. Just a two-bedroom."

A slow grin almost splits my face in two. "I know, I met you outside of that apartment. Are you saying you like our living arrangement so much right now, you want to continue it when we get out of here?"

Her expression goes shy. "I'm not sure if you're going to want that. Let's wait and see."

Confusion clouds my brain. "Nothing's gonna change how I feel about you between now and then. We can get a place together. Something that's right for just the two of us. Yeah?"

Her expression falls again. "I—"

My phone vibrates on the side table. I reach for it. "Hold that thought, sweetheart."

Glancing at the screen, I frown and sit up. My chest tightens as I swipe across to answer the call. "Nevaeh? What's going on, honey?"

The young girl's voice on the other end of the phone sounds terrified. "Mr. Ryder? He—he's back."

Swinging my legs off the side of the bed, I put the phone on speaker so that Frannie can hear. I don't want to have to explain it to her when I end the call. "Where are you, Nevaeh?"

Her voice sounds muffled, quietly horrified. She hiccups, like she's been crying. "I'm in my closet, like you told me to do. I have the phone that you gave me. H-he doesn't know that I'm here yet. But my mom…" She hiccups. In the background, I can hear a man's voice shouting, and then a woman's voice replying in kind.

Frannie's quiet gasp and "Oh my God" have me glancing at her with a grim expression.

"Nevaeh, listen to me. You did good. Very good. I want you to hang up with me and call 911. And I promise you I'm on my way. Don't come out of the closet. Don't make a sound. And if he comes for you before I get there, do exactly what he says. I'm coming, honey. It's going to be okay."

I end the call and pull on my jeans. I immediately dial Bain.

"Need you to get over here *now* and stay with Frannie. I have a situation with one of my kids that can't wait."

Bain grunts and ends the call, which lets me know he's on his way.

I turn to Frannie, who's staring at me with wide eyes, her hands to her mouth. "I'd take you with me if it weren't for the fucking Eli situation. As it is, I'm not bringing you into another dangerous situation. Nevaeh's old man is an abuser, and he's apparently just gotten out of jail for the third time. He hits her mother, and sometimes her too. When he's drunk, he's a mean asshole. I'm going over there. There's a chance her mom's high on something, and I have no idea what I'm walking into."

I place my Glock into my holster and pull my shirt on over it. Placing a kiss on Frannie's forehead, I look her in the eye. "Don't move a muscle until Bain gets here, you hear me?"

She nods. "Please help her, Ryder. I feel for that girl. Get her out of there."

My expression is grim. "This time, I think that's going to be the only thing I can do."

Grabbing one of Frannie's guns from where we placed them in the kitchen drawer that first day, I put it on the nightstand beside her. She grins at me. I smile back at her. "You won't need that. Bain's coming. But I know you like to be armed."

I kiss her hard on the lips before turning and walking out of the bedroom and onto the elevator. I'm in the BMW and driving toward the wrong side of town, trying not to let the memories of a similar phone call nine years ago mess with my head.

It's not the same. It's not the same.

Nevaeh is not Echo. Nevaeh isn't spiraling out of control. She called me for help because she wants it, not because she wanted to see if I would still come running when she needed me. I've known about Nevaeh's situation for a while. There just hasn't been anything I could do, because she isn't yet a ward of the state. Her mother and father still have parental rights, somehow. But I know that this time, this incident, as long as she calls 911 the way I instructed her to, will get her removed from the home.

And that's what I've been waiting for.

On the way to her house, I call Lawson on Bluetooth.

"What's up, man? If you're calling about Ward—"

I cut him off. "I'm not. Not right now, anyway."

Lawson goes quiet.

"I need a favor."

Lawson must hear something in my voice, because his answer is immediate. "Name it."

"Call your sister for me? One of the kids I work with at the club is having domestic issues with her parents. I think she's about to get removed from the home. I've already had paperwork done so I can become her foster parent. But I can't take her with me right now because of everything that's going on with Frannie. Do you think Lilliana can find a place for her to go tonight?"

Lawson's sister runs a nonprofit agency for battered women who are running away from abusive husbands; it's called the Underground. She's actually the one who helped Frannie when she first arrived in North Carolina, although none of us knew it when Frannie first met Lawson and Indigo.

There's a smile in Lawson's voice when he answers. "If Indy and I weren't hot on Ward's trail right this minute, we'd take her ourselves until this mess was all over. Meantime, I'll send Lilliana with the social worker she knows. They'll get your girl all straightened out. You on your way there now? The little girl gonna be all right?"

I expel a breath as I blow through a yellow light, entering the rougher side of town. "God, I fucking hope so, Sleuth. I'm scared. And I left Frannie with Bain, which I don't exactly feel good about either."

Lawson's voice is calming, like it always is. "Bain's got your girl. She *is* your girl now, right?"

I don't say a fucking word.

Lawson chuckles. "Yeah. Thought so. We all saw it that day at the house. Bull's-Eye will keep her safe for you while you go handle your business. And Lilliana will meet you there. Text me the address when we get off here."

"Will do. Thanks, Sleuth."

We disconnect the call, and five minutes later, I'm turning onto the block where Nevaeh lives. It's a neighborhood of run-down town houses, mostly rentals, cars taking up spaces in the lots on both sides of the street. The front door at Nevaeh's house is wide open, and there's no sign of police yet.

Leaving the BMW parked by the curb instead of in a parking spot, I draw my Glock and jog to the door, sticking close to the front of the house. All the lights are blazing, and I can hear Nevaeh's drunk father yelling as I walk into the home.

Kitchen.

Stealthily bypassing the two adults yelling in the direction of the kitchen, the sound of breaking glass raising the hairs on the back of my neck, I move silently up the stairs. Nevaeh's described the house to me enough times that I have the layout memorized, even though I've never been here. Going directly to her room at the end of the hall, I whisper her name instead of turning on the lights.

"Nevaeh. It's me, honey. I'm coming to the closet. Don't be afraid…I'm getting you out."

I'm two steps away from the closet door when it's flung open and she hurtles out of the darkness and into my arms. Moonlight from the window streams onto her face, shining a spotlight on her fear.

Quiet sobs rack Nevaeh, and I just hold her close to my chest. "Hey, it's okay. I've got you. I've got you."

I smooth her hair, then lean down to look in her face. "You hurt?"

She shakes her head, almost frantic. Another scream erupts from downstairs, and the sound of furniture being knocked over.

Shit. She's been sitting in that closet, listening to this for half an hour.

The unmistakable sound of a fist hitting skin, and a woman's cry. Nevaeh looks up at me, terror bleeding into her expression. I place a finger to my lips, even though fury threatens to explode my chest.

We're leaving, I mouth silently.

She nods. I push her behind me and we walk quietly down the darkened hallway until we reach the stairs. The sound of sirens outside alerts us to the fact that the police have finally arrived. Relief floods me, but I still have to get this girl out of the house before—

A gunshot rings through the house. The sound of a body slumping to the floor. Behind me, Nevaeh's high-pitched scream rings in my ears.

Turning, I grab her and pick her up, holding her against my chest. Neither of us saw what happened, but we both know.

Her father just shot her mother.

We're halfway down the stairs when two things happen simultaneously. Her father comes stumbling out of the kitchen, a shotgun propped in his hands. And two police officers burst through the front door, screaming at him to put the weapon down.

Instead of doing that, the drunken coward raises that shotgun.

I whirl with Nevaeh in my arms and turn toward the top of the stairs. Another gunshot rings out, and I hope to God one of the officers was able to bring him down without a fatal shot, before he brought that shotgun to his own head.

19

FRANNIE

When the elevator doors slide open to reveal Bain's presence, I've been pacing the wood floor in the wide-open main room for what feels like forever. But in all honesty, Bain arrived at the penthouse so quickly, he must have already been in the vicinity.

I stop midpace. "Have you heard from him?"

Bain steps into the penthouse, his crystal blue eyes seeming to assess everything at once. The last thing they land on is me. Finally, he answers my question. "No."

Covering my face with my palms, I scream into my fingers. "This is so frustrating! What if he's not okay? What if Nevaeh's hurt? What if—"

Bain stalks toward me, placing both hands on my shoulders, and stops me cold. I'm so shocked by his touch that I freeze on impact. He stares at me, his expression firm. "In our business, we don't deal in what-ifs. The White Wolf is a trained killer. Do you understand what that means? It means he didn't walk into that situation without being completely prepared to walk out of it with that girl in his arms. Alive and well."

Those are the words I needed to hear. The first deep breath I've taken since those elevator doors slid closed on Ryder enters and exits my lungs.

"Thank you," I say quietly.

Without another word, Bain releases me and walks away, going to stand in front of the bookcase beside the fireplace. I watch as he selects a book from the third shelf, then sits down in an armchair that neither Ryder nor I has ever sat in and opens it up to the first page.

He begins to read.

Huh. So Bain is a reader. Wouldn't have guessed that one.

I pause by the dining table, planting my fists against my hips. "So you're just going to sit there and read?"

Bain doesn't even glance up. "Reading is how I pass the time. Quiet. Allows me to listen. Which is a big part of protection detail."

I stalk to the bar and grab my phone from where I left it the last time I checked it, right before Bain walked in. Still no call or text from Ryder. My Photos icon catches my eye, and I click on it. The first photo that comes up in my camera roll is the selfie that Ryder and I took today sitting on a lounger together at the pool. I was between his legs, and we were both wearing sunglasses. The plant of his lips on my cheek, his chiseled cheekbones, and the big smile on my face give us the illusion of being any normal, happy couple.

Emotion, raw and real, stabs at my heart.

I want that. I want this life with him.

Whatever happens when this is all over, I know that I want to move forward in a life with Ryder. He loves me. And even though I haven't said the words yet, I know I love him. The only reason I haven't told him is because I know it wouldn't be fair to tell him that truth when I'm still keeping the most important part of my life from him.

My daughter.

But that's all going to change. Soon.

What if he doesn't want a daughter? What if he isn't ready for kids?

The nagging voice in the back of my head pokes a finger at me, shoving doubts into my consciousness.

But if I want a life with him, I have to go for it. All I can do is put myself out there and try. Dove is amazing…who could resist her?

The chime that announces the arrival of a visitor from the lobby sounds through the penthouse. I shoot toward the elevator, but Bain moves faster than I thought possible, blocking my forward motion and bodily moving me into the hallway leading toward the bedroom.

"Stay. Here," he growls. "We're not expecting anyone."

"But it might be Ry—" My voice trails away as I realize too late how ridiculous I sound.

Immediately, I whirl on my heel and walk to the bedroom. Listening as Bain asks who our visitor is over the smart intercom system, I pull my pistol from the nightstand and carry it with me back out into the hallway.

By time I make it there, pistol gripped in both hands and ready to use if needed, the elevator door is sliding open.

Lawson and Indigo walk into the penthouse and take one look at me with my gun aimed at the floor by my side. Indigo gives me a huge grin and a thumbs-up, and Lawson lifts his chin in approval. "I'm assuming Thorn knows about this?" He gestures toward my gun.

I nod, glancing at it. "He made me put them both away at first."

Bain turns toward me, eyes my gun, and an incredulous expression crosses his face before irritation quickly follows.

"You know I'm here to protect you, right?"

I raise my chin an inch. "I protect myself."

Lawson chuckles.

Bain rolls his eyes. Indigo jabs her elbow into Lawson's ribs. I turn and walk back down the hallway to put my gun away.

When I return, Russ has appeared from the elevator just before the doors slide closed.

Bain scowls. "What's he doing here?"

Lawson glances behind him. "Jacob knows he's here. We had a breakthrough in the Ward case—"

Russ interrupts, stepping forward and glancing around the penthouse. "The Ward case you aren't actually supposed to be working, you mean."

Indigo puts her hand on Russ's shoulder. "Russ, please. You know how good Lawson is at this stuff. You said you'd keep an open mind."

Lawson shoots both Bain and I a *look* before heading for the couch. "Let's sit. I have some things to say. Bull's-Eye, you can fill Wolf in when he gets back."

Bain nods, moving back to his chair. I notice his eyes don't leave Russ, though.

Lawson leans forward. "This is a quick visit. We just thought Frannie deserved to know that Indigo and I found where Ward's been hiding."

I sit up straighter, my mouth dropping open. "Really? Where?"

Indigo rolls her eyes. "Are you ready for this? He's been holed up at the Four Seasons. He's been staying under a false name. He's there as we speak, and the cavalry is getting ready to ride in."

The air deflates out of me. "I knew it. I knew he wouldn't be hiding down in some underground, seedy world. That's not Eli. He's always thought he deserves better than he actually does."

Indigo squeezes my knee. "You told us."

Lawson nods, clasping his hands together. "Yeah, you did. Planting that bug in our ear during that meeting made Indy and I start looking in some different places. Checking out some aliases."

I nod slowly. "So this could be over tonight?"

Russ shakes his head. "This is far from over. We're just getting started with Eli Ward. Posting charges, the whole nine. It's going to be a long road."

I sigh. "Yeah, I guess so. I don't really want to be a part of it."

"I can understand that," Russ states. "But eventually, we might need you to testify. So we'll be in touch."

I'm suddenly really missing Ryder. I'm missing his warmth, his arms around me, and the way he always has my back, no matter what.

"Whatever you need to make him go away for good."

Russ's eyes flash. "That's all I've wanted to do since he first came to my town. Make him go away for good."

Indigo leans back against the couch cushions. "Shit. That's all any of us wants. Eli Ward has been like one long horror movie I just want to end."

Lawson grabs her hand, intertwining their fingers. "We're approaching the credits. Let's go."

Russ, Lawson, and Indigo stand, and Bain walks them to the elevator. I stay seated on the couch, still stewing in shock at the fact that Eli is about to be caught and sent to prison for what I hope will be the rest of his life.

Dove and I are about to be free.

All I can think about is the life I'm going to live with Ryder, and introducing him to my little girl.

When the elevator doors slide closed behind our visitors, Bain stares at me with an assessing glare.

"What?" I finally snap.

"*Two* guns?"

20

RYDER

Nevaeh won't leave my side. Not while she's being questioned by the female police officer about what she's witnessed between her parents, or after Lilliana arrives.

She flinches every time someone comes near her, and I know the long road to recovery after the trauma of this night is going to be hell.

We're sitting in the back of an ambulance at the end of her street. I have one arm around her shoulders, while the paramedic takes her vitals and makes sure that there's nothing more serious than shock going on for her, healthwise.

Finally, the investigator's questions are finished. Nevaeh turns her head into my neck and sobs ensue. Big, racking sobs.

"My mom's dead," she wails. Her tears soak my shirt, and all I want is to wrap her up and carry her far, far away from here.

Far from the life that caused a child of eleven to deal with a burden like this. With a loss like this. With an upbringing where she spent a second feeling unsafe, unloved, unsure of what was going to happen next. She deserves so much more than that.

And I'm hoping Frannie and I can give it to her.

I haven't told Nevaeh yet that I've filled out the paperwork to become her foster parent. And there's no way that I plan on that being temporary. Once she becomes mine, to me, that'll be forever. It doesn't matter how long that paperwork takes.

I let her cry, rubbing her back and whispering soothing words in her ear. I meet Lillianna's eye and see the heartbreak there. Lawson's sister is used to dealing with battered women, but children who've been through the kind of shit Nevaeh has just endured aren't her norm. The sadness in her eyes reflects the shattering I feel in my chest.

"Listen to me." I pull back once Nevaeh's sobs have subsided. "You're gonna be okay, Nevaeh. You have me. There are people who care about you."

She sucks in a shuddering breath. "What about my dad? Is he going back to jail?"

Nevaeh's dad was shot in the shoulder by police officers. He was then taken away in an ambulance. I kept Nevaeh shielded from the entire scene on the stairs and didn't let her come down until her mother was wheeled out of the house on a stretcher and her father was out of the home.

"Your dad will be incarcerated again, yes," I admit to her, my tone serious. "But that doesn't mean you're alone. Nevaeh, would you like to come and live with me?"

She looks at me in shock. "You…you want me to live with you?"

I nod. "No doubt. I've already filled out the paperwork to make it happen. It can't happen right away, but if we give it a couple of weeks, you should be able to come and live with me and Frannie. How does that sound?"

She throws her arms around my neck. My heart does that thing again where it goes all warm and mushy. "Thank you, Thorn. For everything."

I lift her chin. "But you gotta do something for me. Tonight, you need to go with Lilliana here. She's a good friend of mine. Her brother works with me, and I trust her. You'll be safe with her. Deal? I'll come and see you soon."

Nevaeh takes a deep breath. "Okay. I'll do that for you."

I nod. "Good girl."

When I walk back into the penthouse, Frannie rockets into my arms. I catch her; my arms wrap around her back while her legs wind around my waist. My holster thuds against the cement countertop as I remove its weight from my hip, and she settles more firmly against me. She squeezes my neck so hard it hurts, but I don't care. She feels so damn good in my arms, and in all the commotion of the last two hours I spent with Nevaeh, I'm just relieved to have Frannie safe in my sight again.

Bain clears his throat after a minute, and Frannie slips down my body but stays beside me, leaning into my long frame. My arm snakes around her slim waist and pulls her even closer to my side. She sighs, the same relief that I'm feeling pouring out of her.

I extend a fist to Bain, who bumps it. "Thanks for keeping her safe."

Bain lifts his chin. "We had some visitors while you were gone."

Every muscle in my body goes rigid. "What?"

Glancing around the penthouse, I zero in on every surface, checking for signs of trouble. A fight, a struggle, anything out of place. But everything looks exactly the way I left it, even though now it's the middle of the night.

Frannie rubs my arm. "Not like that."

Bain meets my gaze head-on. "Sleuth and Indy brought Russ Walker with them to let us know that they'd found Ward. WPD is probably going into the Four Seasons where he's been staying and arresting him as we speak."

Elation bubbles up inside my chest and I toss my head back and roar with laughter. Picking Frannie up again, I whirl her around in a circle, looking up at her with triumph in my eyes. "Did you hear that, Pistol Annie? Tomorrow, you, me, and our guns are all going house hunting!"

She squeals, her eyes crinkling at the corners from the laughter and joy telling a story all across her face.

"Oh my God," she cries. "I can't even believe this is finally over. Ryder…"

Frannie's plump bottom lip loses color as her teeth clamp down gently on it, and her eyes go hooded the way they always do when…

She slides down my body just before her feet hit the floor, electricity and need following with every brush of her skin against mine, and I slam my lips against her. I don't need to hear the next part of her sentence. In the background, the elevator doors slide open.

A quiet "Be ready to debrief tomorrow" comes from Bain right before the doors close on him and Frannie and I are alone. Our mouths still fused together, our hands are frantic as they move over each other, not knowing where to touch first. Her hands slip up underneath my snug-fitting T-shirt, and my body shivers in response. Her touch is everything I need; maybe it's everything I'll ever need. The prospect of our lives together flip and flash in my brain like a movie, and it's the most perfect fucking thing I've ever seen.

Cock hard and throbbing, I unzip my jeans and walk us backward until we're falling over the side of the couch, me softening Frannie's fall with my body.

She straddles me, planting her hands against my chest to sit up and pulling the hem of her T-shirt over her head. With a tender smile that steals my breath, she glances down at me. "I have something important to tell you."

As I look up at her, one side of my mouth kicks up because *damn*, this woman is beautiful. The shine from the recessed lighting behind her leaves her blond-and-pink hair backlit, and as she stares down at me I swear I'm looking at an angel.

I lay both palms over her full breasts. Pulling the cups of her lacy black bra down, I lift up on my elbows and suck one strawberry nipple into my mouth. She moans, arching into me, and my hands caress her bare back. She rubs her hips restlessly against the rough fabric of my jeans, trying to feel the friction against her needy pussy.

"Same, sweetheart. But I need to be inside you first."

The elevator doors slide open again.

Frannie dives for the floor in front of the couch, blocked from view of the elevator, to search for her T-shirt.

"Goddamn, Bull's Eye—"

But it isn't Bain who walks through those elevator doors.

The doors slide closed behind Russ Walker.

From the somber expression on his face, I know that either the arrest tonight didn't go as planned, or something bad happened to someone on my team. I shoot to my feet, moving faster and more efficiently than I should be able to. I glance to make sure that Frannie's okay on the floor, and she offers me a sheepish thumbs-up as she throws her shirt on in the privacy the couch gives her.

"Walker? What's up? I thought you were supposed to be arresting Ward tonight."

He stops walking just inside the foyer and pulls his gun.

All of my instincts, the ones I developed during my training as a SEAL and the ones I was born with, whir and communicate with one another at once. And nothing good can come of this situation.

Nothing.

My voice is calmer than it should be when I place both hands in the air. I shift to one side, positioning myself in the opening between where Frannie is still on the floor and Russ Walker. "What's going on here, Russ? What do you want?"

Frannie's looking up at me with a mixture of confusion and panic. I shake my head slightly at her, because from his angle by the elevator, Russ hasn't seen her yet, unless he caught her rolling off the couch when he first came in.

My mind goes to my holster, sitting on the kitchen island mere feet away. I walked into the penthouse. If I could get to it now, I could take Russ out before he could make any stupid decisions.

But I still don't know why the fuck he's here.

Russ doesn't move. His revolver stays pointing solidly at my chest. "You can't Night Eagle your way out of this one, Ryder. You can't protect her this time. Not this time."

My skin goes clammy, my blood running slower in my veins. "What are you talking about?"

Russ raises his voice, keeping his eyes and his gun locked on me. "Frannie? We need to go now. Eli's waiting, and he wants his daughter and his wife back before he heads to the Swiss Alps."

Frannie cries out, and before I can make a move to stop her, she flies to her feet. I move to block her from rounding the couch, but Russ shakes his head at me, slowly turning his gun on Frannie.

I freeze.

I glance back and forth between the two of them, and my mouth moves faster than my brain does as I try to catch up. "Is Ward fucking batshit? She lost their baby. What, he wants to kidnap her and pretend like that never happened? Like he didn't *beat a damn pregnancy out of her*?"

Rage, so hot and so dangerous it bleeds into my vision, blooms through my entire body. Frannie and I have never gone there, never talked about the baby she lost. I'm not even sure if she's finished grieving, or if she ever will be. It's one of the reasons I've been so hesitant to bring up the fact that I want to adopt Nevaeh, because I'm not sure if she's ready for kids after everything she went through with losing her own child.

Russ's eyes widen a fraction as he looks between Frannie and me. Frannie is standing there in front of the couch, out in the open, and every instinct I have tells me to grab her and throw her behind me. I want to go after Russ with everything I have, not caring if I take a bullet in the process. But I can't do that when she's standing between us.

Goddammit, Frannie!

"She didn't tell you?" True surprise colors Russ's tone. "I thought you two…"

The words explode from me in a roar I can't control. "*Tell me what?*"

Russ offers Frannie a sympathetic smile. "When were you gonna tell him? We're on a short time frame here. You have thirty seconds to say what you need to say, and then we're leaving. I'm sure that little baby of yours would rather have her mommy than the man I have with her right now."

A cry of fury escapes Frannie's small frame, so big and angry it shakes her whole body. "You *bastard*! Where is my little girl?"

I want to take a step back. A big one. My mind is reeling with questions, with disappointment, with regret. Because I can't believe the words that just came out of the mouth of the woman I love.

Russ points to his watch. Frannie turns to me.

"I have to go with him, Ryder."

I'll be damned if I watch you walk out that door.

My voice is flat. "You're not going anywhere. And he's not getting out of this penthouse alive."

I mean it. She has a lot of explaining to do right now, but there's no fucking way I'm letting her leave with him. And no one walks into my house and tries to walk out of it with my girl. I'm going to make him eat bullets. And I'm going to enjoy it.

She shakes her head, the urgency plain on her face. Walking over to me, she places her hands on either side of my face. "I was going to tell you. I wasn't sure that she'd be safe…not with Eli out there. But tonight, after I found out that it was all over…God. Now it isn't, is it? And she's not safe."

Her words are coming out in a jumbled mess, but her hands are hot on my cheeks and there are tears pooling in her eyes.

Fuck me, I don't want her to cry. And I don't want that bastard pointing a gun at her right now!

She sniffs and takes a deep breath. "I'm walking out of here with him, Ryder, because I didn't have a miscarriage. I faked it after Eli beat me up. I pretended I lost the baby, and then I ran. I disappeared, found the Underground, and made a life for myself here in Wilmington. Then I had Dove. She's my little girl."

I blink, staring at her. Frannie's a mom? She has a baby? The miscarriage was a lie? My mind is spinning, and I want to sit down, but I can't fucking sit down right now.

"It doesn't fucking matter." I grit my teeth. "Do you know what I do? Do you know who I work for? We take him out." I tilt my head toward Walker, who stiffens. "And then we find your little girl. It's *what we do.*"

She drops her hands from my face. "I can't do that. Not when it's *my* little girl."

She turns to Russ. "I have her diaper bag in the bedroom. Do you want to walk with me to come and get it, or can I just go?"

He shakes his head. "No diaper bag. Let's go."

Frannie's lips thin and her eyes flash with irritation. "You and Eli know nothing about Dove, do you? She's diabetic. She needs insulin injections. I keep them in the diaper bag, and I'll also get them from the woman she's staying with so we'll have plenty for travel. If you don't let me get the bag, we won't have enough. How's Eli going to react when he finds that out?"

Russ pauses and then scowls. He gestures toward the bedroom. "Make a move, Frannie, and your bodyguard gets a bullet to his brain."

A growl rumbles in my chest. "Not even going to give you the courtesy. I'll kill you slowly."

She turns back to me. "You know me, Ryder. You need to trust me."

Her eyes are full of sincerity, but I can't see any of it. She didn't trust me enough to tell me that she has a *child*. I've been protecting her for weeks, and this little fact never came up.

It's Echo all over again.

And I'm going to lose her, the same way I lost my sister.

21

FRANNIE

I know for a fact that Ryder won't let me walk out of this penthouse with Russ Walker. He'll throw himself in front of a bullet for me first. But I *need* to go. For me as a mother, it isn't an option. And I can't live with myself if something happens to Thorn Ryder as a result of my decision.

I hope he understands what I'm about to do.

Russ and Ryder are still facing off as I walk past the coffee table toward the hallway. Picking up the heavy dish that sits in the middle of the table, I swing it hard at the back of Ryder's head.

When it makes contact, the sound of metal against bone makes my stomach roll. Ryder pitches sideways onto the couch and lies still. Nausea roils, threatening to overtake me. Hurting Ryder is the last thing I want to do, but he would have done anything to stop me from going. And I know, beyond a doubt, that I have to go.

The sick feeling doesn't go away as my eyes take in Ryder's unconscious form, worry gnawing at my gut. *He'll have a concussion...he'll need medical attention.*

Russ Walker looks impressed. "I can still shoot him, you know."

I glare at him over my shoulder on my way down the hall. "But you won't."

Once I'm in the bedroom, I move quickly in case Russ decides to make a trip down the hallway and check on me. Dove isn't diabetic, but I throw in my medical bag with needles and syringes and hope that's enough to convince him for a short time. I tuck the pistol from the nightstand into a secure double-zip compartment in the side of the diaper bag that's meant to keep bottles refrigerated. This bag appears, from the outside, to be an ordinary backpack. No one would know its true purpose unless they opened it, and Ryder never did. I slide two burner phones into the opposite zipper compartment on the other side.

I might be going to get my little girl a bit earlier than expected, but I won't be leaving the country with Eli Ward tonight. Not if I can help it.

Slinging the bag over my shoulder, I head back out into the living room. "Let's go."

He uses his gun to gesture toward the elevator, which means I should enter before he does. I take one last glance at Ryder, unconscious on the floor, and send up two prayers toward heaven: *Please don't let me have hit him too hard. Please let him wake up. Please let him forgive me. For all of it.*

The elevator ride into the parking garage is silent. It's surreal: I've pictured something like this happening a million times since I left Eli. Only it was always Eli who came to call, never a police officer I trusted with my life.

Even though he's taking me to meet my abusive husband, whom I fled from more than a year ago after he nearly killed me, Russ Walker is acting like this is a part of his daily duties. He's not hurried, he's not agitated. He does glance around him often as we enter the parking garage.

"Any other NES operatives on duty tonight?" he asks as we walk down one of the aisles.

I shake my head. "The only one assigned to protect me is Ryder. He was gone earlier this evening to handle some personal business, so he asked Bain to look after me. Bain left before you arrived."

"I know." Russ leads us to a Ford SUV and opens the driver's side. "Get in and climb over."

I do, mindful of the fact that I'm wearing super-short cotton shorts meant for sleeping, and then realize how stupid that is. There's more at stake here than Russ catching a peek of my ass. I drag the navy paisley-patterned diaper bag with me.

Russ gets in the driver's seat and guns the engine, keeping his revolver in his hand as he pulls out of the space. "I was watching. And then I walked right onto that private elevator and used the security code I stole when I cloned Snyder's phone. Being close enough to Indigo to gain access to that phone was all I needed, along with the location of the safe house." He glances at me, no regret in his eyes.

"Why are you doing this?" The words blurt out of my mouth before I can stop them. I don't want to be the heroine in some action flick, asking the bad guy why he's being the bad guy.

Why do any of them do it? Money. Right? Why else?

So I answer my own question. "Eli's paying you."

Russ swings the SUV left out of the luxury complex, heading away from the oceanfront and the main part of town altogether. "We'll talk about that if you want to, Frannie, but right now I need you to get on the phone. Tell whoever has your daughter to meet us at the gas station across from the entrance to the Ellis Airport in Richlands. We're about forty miles away, so that'll give her time to get there. When Ward located information on you, tracing you to Wilmington, he did everything he could to figure out what made you come here, of all places. He was pleasantly surprised when one of the women you went to high school with back in Oklahoma remembered that you were friends with a women who now lives here. After that, it was easy to find an address. But when he found her, he never imagined that the baby living with her was his own daughter. Until the man he has watching the house in Jacksonville saw you show up. It's just too damn bad he lost you before he could follow you back to that fancy penthouse."

My pulse races hot underneath my skin. "If you already know where she is, then why didn't you grab her the way you said you did?" My voice trembles with underlying fury and fear and the injustice of this entire situation.

Russ turns onto the highway that will lead us out of Wilmington. I bite back my panic, fighting the urge to glance behind us. I'm on my own now; it's up to me to save myself. Ryder did a great job protecting me while he had the chance, but this is between Eli and me. The way it always has been.

I tried to keep Dove out of the middle of it, but her involvement was unavoidable. I swallow down foul-tasting bile and focus on Russ.

When Russ speaks again, his voice is quieter. "Money. It's always going to be an issue for people like me. People like you. We serve. We work our whole lives for a pension. And me...I happened to have a weakness for sports. Gambled away my retirement money on football games. Made some bad bets. I've been trying damn hard to make that right."

I clamp down on my response. *Don't compare yourself to me. I'm nothing like you.*

"I'm doing this because I'll never make the kind of money doing what I do, protecting and serving, in a whole lifetime on the force that I will on this one job for a scumbag like Ward. I wanted him out of my town, and this is the way I'm going to do it and allow some of my officers to cash out in the process. He made millions off of those cars, do you understand that? I only need some of it to pay off my debt."

"I understand the kind of dirty money he made," I spit. "It cost me everything. My parents were blinded by that money too. It allowed them to overlook the fact that he treated their daughter like shit, just so they could be filthy rich and live the lifestyle they always wanted."

Russ turns sad eyes on me. "Well, I'm sorry for that. I truly am. I don't want to hurt you or your daughter. In all honesty, I'm hoping that once you all get to where you're going, you can find a way to get away from him like you did once before. But I have to get a job done here. My officers will 'lose' Ward on the way from the hotel to lockup, and one of them will bring him to the airport in Richlands. It's the middle of nowhere. There's a private plane waiting, ready to fly you straight out of the country. Ward will be gone. The money will be transferred into my account from the plane. And I told Eli I wouldn't do this unless he swore to me he wouldn't hurt you or your little girl—"

I slap him. The car swerves left as his head is forced to one side at the impact of the blow, and my hand stings. It doesn't matter, though.

I'm numb.

"Stop talking," I order.

He obliges, using the back of his hand to wipe the spittle running out of the side of his mouth. It's the first time I've seen him show any emotion other than his fake-ass fatherly sympathy for me. Anger seethes just beneath the surface, and I'm happy to see it. It means he's exactly the monster he's trying to pretend he isn't.

He hands me a cell phone. "Call her," he orders, his voice indicating he's run out of patience with me.

Snatching the phone from his hand, I dial Lobelia's number from memory.

She answers right away, and I know she assumes I'm calling from one of my burners.

"Get Dove ready, Lo. I want you to meet me at the gas station across from the Ellis airport in Richlands in thirty minutes."

Lo is silent for a beat. Then: "Why? What's wrong, Frannie?"

"Eli's found us. He knows where she is. I need you to throw some of her things in a bag and *go*. I'll meet you there." I end the call before Lo can say anything else and toss the phone back at Russ.

"You won't hurt her. You let her go as soon as she hands over Dove, do you hear me? She's done nothing to you. She's innocent here." The threat in my voice is real, because at this point I'm ready to run this car off the road and send both of us down in flames.

The only thing stopping me from doing that is my little girl and the knowledge that Eli knows she exists.

Russ doesn't even look at me. "She behaves, she lives."

"You know you won't get away scot-free the way you think you will. Everyone back in Wilmington will know what you did. You've been feeding Eli information all this time, keeping him hidden. If

NES hasn't already figured it out, Ryder will be coming for you the second he wakes up."

Each word seems to bounce off Russ's perfectly layered armor, like he's prepared for all of it. Every contingency, every kink in the plan, he's ready for.

"I'm going to be out of the country by dawn, just like each of the four officers who helped Ward with this plan. All of us will be very rich men after tonight."

The car's dashboard says it's just after three a.m., so that doesn't give us long.

That doesn't give *me* long.

One more question. "How could you do this to Indigo? You've been a mentor to her…like a father to her. She's trusted you since she was a teenager. Do you know how she's going to feel when she finds out what you've done?"

I watch Russ carefully, looking for the chink. And I see it, in the brief shutting of his eyes before he opens them again and stares straight ahead at the road. In the clench of his hands on the steering wheel as he continues the drive toward Richlands.

"I love that girl like a daughter. Always have. But this is bigger than that. This will set me up for my retirement, for the rest of my life. That's an attractive offer for someone like me, who's been working my ass off my whole life to face nothing but pennies in my old age. You don't understand that, and Indigo won't either. I can only hope that one day she will."

I lean back against the seat and stare out the window again. My thoughts turn to my baby girl, who I'll get to see again in a matter of minutes, and to Ryder, who I'm hoping is waking up by now. *God, he's going to be so pissed.*

My answer for Russ is simple. "She won't."

We're both silent as we pass the green sign in the darkness by the side of the road:

RICHLANDS 20

22

RYDER

When my eyes peel open, I immediately slam them shut again. What I want more than anything else in the world is for my eyes to be *closed*. But I have this nagging feeling that I shouldn't let that feeling take root, like there's some reason I need to be awake.

Forcing them open, I groan, squinting against the bright lights of…

Where the fuck am I? And why the hell does my head hurt so damn bad?

Something's wrong. Very, very wrong. I'm in pain, and I'm…alone. I squint, trying to think, but it's too hard right now.

Fuck!

I must have a concussion. *How?*

Activating the voice command on my phone through the speakers wired through the penthouse, I instruct it to call Bain.

He answers on the first ring. "It's three a.m."

I groan again. "Bain."

His voice changes immediately. "Wolf. Talk to me."

"I…I don't know. Something happened. Get here."

I'm starting to wonder if Bain ever sleeps.

"About to jump in the truck. Just me?"

"Whole fucking cavalry."

Bain is quiet for a moment, and I take the time to realize that the top half of my body is lying on the couch while my legs are slung on the floor. My feet are bare, my jeans zipper undone. Bits and pieces of memory start to zap into my head, but that shit hurts so bad I groan again.

The rev of Bain's truck sounds in the background. "You need medical attention?"

"No. Maybe. Fuck, I don't know. Bain…Frannie's not here." I push myself off the couch, trying to stand, and immediately face-plant onto the floor.

"Fuck!" I roar.

Bain curses. "Stay put. You don't sound like you should be moving. I'll be there in ten. The rest of the team will be there soon." He ends the call.

I lie still and quiet, my head turned to one side. Assessing, I move one limb at a time, trying to find injuries.

There are none; my body is fine. Nothing hurts, except for the insane pounding in my head. Slowly, I reach up and touch the back of my head gingerly. It hurts, and my hand comes away bloody.

Hit. My eyes land on the heavy decorative dish that used to sit in the middle of the coffee table, now lying on the floor a few feet away.

Hit with the goddamn decoration.

I laugh, dark and humorless, but that shit hurts so I stop.

Okay, so I've been hit in the head, but I'm awake and I'm talking and I'm thinking, so I'm going to be okay. Concussion.

I can do a concussion. I've had them in the field, worse than this.

Using my arms, I grit my teeth and slowly push myself to my knees. Breathing heavily, I sit there for a few seconds, staring at the couch in front of me. When I've caught my breath and the pounding subsides enough for me to keep moving, I pull myself to my feet and go toward the kitchen. I catch sight of the elevator and my feet grind to a halt.

Everything, *everything* floods back into my mind.

Returning from Nevaeh's house. Learning that Eli was about to be arrested. Celebrating with Frannie. Bain leaving. Getting ready to *celebrate* with Frannie right there on that couch. The elevator door opening.

Russ walking in with a gun pointed at us.

Frannie admitting that she has a *fucking baby* because she never actually miscarried. Frannie telling me that she's going to leave with him.

Dizziness swirls, and I grab on to one of the dining chairs so I don't collapse.

That happened. The woman I love has been lying to me. And now she and the baby I never even knew existed are gone.

Nausea rises in my gut, and I lurch toward the sink. I make it there just in time to throw up the contents of my stomach. I'm still coughing and sputtering when the elevator door slides open. I don't bother to reach for my gun, which is still sitting in its holster on the counter.

"Damn. What the fuck happened to you?" Bain rushes to my side, and he's holding an ice pack to the back of my head within seconds of entering the penthouse. After rinsing out my mouth, I grab it and head for the couch.

"I need to go." But I sway on my way there, and Bain has to catch my elbow to help me keep my balance.

"Fuck that. You talk first. Where's Frannie?"

"How long till everyone gets here?" I need to know if I'm going to have to repeat this story over and over again, or if I can wait until the rest of my team arrives.

"Within a half hour."

My fists clench. "Fuck. That's too long, Bull's-Eye. I need to go after her."

I attempt to stand, but this time it's Bain who shoves me back down on the couch. My brain swims, my vision blurs, and I shake my head to clear it. The pounding gets worse for a second, and Bain shakes his head at me with a dark scowl. "Listen, asshole. You sit there, and you wait. You need strength. Fill me in on what the hell happened while we wait, and we'll try to strategize. Then we'll have a skeleton plan by the time everyone else arrives. You need to ice your head and see if there's any possibility of you *not* being benched tonight."

Panic lifts my eyes to his, circling in my veins like poison. "That can't happen. I need to be out there. I have to bring them home."

Bain lifts his brows at the word *them*.

I might be pissed as hell at Frannie. I might be confused, and all the feelings from the past that had me running for the door whenever I got close to a woman before her might be rearing their ugly heads again. She didn't trust me. For me, it's a deal breaker; it's the one thing I can't handle. I lost my sister that way, and tonight, there's a chance I might have lost her.

This is why I can't sit on the sidelines. There's a child involved. I've never even met her baby girl, and I already know that if she belongs to Frannie, she's the most precious little life in the world. Her daddy is a monster, and he needs to be put down. For both their sakes. And I'll be the one to do it.

I'm going to be out there with my team. I have to be.

"I can't believe he did this!" Indigo shoots off the couch despite Lawson's attempts to keep her beside him. She paces toward the balcony doors. Just before opening them, she turns back to the rest of us.

"Are you sure?" she asks me, and the only way I can describe her voice is *anguished*. She's destroyed by the news that her mentor is the one who betrayed one of her closest friends. It's written in the broken way her shoulders hang, the tortured expression on her face.

Indigo trusted this man. Russ rescued her from the streets when she was a teenager, gave her a purpose and someone who loved her. He gave her drive and passion for life. Then, later on, he inspired her to become a cop. He was her mentor and then her boss. She loves him like a father. Like blood.

They both worked with us on the task force that was initially put together to take Eli down. We had no reason to suspect Russ Walker of any wrongdoing.

Until tonight.

I look Indigo straight in the eye, because she's one of us. Has been since she went undercover with Lawson months ago. "I wish I was wrong, Indy. But it was him. He stood right here in this room and pointed a gun at me and Frannie. He's working for Eli."

With a strangled cry that's halfway between a sob and a roar she disappears out onto the balcony, sliding the door closed behind her.

Lawson stands. On his way past me, he lays a hand on my shoulder. I glance up at him. "I'm sorry, brother."

Lawson nods. "She just needs a few. She'll be okay eventually. But damn…Russ?"

Shaking his head, he follows her onto the balcony.

When the door closes behind them, I turn to the rest of the team. Jacob brought Grisham Abbott, who's been stepping up as a leader for the company more often than just his own Rescue Ops missions require. Grisham's married to Jacob's oldest daughter, Greta, and I have a feeling Jacob's grooming him to take over the entire company someday. Not anytime soon, but one day.

Grisham was on the same SEAL team as Lawson and Ben, and the three of them work together like cogs in a machine. Grisham fits well into our team, and I don't have any complaints about having him on board to help find Frannie.

I need her home.

And then I can deal with my feelings about what she did.

We're all sitting around the living room, minus Lawson and Indigo, and I speak first. "Bain and I want to go after them. Immediately."

Grisham, also known as Ghost when he's on a mission, frowns. "How do you plan to do that? Do you know where he took her?"

I shake my head, the fogginess still a distinct, damned frustrating cloud hanging over me.

Bain speaks up, leaning forward in his seat and placing his elbows on his knees. "When he was here, Wolf remembers Walker mentioning something about meeting up with Ward. We figured out that meant he had other cops on the payroll. There's no way that arrest is going down tonight the way it should."

Jacob checks his smart watch. "I can check with my contacts, but I bet it's too late to be there when the arrest goes down. If the dirty cops were going to take Ward off the scene, they've already got him."

My hands go to my hair, tugging on the short strands. "He can't get to Frannie and the kid. He can't."

Ben claps a hand on my shoulder. "Working on it, dude. Settle."

Being halfway out of commission is driving me fucking insane. My brain isn't working the way it should be. What if, out in the field, my instincts aren't working either? What if my responses are slow? What if I can't get Frannie out of danger when she needs me to?

Grisham is talking, and I focus in on his words even though my heartbeat is racing and my head throbs with pain. "If he has his wife—"

My whole body bristles, and I feel Bain's eyes on me.

"—and his child, and he's free, the only thing he's going to want to do is flee the country. He's gonna bounce."

Jacob nods. "But not from the Wilmington airport."

I never heard the sliding glass door to the balcony open again, but Indigo speaks. Her voice is deeper than usual, husky with sadness. "Russ is smarter than that. He would have advised Eli to use a private plane at one of the smaller, less public airports outside of Wilmington."

Grisham nods. "So we need to narrow those down. Figure out which one has a small private plane leaving tonight. Maybe even within the next couple of hours, before dawn. That's how we'll get him."

Ben glances at me. "That's how we'll get your girl back."

I suck in a breath. "We'll be cutting it too close."

Jacob shakes his head. "No choice. We're going to work the case, Wolf, just like we always do. We know you've grown to care about her. We're all aware that this isn't just another case for you. Seems like my boys fall faster than chess pieces when you have to protect a beautiful woman." He offers me a wry smile, but I'm too tense to return it.

My brain clears. This has to happen. There's no way my Pistol Annie is getting on a plane to God knows where with her abusive estranged husband tonight. I won't allow it to happen. "Get Sayward Diaz out of bed and get her miracle fingers tapping on her motherfucking keyboard. The rest of us can arm up and load up. We're going hunting."

23

FRANNIE

I recognize Lo's car waiting in a remote corner of the gas station parking lot as soon as we pull in. I point it out to Russ, my heart hammering a rhythmic drumbeat in my chest.

Russ has already told me the plan, the point of being that Lo doesn't panic and drive away with Dove.

Which is exactly what I would want her to do at the first sign of trouble. She knows that I would never want Dove anywhere near anyone who seems dangerous, or want her in a compromising situation. It's the whole reason Dove is staying with her in the first place. I've trained her for it. She knows what to look for.

It's the whole reason I told her over the phone that Eli already knew where Dove was and that he was coming for her. Hopefully, now she'll turn Dove over to me. Even though a part of me hopes she'll just take Dove and get as far away from here as possible.

I just don't trust that Eli won't find her.

I have to make sure Dove is safe. That's my first priority.

As we drive into the parking lot, Russ's low voice is a threatening reminder. "Remember, none of this works without the baby. Eli is getting on that plane with his family in twenty minutes. Grab her and let's go."

I put one hand on the door handle. "What if she runs?"

Russ exits the SUV and walks around to my door. He pulls it open and glances around the deserted parking lot. Then he shoves a gun into my back. "Let's hope she cares enough about her life not to do that."

I briefly close my eyes, and then Russ nudges me with the butt of his revolver. I walk like it's my last mile, my blood simmering all the while because this is a reunion with my daughter. The day that I usually look forward to above all others. But it's been tainted by Russ and Eli and the ax hanging over my baby girl's head, and I'm *pissed*. Even more than I am scared.

As we approach, Lobelia exits the Rogue. The gas station is surrounded by forest on three sides. Directly across the street is a two-lane highway and then the long road leading into the Albert J. Ellis Airport. The red lights from the runways blink on and off in the distance, and the neon signs from the gas station create an eerie ambience for our meeting.

Lo takes one look at Russ and narrows her dark brown eyes. Hair tossed in a messy bun, she practically vibrates all over from a mixture of fear and loathing. "What do you want me to do?"

"Get the baby out of the backseat and hand her to her mother." There's no give in Russ's voice, no room for argument or error.

Lo looks at me like she's waiting for a Hail Mary pass, but I don't have one. I nod at her to do as he says.

My heart sinks as she turns and opens the rear door of the Rogue. She turns back to Russ. "She needs her car seat for the pl—"

"No." Russ cuts her off, voice flat. "Eli will get his kid whatever she needs when they get to where they're going."

I swallow. *Over my dead body will Eli ever get Dove anything.*

Lo looks like she wants to say the same thing, but she buttons up her lips and reaches in for Dove. When she pulls out my sleeping baby girl, clad in yellow onesie pajamas with her head lolling on her shoulder, my chest aches. Lo cuddles my baby to her chest, and my eyes cloud, because I know how much my friend loves Dove. The last thing she wants to do right now is hand her over. I reach for my baby, leaning in close to Lo for the exchange.

"Use the number."

It's barely a whisper, but Lo hears it. Aloud, I say, "Can I have the bag you packed her?"

Lo nods and grabs it from the seat. When she hands it over, Russ jabs me again. This time, I bristle because I'm holding Dove. He can shove me with a gun all day long, but it's a different story when I'm holding my child.

I take one last glance over my shoulder at Lobelia as we walk away, back toward the SUV, and the look on her face is one I'll never forget. Sympathy, pain, and gut-wrenching sadness fuse together to plaster an expression of horror across her features.

I hope to God it's not the last time I ever see her.

Climbing in the front seat with Dove in my lap, I nudge the bag I packed with my foot. As Russ pulls out of the parking lot, probably relieved that his job here is almost done, I use my foot to turn the bag so that the refrigerated side pocket is closest to me. I don't want to waste a second of time trying to rotate the bag.

When I have a moment to grab my gun, I'm going to take it, and every second will count.

My mouth suddenly goes dry as my mind flips through all the possible scenarios of what could happen. I lean forward and inhale Dove's clean, light baby scent. Lavender and rain. The smell soothes me, makes me believe in doing whatever I have to do to keep her safe.

No matter what.

Russ pulls across the street, leaving the gas station behind, and turns onto the airport road. A film of sweat grows over my skin, cool and slick.

I can do this. I can do what it takes to save my child.

I press my lips against Dove's downy smooth hair. She stirs in her sleep, tipping her head back. And when her eyes, sleepy and bright blue, blink up at me, her lashes flutter and a baby-soft smile crosses her lips.

"Fobba," she gurgles.

Joy fills my heart, mixing with the fear that forces me to glance at the man driving the car.

"The princess wakes," he muses. "Guess her daddy will be happy about that."

"Don't call him that," I snap.

Russ doesn't even glance at me. "Facts are facts. Blood is blood. The man is who he is, and I know how you feel about him. But the truth is, he's her father. What if meeting her, having the chance to be a dad and do things right, makes him change?"

My palm itches, because all I want to do is slap him again. "You've met Eli Ward. Do you really believe change is something he's capable of?"

Russ shrugs a shoulder as his phone chimes, sitting in the cup holder between us. "What I think doesn't matter."

Pulling Dove closer to my chest, I use the toe of my black Nike to slowly unzip the side pocket of my bag. I'm still counting on the fact that Russ has no idea that I even know how to use a gun, much less that I carry a concealed weapon with me regularly and am trained to use it.

The airfield comes into view, a few small private planes sitting on the runways sprawled out before us. There are no other cars in sight, which I guess isn't unusual for three thirty in the morning.

I breathe a sigh of relief, because it also means that Eli hasn't arrived.

Russ pulls to a stop and leaves his engine idling, then picks up his phone and checks the message he just received. He glances at me, but it appears all his empathy is gone. His expression is blank, even tired. Lines pull at the corners of his eyes, and his mouth turns down slightly.

Leaning his head back against the seat, he glances down at Dove. "They'll be here in less than ten minutes."

I sigh. "That gives me enough time to change Dove's diaper and give her an insulin injection."

Russ nods. "I'm watching you."

With my heart thudding against my rib cage, I nod. "I'm going to climb out and lay her down right here on the seat. You can watch."

He snorts. "Gee, thanks."

I pull the backpack Lo packed for Dove onto my shoulder as I climb out of the car, having no idea what's in it but thinking I might need it later. As if she senses my own tumultuous emotions, Dove doesn't make a sound as I open the car door and then lay her down on the seat to change her. After she's dressed, I reach deep down inside my soul and find the nerves of steel I need, keeping my eyes trained on my baby girl as I reach for the gun I have stashed in the diaper bag.

Pulling my pistol and aiming it at Russ's face in one swift motion, I pull the trigger with my right hand. With my left, I sweep my daughter from the car, turning and running with her even as the hollow ringing sound of the bullet rips through the air behind me.

Dropping the gun so I can hold tightly to Dove, I run.

Toward the cover of trees at the forest line about thirty feet away from the runway down toward the airport road.

There's no movement or commotion from the car behind me, no indication that Russ is in pursuit. The only sound is the whistling, wheezing sound of a nearly hysterical cry coming from all around me. When I realize I'm the one making the sound, I swallow hard around the golf-ball-sized lump in my throat and tighten my hold on Dove.

She doesn't make a sound. Not a cry or a whine, just nestling to my chest and hanging on to my neck like she's holding on for her life.

I don't breathe until I reach the cover of the trees, and the pitch-blackness slips over both of our bodies like oil spilling into the ocean.

It feels like freedom. Like safety.

Not yet.

I turn into the woods and keep walking, cuddling Dove and speaking softly into her ear.

"Mama's here. You're safe. I'll never leave you."

24

RYDER

My head still throbs, but it's much clearer as the five of us raid the weapons bunker at NES headquarters in Wrightsville Beach. We left for HQ immediately following our discussion at the penthouse, with Jacob's stern admonishment to me before I stepped onto the elevator: "If this were any other case, with any other victim, you'd be benched. But when it comes to the women in our lives, I've learned I can't stop my men from going after them. So you follow your instincts, but listen to your team. Be smart and be safe."

I couldn't make him any promises before stepping onto the elevator with my team and leaving the condo.

We're armed with typical Delta Squad mission weapons and gear. Each of us wears black or dark green cargo pants with pockets for extra ammo. Lightweight backpacks stocked with knives for hand-to-hand combat, flash-bangs, grenades, night-vision goggles, and binoculars. Kevlar protects our torsos underneath black shirts and vests with more pockets lined with extra refills and supplies.

And each of us has a rifle we can carry and two pistols in holsters.

So it doesn't matter if my head feels like I got hit by a train instead of a five-foot-three woman who thought she was protecting me.

I'm more than ready for Eli fucking Ward, and if he puts one finger on Frannie he'll get a bullet between his eyes for his trouble.

We don't know where we're going when we load into one of the NES Suburbans, but we want to be on the road when a call comes in with a location, so we pull out of the parking lot and onto the streets of Wilmington.

"Everyone clear on the plan?" Grisham asks from behind the wheel. He glances in the rearview, his eyes meeting mine from my captain's seat in the middle row.

All I do is nod, glancing out the window. Adrenaline surges, my blood heating up and causing my left foot to jump in anxious impatience. The waiting is killing me. I want to do something, but we need Sayward to call with the intel.

From the seat beside me, Cowboy speaks up. "Bull's-Eye finds sniper position and stays there. Gives us intel via communication devices on enemy location and movements. Gives us the lowdown on terrain, possible complications that we can't see. The rest of us partner up, try to come up at them from two sides. Ghost and Wolf take point, me and Sleuth at the rear. Close in and find an opening to grab our targets. Rescue Ops team is our backup and will clean up after we get Frannie and the baby out because we don't know which cops we can trust. WPD can sort their shit out when we're done."

Frannie and the baby.

Frannie and the baby.

Frannie and the baby.

The words repeat themselves over and over again inside my head, like a fucking prayer. I squeeze my eyes shut, rubbing my forehead.

When Ben's done talking, he glances at me and grins. Then he lifts his voice, talking to Grisham and Lawson up front. "That about cover it?"

Grisham's mostly a serious guy, but he cracks a smile. "Yeah. I think you got it down."

Sleuth peers over the front seat, pinning me with a shrewd look. "It's not a question that you're gonna be able to pull this off. But if there's anything you want to air out before we go in hot…we're right here, man. We all know how you've been feeling about her. Some of us have been there."

Grisham lifts his chin from the driver's seat. Once upon a time, he fell for the woman who's now his wife, Greta, when she was being stalked by a former NES employee. I heard the stories about how he was the one to figure it out and save her, and I always wondered how that would have felt. And then everything went down with Lawson and Indy and I thought it was crazy that Lawson had to do this kind of job with this kind of pressure when the woman he was clearly in love with was in danger.

And now it's me. And it's not just the woman I love. There's a child involved.

"Are we all just gonna tiptoe around the big-ass elephant in the Suburban?" Ben blurts out.

A quiet groan emits from Bain in the backseat.

"Because Frannie has a baby. She didn't tell anyone. You didn't know, right, Wolf? Isn't that shit messing with your head?"

The air whooshes out of me like I've been punched in the balls. My teeth grind together. Lawson cranes his neck, trying to stare Ben down, but he isn't done.

"I mean, fuck, man. Do we even know the baby's name? How old is it? Is it a boy or a girl?"

"Shut the fuck up, Cowboy." Bain's words are a growl. "Just...chill for once in your life."

Ben glances at me, probably seeing the rage seething just beneath the surface. "Fuck. Sorry, man. I didn't mean to screw with your head. But weren't you already...?"

I sigh, leaning forward and scrubbing my face with my hands. "Yeah. I was. Everything you just said has already been running through my mind every second since she knocked me out. I can't fucking stop thinking about it, Cowboy. But if I let it consume me now, I can't save her. Them. God. And all I want to do right now—all I *need* to do—is save them."

Ben nods. "Roger that."

Lawson touches two fingers to his forehead and dips his chin before turning back around. "We got you, brother."

Two things happen almost simultaneously. My phone rings on the console beside me, and Grisham's lights up the car's synced Bluetooth system.

I snatch mine up. Not recognizing the number on the screen, I answer it like a work call. At three thirty in the morning. "Thorn Ryder."

"Oh, thank God!" The woman's voice on the other end of my phone is urgent, and the hairs on my arms stand up. I look at Ben, and he tries to read my facial expression.

"Mr. Ryder, my name is Lobelia Novak, and I'm calling you because Frannie told me to. She's in trouble."

Her words tumble over each other in her rush to get them out, and I try to calm my racing heart and act like this isn't about the woman I love. Like this is just a regular mission I'm working.

"Lobelia, can you slow down for me? I'm looking for Frannie right now. Do you have a location on her? And are you safe?"

A strangled sob comes through the other end of the line. Ben shoves me from the other seat. His voice is urgent. "Hang up. Sayward knows which airport. We're on our way."

I shake my head, putting Lobelia on speaker. She keeps talking. "She met me with some man at a gas station across from Ellis Airport in Jacksonville. They made me give them the baby, and I think they were going to meet Eli at the airport and fly away with her! Oh God. I did the wrong thing. I did the wrong thing, didn't I?"

I swallow. "You did the right thing calling me. And now we know where she is. We're on our way there now to get her, Lobelia. I want you to call the number I'm about to give you. It's my boss, Jacob Owen. He's going to pick you up and make sure you're safe. Okay?"

She's crying in earnest now. "Okay. Please find them. Frannie's my best friend and that baby…she's been my whole life."

I allow my eyes to drift closed and hope I'm not telling her a lie. "I promise you, I will find them. And I'll bring them home."

While Grisham drives, Lawson evaluates the aerial-view map that Sayward sends us of the area surrounding the Ellis airport. The area is heavily forested, and there's a back access road that can be used to access the airport apart from the main entrance. Lawson holds up the map on his tablet, pointing to the back road.

"This is where we enter. We're going in hot, because Ward wants Frannie and the baby on that plane and he wants it to happen yesterday. We don't have time for anything once we get there but to act."

The words he doesn't say hang in the air between us all, heavy with unspoken meaning.

If it's not already too late.

"When's that damn call coming in?" I growl, my leg bouncing even more furiously as the miles fly by out the window.

"Any minute now. Sayward should know whether or not the flight has taken off." Grisham's response is immediate. "Ten miles out. Everyone ready?"

Grisham's phone rings, and he answers the call through the Bluetooth. Sayward's voice comes through the Suburban's speakers.

"Eli Ward is Interpol's problem now. That flight took off eight minutes ago."

Something inside me curls up and dies. My chest just…deflates. It feels like someone dropped an anvil on my chest and left it there; breathing is impossible. Leaning forward, I lower my head between my knees, not sure if my next breath will come.

"Sorry, guys," Sayward is saying. "We were just at a time disadvantage. But something happened out there at that airport, because there's no woman and baby on the manifest. *Frannie's not on that flight.*"

I gasp for air, my head coming up and my eyes going wide. "What'd you just say?" My voice is hoarse.

"You heard me," she answers, voice triumphant. "Your girl's still out there somewhere, Wolf. You need to go and get her."

Grisham ends the call and takes a quick look into the rearview. "Change of plan, then. Kind of sucks we don't get to shoot Eli Ward in the balls, but the plan was always Frannie, right? We're going in on the main airport road. Let's just see what we find."

Determination sinks into my bones, spreading a new energy through me like an injection. "Place is gonna be crawling with cops soon. I want to get Frannie and get out before that happens. The last thing she needs is to be interrogated tonight. Especially when they're the ones who fucked up. Let them figure out what the hell happened with Ward."

Next to me, Ben lifts his chin. "Agreed. Search and rescue, then."

A few minutes later, the Suburban is flying up the road leading to the small airport. When we pull up to the parking lot in front of the terminal entrance, we can see several small planes sitting in hangars and a couple waiting on the runway. There's another SUV in the parking lot, and the passenger-side door stands open.

There's no sign of Frannie or anyone else.

"This being such a small airport, all the shady shit that probably went down here tonight hasn't even been called in yet," Bain mutters under his breath as we pile out of the Suburban.

We move in formation, Grisham staying behind the wheel of our vehicle, eyes open and engine idling. He's ready to pull us out if he needs to, but everything is quiet around us. Too quiet.

Ben and Lawson fan out, rifles lifted while they turn in every direction, searching. Bain and I approach the SUV. Walking up to the passenger side, I notice a diaper bag on the floor. Then I take note of the man sitting in the driver's seat. Nodding at Bain to indicate he go around to that side, I take him in.

It's Russ Walker. He's been shot, a bullet hole in his neck just under his jaw. His eyes are closed, head lolled against the seat. Bain opens the driver's-side door and checks for a pulse.

He shakes his head. "Dead."

I blow out a breath. "Frannie. Fuck."

I swivel around, searching. *Where are you, baby?*

We reconvene at the Suburban.

"She killed him," I said. "That's how she escaped. He didn't know who he was messing with. She shot him so she could run with the baby." I glance around me, taking note of the tree line about thirty feet away.

Inclining my head in that direction, I can almost see Frannie running with her baby clutched to her chest, scared out of her mind and sobbing. If she'd just shot a man, not sure if she'd taken his life or if he'd come after her, she'd be running for her life.

"She's in the woods." My adrenaline ramps up a notch. "She's got the baby, no supplies. We need to get to her, and soon."

Lawson shoulders his rifle. "Then let's do that. She can't have gotten far. We'll fan out. Ghost can take the Suburban out and follow the road around the woods, in case she made it back out there. We'll stay on comms and speak up as soon as one of us finds her."

"Them," I correct him. "We're looking for my girl and her baby."

They all look at me, serious expressions on their faces. They understand exactly what I mean.

25

FRANNIE

When the sun crests the horizon, I know Dove and I might be in trouble. There's no way I can hike for very long on a ninety-plus-degree day carrying Dove with no food or water.

There's one positive thing, one thing that lets me know I did what I set out to do: I saw a small private plane take off from the runway a mile behind me. It lifted over the tops of the trees, sweeping into the still-dark sky and off into the distance, its lights fading into the navy expanse until they blended in with the dots of stars blanketing the horizon.

Laughter bubbled up inside me, and a whoop of triumph escaped my throat as I brushed a gentle hand over Dove's silken curls.

I'd kept her away from Eli.

"We're safe, baby girl. He can't hurt us anymore." I dropped a kiss on top of her head and kept marching forward.

But I had no clue where I was going. And although I grew up in Oklahoma, I grew up in the *suburbs*. I might know how to use a firearm, but I have no clue how to keep myself alive in the woods. I don't know if I've been hiking deeper into the huge forest surrounding the airport, or whether I'm heading toward civilization. As the sun dances higher toward the clouds, I remember the backpack on my shoulders.

"Let's stop and take a breath, okay, Dove-girl? I want to see what Auntie Lo put in your bag."

Coming to a halt, I spot a fallen log and sit, pulling the pack off my shoulders and placing it on the ground beside my feet. Holding Dove on one knee and securing my arm around her waist, I use my other arm to unzip the bag and start pulling out the contents.

Diapers and wipes. Water bottles. Crackers. Empty baby bottles for Dove. An extra outfit and bibs for Dove. Pouches of baby food, the formula she drinks. The sling wrap I can use to carry her without having to hold her.

And down at the bottom of the bag...a burner phone.

Tears. Actual, real tears of joy spring to my eyes.

The woods wake up with the sun, birds beginning to sing and chatter in the trees overhead. The day is warm and heavy and still, sticky in the Carolina summer. As the day goes on, my clothes will stick to me, and I'll worry about sunburn and dehydration. The tree cover of the forest will be a good thing.

My head drops back and my eyes burn. Blue patches of sky peek through diamond-shaped holes in the canopy.

"Your auntie is a real savior, baby girl. You know that?" My whisper disappears into the humid air and I swipe at the moisture clinging to my eyelashes.

Dove coos, one of the first sounds she's made in a while. She's been quiet as a mouse since we've been hiking through the forest. At one point, I thought she'd fallen back asleep, but when I checked, her eyes were wide open, taking everything in.

I pull out one of the bottles, and she immediately starts to squirm in my lap. Her eyes widen, and her little hands turn to fists as her fingers open and close, trying to grab for the bottle.

"Ah. There's my hungry girl. Let Mama make it."

Dumping the formula pack into the bottle, I pour in some water and shake it. Then I hand it to Dove. While she drinks, settled against my chest, I pull out the phone and turn it on. The screen flashes, telling me that I have no signal.

"Damn," I murmur. "We're going to have to walk a little farther, sweet girl."

My legs protest at the thought. I'm in decent shape, but running a mile through the woods at a clip in the dark was about all I had in me for today. I'm not a runner by nature, for Christ's sake.

I pull the changing pad from the back of the bag and spread it on the leaves, then lay Dove on top of it. It takes me a couple of minutes to change her diaper and then wrap her in the sling against my chest. I face her forward so that she can see, her legs hanging out. Her pink feet bounce happily in their pink socks, and I place her empty bottle back in the pack. As I hand her a pouch of baby plums, she makes happy slurping noises as she eats. I take a pack of crackers and eat, chugging a bottle of water.

"In a little bit, Mama's going to have to use nature's bathroom. But I can wait."

"Coo," answers Dove.

"Yep. We better get walking. We might have a long way to go today." Placing the bag back on my shoulders, I turn to lead us in the direction I hope will take me to a road.

And out from behind a tree steps Eli Ward.

I stumble backward, almost falling over the log that just gave me refuge.

Oh, shit. I'm hallucinating. I didn't think I was that tired. Eli isn't here, Frannie. Get your shit together, and do it now. Dove needs you.

Somehow saving myself from falling, I right myself and stand completely still, frozen in place on the forest floor. The forest that seemed so awake moments ago now lulls, all movement and sound coming to a halt around me. The bird conversations drift away on the breeze; the rustling of animals in the trees and bushes nearby goes silent.

The wood is watching, waiting for the apparition in front of me to disappear.

Just like I am.

But Eli doesn't move. He stands there wearing an expression on his face that I've never seen before.

Eli looks the same as he always has, except for the fact that he's more dressed down than I can recall seeing him in a long time. Eli was already running a business when we met. He swept me off my feet with dinners and expensive cars and fancy trips, and he was almost always in a suit. He liked to rub elbows with legitimate corporate players, even though he wasn't one. He looked the part.

Here, in the woods, Eli's wearing dark jeans and a plain gray T-shirt. His feet are clad in sneakers, and I'm guessing that whoever brought him clothes to change into didn't think a suit would be practical for a jail escape. Eli was probably pissed.

He probably planned to change as soon as he arrived in Switzerland.

Oh God, why isn't he disappearing?

Eli's dark brown hair has grown out longer than he used to keep it, long enough for slick curls to form on top. His golden complexion is thanks to his Italian heritage on his mother's side, and he's always prided himself on his handsome face, the muscular body that he spends hours working on in the gym, and his stellar sense of style.

I blink rapidly, trying to force his image away. The day is only going to get hotter, and Dove and I need to keep moving. I need to find a road or a place where there's signal so I can call Ryder for help.

Ryder.

Just thinking of him sends a jolt of pain arcing through my body. I want his strong arms wrapped around me and my daughter so badly right now it physically aches to think about it.

"You're not here," I rasp. My voice has suddenly stopped working. "You got on a plane to Switzerland."

I realize Eli's eyes aren't aimed at me; he's staring at our daughter. Glancing down at Dove, I find that she's fallen asleep. She's dropped the pouch of plums and her head lolls to one side as her arms and legs dangle.

Eli finally meets my eyes, his dark brown ones bringing an intensity I can't handle. There's hunger in his gaze, mixed with ferocious anger and his usual impatience. But there's also…*wonder*?

"That's our baby." There's an accusation in his words. "You lied to me. To everyone. You said she died. But this is our baby…*right here.*"

I take two tiny running steps backward, my eyes wild. My heart hammers, trying hard to escape the cage in my chest.

"Why aren't you on that *fucking plane*?" My words are a whisper-shout.

He looks down at Dove again, and now I pinpoint the expression that settles in his eyes again. It's love.

Eli *loves* our daughter.

And I can decipher it because it quickly changes from love to possession. It's penned all across his expression like words in a diary; he couldn't hide it from me even if he wanted to.

He loved me once too. In the beginning, he loved me enough to put me up on a pedestal and buy me pretty things. He loved me the way he thought a man was supposed to love a woman. But somewhere along the way in his life, the concept of love was twisted, ruined. He never shared himself with me, never allowed me to become his partner in three years together the way Ryder had in mere weeks. He never showed me his soft side, never let himself be vulnerable with me.

And when I didn't behave the way Eli thought I should, or when something wasn't absolutely perfect the way he expected it to be, he hurt me. It was consequential in his mind. And Eli wasn't the kind of man who apologized for it later. He forced me to accept my consequences, and he explained why it was happening. And later, he spoiled me harder to show what a good provider and husband he was.

This can't happen.

This can't happen.

Not again.

Eli takes a step forward. "She's mine. You both are. I would never leave the country without you, Francesca. My name is on the flight manifest, along with one of the officers who were on my payroll. They'll think I'm gone."

My heart sinks. "You can't have her, Eli."

He steps forward again, this time walking until he reaches me. I could turn and run, but he'd just catch me. I have Dove strapped to my chest, and Eli's much-longer strides would cut mine in half.

He stops just in front of me, staring down. He's not quite as tall as Ryder, but he's over six feet and dwarfs me. Old habits die hard, and I cringe, waiting for a blow that doesn't come. Eli just stares down at me, his deep-set eyes unblinking.

"I can have you. I've always had you. You've just been lost. We're going to start all over in Switzerland. We'll be a family. It'll be perfect. We can have more kids."

Every part of my body trembles with his words. Because I can picture it in my head. Everything he's saying. The life he's talking about would be stunning. A picture-perfect, beautiful nightmare. I can't go with Eli. I can't have a life with him. I can't live with a man, build a life with a man, *start a family* with a man who loves me by hurting me.

I'm too strong for that now.

I'm not Francesca anymore, I'm Frannie. And Frannie knows how to defend herself. She's not a doormat. She doesn't get her head turned by pretty things. She doesn't let her parents tell her what she should and shouldn't do. She doesn't let her image and a town's opinion of it influence her. And she damn sure doesn't allow a man back into her life who beat the ever-loving shit out of her and almost made her lose her baby.

I look up at Eli and plaster the most sincere expression I can on my face. I channel Francesca, way, deep down where I locked her away. And I nod. "Okay, Eli. It's going to take me a while, but I can get back to a place where I trust you again. But you have to promise you won't hurt me or Dove. That's the only way this will work. Otherwise I'm always going to want to run away."

Lies. Give him lies, but make them sound like your truth.

He flinches like I've slapped him. "Is it too late to change her name?"

My hands ball into fists and I wish I had my gun. Either one of them. I close my eyes briefly to steady myself and to keep the anger from exploding out of me.

Because where Francesca used to be laden with fear, Frannie seems to be chock-full of hissing, boiling rage.

And Eli is what brings it out of me.

So I just open my eyes wider and nod. "Yes, it's too late. Why, don't you like it?"

He squints down at her. "I, uh...Sure, babe. I'll get used to it. And your little deal? You know that's not how life works. You get what you earn. If you behave the way you're supposed to..."

I heave a big fake sigh. "You're right. I'm sorry. We'll work on it. Do you know how to get us out of these woods?"

Eli grabs my hand and turns us in a slow circle, frowning. "We must have pulled up not long after you shot Walker. You dropped one of the baby's blankets, and I figured out which direction you ran. I followed you into the woods and caught your footsteps in the ground. I just followed you and heard you talking to the baby. Watched you for a while. I'm not a woodsman."

I bite my lip, looking around. "So you don't know how we're getting out of here either."

Damn. I was hoping that he'd lead us to civilization so I could get away from him. Call for help. I don't want to be alone in the woods with Eli Ward.

He tugs on my wrist, his voice commanding. But not in a sexy way like Ryder's. In a slimy, douchey way that makes me want to punch him.

But if I punch Eli, he'll punch me back.

Twenty times harder.

We've walked only fifty feet when he grinds to a halt. "Walker's dead."

I gasp, one hand flying to my mouth. Nausea rolls like thunder; my head swims as a wave of dizziness threatens to overtake me.

You did what you had to do. You did what you had to do.

"Must have been a lucky shot," Eli remarks, watching me sideways.

Without warning, he yanks me close to him. Dove startles in her sleep and her eyes pop open. She sees Eli staring down at us and immediately starts to cry. The sound almost breaks me, because crying is such a rarity for Dove.

"Guess we'd better check you out to make sure you're not carrying any surprises. I don't want to end up like Walker."

He whips me around and unzips the backpack. Dove's wails grow louder, her arms reaching out in front of her. I grab her hands, rubbing the backs gently with my thumbs as I murmur in her ear.

"Mama's right here, baby. Right here. Don't cry."

"Did you try this?" Eli holds the burner phone in front of my face.

Regret stabs me through the heart. I nod. "No service."

I feel his hands cup my breasts and I stiffen, my hands going frozen as they grip Dove's. Eli palms my breasts roughly for just a moment before he slides them down my rib cage until he reaches my hips.

"What are you doing?" This time, it's impossible to tamp down the fury in my voice.

He moves his lips to my neck and cups my ass. All while our baby cries against my chest. The nausea from earlier returns, and I squeeze my eyes shut as Francesca peeks out from her box. Fear engulfs me.

He can do anything he wants out here in these woods. Anything.

He could even decide Dove doesn't need a mama, bury me, and run away with my baby.

Jesus help me.

"I'm patting you down," he whispers against my ear. He presses his hips against my ass, allowing me to feel his hard cock straining against his jeans.

Bile rises in my throat.

"Stop," I murmur. "Dove is upset."

"Make her stop."

He releases me, coming back around to stand in front of us. He stares down at Dove, cocking his head to one side. "Let me hold her."

My heart goes up in flames. "Maybe later."

Dove takes one look at Eli and her cries grow ten decibels. They seem to ricochet off the trees, sending her own set of echolocation signals bouncing off the leaves. She tilts her head back and squeezes her eyes shut, her face now scarlet.

Eli's eyes darken. He lifts his voice to be heard above our daughter. "Francesca! I said let me hold her."

I lift my voice too. "I said not right now!"

There's no warning. Eli raises his hand, palm open, and slaps me hard in the face.

26

RYDER

My boots barely make a sound on the soft forest floor. It rained yesterday, and the ground is still spongy and damp. It also means that if I'd known exactly where Frannie had entered the forest, I might have been able to track her. Silently, I wonder how long it'll take the police to figure out what happened to Eli Ward. When they do, the airport will be swarming with cops, and I'd really like to be gone when that happens.

Gone, but not without my girl.

And her baby.

Christ. The thought still kicks me in the chest, heel first, every time I think it. She has a child. The life I thought we'd build together, if we're even still able to build it, is going to be completely different from the one I imagined. So many what-ifs knock on the door to my mind, but I slam it shut, blocking their entry.

This isn't the time.

Later, after I get Frannie home where she's safe, I'll confront this.

I'll figure out why it hurts so damn much. I'll face the fact that she completely mind-fucked me head-on.

First? I'll find her.

Glancing up, I note that the sun's rays have forced darkness back from the horizon. Now that the sun is up, the day won't do anything but heat up. And a summer day in the Carolinas isn't one you want to be out hiking in without supplies. And Frannie has none.

She's also carrying a baby, and she's scared and alone. I move forward, the hard press of conviction slamming into me with new vigor.

I've walked due north for about a mile when Bain's voice comes over my earpiece. "Everyone stop and listen."

We all started out in the same spot and branched out diagonally from one another. That way none of us would be too far in case we found Frannie, and we could get to one another's location quickly.

I hear the faint whimpering first, because I'm the first to respond. "I've got sound."

Bain's voice crackles through the comms. "I'm climbing a tree. Gonna set up my scope and rifle, and I'll let you know what I see. Just keep walking forward and tell us what you hear."

Lawson's voice comes through. "The rest of us will stay put."

I move, my ears straining. A sound breaks through the trees, suddenly becoming clear. "It's a baby crying. I'm close."

Frannie's nearness, the fact that I'm close enough to hear the baby, pushes me forward at a quiet run, and I don't stop until I hear Frannie's voice. And then I'm forced to stop, because she sounds scared.

I can't make out what she's saying, but she's talking to someone, and I can't understand who that would be. She shot Walker; his body is still lying in his SUV. So who's out here with her and her baby in the woods?

I speak softly into my comms. "Need that visual, Bull's-Eye. Frannie isn't alone. Staying hidden."

I wait, holding my breath while I listen to my girl. Her agitation ramps up; it's like I'm standing right there next to her. I can feel her emotions rising and swirling around me like I've been pulled into an ocean undertow.

I've never been able to control what Frannie does to me. But right now, I'm glad for it. Our connection brought me straight to her side, and now I can feel her mood and mind-set as easily as if they were my own.

"Got her in my sights. Prepare yourself, Wolf."

The beating of my heart is a continuous collision with my ribs. "What's happening?"

"It's Ward. Guess he didn't get on that plane after all. He's got his hands all over her."

A growl rips from my chest as my weapon comes up automatically. My feet creep forward before I tell them to, silent footfalls meeting damp, fragrant earth.

I don't stop moving until they come into view, and I find a spot to take cover behind a tree nearby. Speaking softly into my comms, I talk to the boys. "If you're headed in my direction, that'd be good. Because there's a good chance I'll kill this motherfucker just because he's breathing."

He's standing in front of Frannie, and she's looking up at him. Everything about his stance says that he wants to intimidate her, dominate her. As if he has the fucking right to breathe the same air she does, much less have any kind of importance in her life.

He lost that right the first time he laid hands on her.

He lost the right to keep breathing the second time.

And now? Now he's just deadweight that I'm ready to cut from her story.

The baby must have taken one look at him and decided he wasn't a good guy. She's screaming at the top of her lungs, head thrown back, eyes squeezed shut.

And that bastard is demanding that Frannie hand the baby over to him. As soon as she says no, I take a step forward, out from behind the tree. The look on his face tells me everything I need to know. There's no way he's going to stand for her refusal. He never has before, has he?

But for Frannie, handing over her baby would be a no-go. She's not going to do it. There's no part of her that would be able to place her daughter in that monster's arms.

"You're out of cover." Bull's-Eye, calm and collected, comes over the comms.

I don't answer, watching the scene unfold in front of me.

"You're what?" Lawson's voice, not nearly as placid, follows.

Frannie refuses for a second time, and Ward doesn't hesitate. He slaps her across the face, as forcefully as if he were hitting another full-grown man.

Only Frannie isn't another man. She's a woman, and she's *holding their child*.

"You motherfucking coward." The words spit from between my teeth. I step forward, holding my rifle, until there aren't more than thirty feet separating me from them.

Ward plays the part, pulling Frannie and the baby in front of him as human shields. I curse under my breath, because I acted against every ounce of training I had. He raised his hand to her, again. I saw that he was about to hurt her, and I knew what that would do to her. After all she's done to become strong.

After all she's done to escape him and his abuse.

He'd hit her like she was worthless.

Instead of controlling my fury, I acted on instinct and *moved*. And now her life is standing between me and him.

"You're going to put that gun down and walk away." Ward starts giving orders right away. Like he was born to boss people around. "Because the only other alternative is aiming your rifle at a defenseless woman and child."

Frannie stares at me. Both of her hands come up to protect the baby, and even though she's being held against the man she hates more than anything in the world, I see the sigh she releases.

"Ryder," she says. "What the hell took you so long?"

My lips twitch, and I don't take my eyes off Ward. "Got held up. Some Pistol Annie hit me over the head."

Frannie starts to cry. She's shaking all over, silent tears streaming down her face. She mouths her next words.

I'm sorry, she says.

I shake my head at her, indicating that she'd better not be sorry for a damn thing right now.

Later, I mouth right back.

"What the fuck is this?" Ward glances down at Frannie. "You fucking slut! Seriously? You've been fucking him?"

He tightens his hold on her, and she cries out. "Eli, stop it! I've got Dove!"

My words are bullets shot from a pistol. "You have one chance to live through this, Ward. One. And believe me when I tell you that I don't even want that to happen. Step. Away."

Grisham's voice roars into the earpiece. "Fucking hell, Bull's-Eye! Wolf can't take that shot at that range with Frannie and the baby in front of Ward! If you see a shot—"

"I realize you're not usually on this team, Ghost," Bain answers. There's no give in his words. "But we don't need orders. We've got this."

Grisham curses, and everyone goes quiet on the comms as they listen.

Ward's eyes are slits. "You think you can give me orders, you military spy-guy wannabe? I give orders to the tune of millions of dollars for a living. You don't scare me."

I edge forward. "Yeah? And where'd that get you? Running off to Switzerland, huh?"

Ward grits his teeth, and so do I. Movement catches my eye from behind him. Off his left shoulder, Cowboy salutes me, then returns his hand to his rifle. It sits on his shoulder, aimed squarely at the back of Eli Ward's head.

Bain's voice sounds in my ear. "We've got him surrounded, Ghost. We'll be bringing Frannie and the baby out of the woods from the east. Get the getaway vehicle there now."

There's an edge in Grisham's voice when he answers. "I've got you."

"Fuck you," Ward spits. He brings one hand to Frannie's throat.

Her eyes go wide, and my trigger finger twitches, a twinge of pressure pressing on my weapon where it counts.

Behind Ward, Ben whistles. The sound is so loud and high it can't be ignored, and Ward's body jerks like he's been electrocuted. He turns partway, his hands dropping from Frannie, and I hurtle forward.

She doesn't waste any time, leaping away from Ward and toward me, and I reach out and grab her hand, pulling her into my body and to the left just as Cowboy launches himself at Ward.

I pull Frannie into my side, baby and all, hugging her as close as I can with a now-whimpering little girl with flailing arms and legs strapped to her chest, while Ben smacks Ward in the side of the head with the butt of his rifle.

Ward goes down hard, hitting the ground without a single shot having been fired. Sleuth moves in like an oil slick from behind a tree off to our right, dragging Ward by his legs to another tree and zip-tying him to it by the wrists.

Frannie frantically unties the sling that holds the baby to her chest, grabbing her into her arms and cradling her daughter to her chest. Then she grabs me by the neck and pulls me to them, holding me close. I let my gun slip to the ground and allow myself this moment, wrapping my arms around her waist and holding her close. I inhale her scent, mixed with the fear and the baking heat, and I damn near cry out with the relief I feel.

"You came." It's a sob from her, spoken into my chest as her fingers dig into my neck.

"Always." As the word leaves my lips, I realize that it doesn't matter how fucked up my head is.

When it comes to this woman, I'll always be here.

"Let me see your face." I pull back, noting that the baby goes quiet as she stares up at me, big blue eyes taking me in.

I glance down at the baby. "I'm not ignoring you, angel, but I'm gonna check your mama out first. That okay with you?"

"Duff." She reaches out a tiny finger, lifting it toward my face, and I grab it gently in one of my fists. Something warm and unfamiliar slips and slides inside my chest, but I push it aside and look at Frannie's face.

She's staring down at the baby, something like awe in her expression, but I tilt her chin gently up to look at me. The side of her face is an angry red, the mark of his hand harsh against her creamy skin.

I swallow hard and turn her face, staring at the mark he left on her. "He should be dead."

I glance at Ward, slumped against the tree.

She nods. "He should be. Can I hold your gun for a minute?"

I can't fight the smile that fights its way to my lips, and that's a fucking problem. Because now isn't the time to smile, but when Frannie's around I can't help it.

"No."

She sighs. "Damn. Well, then I guess he'll have to live. Because if anyone deserves to kill him, it's me."

I nod, my throat closing up as I stare down at her. I brush the hair out of her face. *Wasn't I pissed at her only hours ago? Fuck.*

Her eyes, so deep and blue, match her daughter's. And that means I'm going to love that baby girl's eyes with all my heart. Frannie leans into my touch. "Can I ask you something, Ryder?"

"Sweetheart, ask me any fucking thing. Anything you want."

"Can I introduce you to my little girl?" Frannie asks me this with an earnestness I can't quite place. It's important to her, more important than I can even grasp right now.

So my answer is simple. I cup her cheek and let my thumb gently graze that quickly bruising skin. "Yes."

Her eyes go bright. "This is my daughter, Dove." She glances down at the baby, who's still staring at me with big, blinking eyes.

Her tiny little lips part, their perfect pink heart shape forming gibberish words. Her little fist still rests in my hand. She coos and blinks, and my chest explodes as I stare down at her. I'm not an expert on what's happening to me, but I'm pretty damn sure it's love at first sight.

It's a steep slope, one I'm sliding down without a grip on anything solid to keep me from falling all the way.

"Dove. Damn, that's beautiful. It's nice to meet you, angel."

Frannie stares up at me, tears shining in her eyes, some fierce emotion lighting her up from the inside out. Her blond hair's a mess, her face is bruised and dirty, and her clothes are askew, but I'm not sure I've ever seen her look this gorgeous, with her baby in her arms and the way she's looking at me right now.

"I know we have some things to discuss. And I have a husband sitting over there who I need to divorce. Also, I have a baby who you just met. But I love you, Thorn Ryder. That's my truth, and it's been my truth for a while now. And if I know one thing, I know that's never going to change."

Love. It's all I see when I'm looking down at them, and I know that's the truth when my earpiece crackles.

Grisham's voice sounds tired, but also highly amused. "You realize we're still on comms, right, Wolf?"

27

RYDER

For the rest of that day, NES protects Frannie from police and federal questioning. Jacob calls in every favor and uses every connection he has to make sure she and Dove have the time and rest they need to recover from the trauma they endured while being hunted—and found—by Eli Ward.

When we arrived back at the NES office at nearly lunchtime, Frannie was almost dead on her feet. Jacob met us with the keys to the BMW, which was waiting in the parking lot, and a baby car seat. He pulled me aside while Frannie and Dove went into the bathroom to get cleaned up.

"I put in a call to Dare Conners's wife this morning. She's been working on it since then, and I think that by the time you get back to the penthouse you'll find that it's been set up for Frannie and Dove. At least for a little while. You can stay as long as you need to."

He looks at me like he gets it.

I hold out a hand, and my boss shakes it. I pull him in for a short hug and when he pulls back there's a tight smile on his lips. He doesn't give those freely. "Don't thank me, son. Just make sure she and that baby are doing okay. I'll keep everything good on my end here. We'll have to get her in tomorrow for debriefing, but we can do that on Frannie's time, and we can come to her if we need to. I'll tell the WPD the same damn thing."

After the day I've had, my throat clogs with emotion. I don't have the words to thank him, so I just nod. He slaps my back and walks away.

I'm waiting for Frannie in the lobby when my team walks in, along with Grisham. Each one of them grasps my hand, pulling me in for a bro hug before releasing me.

"Glad she's okay, brother." Lawson looks me over. "You look like shit, though. Go home. Take care of them."

I nod. "Can't thank you—"

Ben cuts me off. "Don't do that shit. We don't thank each other. This is what we do. Every time. Frannie wasn't just a client for us. We knew that. We would have brought her home no matter what, but there was extra incentive."

Bain nods. "And now Ward is where he belongs, in a federal prison. He won't get away, and he'll end up in even deeper shit for trying to run." He shoots Grisham a meaningful glance. "And we did it all with no shots fired."

Grisham meets his gaze head-on. "I don't have an itchy trigger finger, Bull's-Eye. That's not who I am. I just wanted to make sure he was down and that Frannie was brought home safe."

Bain lifts his chin. "That's what we all wanted. I could have made that shot with my eyes closed. But Wolf loves that woman." He tilts his head toward me. "Wouldn't take that risk, not with her and the baby's life on the line."

Grisham nods. "I get it. Listen, I'm still learning when it comes to leading the pack. You guys are a tight team. I'm impressed."

Bain shoots me a glance, and I can read it loud and clear. Bain isn't trying to impress Grisham Abbott. Grisham hasn't earned his respect as a leader, and if the day comes when the Boss Man turns the reins over to his son-in-law, I'm not sure where that'll leave Bain and Grisham's working relationship.

Frannie walks out into the lobby, cuddling Dove in her arms, and every single ounce of my attention is immediately drawn to them.

Walking toward them, I wrap an arm around Frannie's waist. "Ready to go?"

She looks up at me, and it's the first time I've ever seen her with a shy expression on her pretty face. "Where exactly are we going?"

"Home," I say simply.

She doesn't ask any more questions, just lifts a curious brow, and I usher them out the front door and into the BMW. Frannie leans her head back against the seat as we drive, but her eyes aren't closed. She keeps checking the backseat, where Dove is turned around in her car seat.

I glance toward the back. "Shit. Guess I'm gonna have to get an SUV. Feels wrong carting a baby around in a sports sedan."

Frannie's lips spread into a beaming smile that brings sunshine into all the darkest places inside me. "Careful, Ryder. You're gonna make a girl think you want this to be a habit."

The fact that there's a question in her tone means that we still have so much to talk about. We'll get there. First I need to get her home. I need to get her fed, and showered, and rested.

Then we'll talk.

When the elevator opens into the foyer of the penthouse, everything looks the same.

And everything looks completely different.

For one thing, there's a stroller standing by the elevator, right beside the entryway table. There's a playpen in the living room, with plush toys littering the floor inside it. In the kitchen, we find a full stash of baby bottles, formula, and baby foods.

Frannie looks at me with wide, confused eyes. "How did you do this? *Why* did you do this?"

I hold my hands up in the air. "I didn't do this, sweetheart. I swear to you, I *would have* done this if I'd had the time. But Jacob called Dare Conners's wife, Berkeley. She's an interior designer, and I guess she put some shit together for us. Some of the Rescue Ops wives are tight, and they have kids and stuff. They must have helped."

Frannie and I walk up the stairs, where we don't usually have much of a reason to go, and peek into one of the secondary bedrooms. The first one, which previously had a queen-sized guest bed, is now fully outfitted as a nursery with a crib and changing table, a shaggy pink rug, and an overflowing box of toys. There's a comfortable-looking rocking chair with a bookshelf beside it, and I just keep staring around the room.

"Fuck me. Do they think we're staying here forever? This isn't our place!"

Frannie's giggle is breathless, and she carries Dove around, showing her every piece of furniture in her new room. I watch as she talks to her, cooing and pointing. That feeling I got in my chest earlier when I looked at Dove returns full force when I watch the two of them together.

I don't understand it. I'm not Dove's father. I didn't watch Frannie carry her in her belly for nine months. I didn't help create her. I don't even want to think about the bastard who did. But when I look at the two of them, with their identical blond hair and blue eyes and the way they both look at me like I belong to them…I feel like I'm home.

They belong to me just as much.

"They just wanted to help us feel safe and secure again. After everything. I get it. It was so nice of them. I'm going to have to meet them…thank them in person."

I nod. "We can make that happen."

Frannie walks toward me where I'm standing at the entrance to the nursery, and Dove blinks, curling her little lips upward.

"Boosh," she says, and extends her arms out toward me.

I go still, and Frannie's footsteps stutter to a halt.

She glances down at Dove, whose arms are still extended. The baby makes an impatient sound, and stretches farther toward me.

"Do you…" Frannie's tone is hesitant. "Do you want to hold her? Just for a minute, while I get her bath ready?"

I've never held a baby before, because I just haven't been around them very often. Some of the guys at work have had them, and I've met them, but I've never held them. Dove isn't a newborn, but she's still fragile and small, and…

She reaches for me again, and I automatically reach back, plucking her from Frannie's hold. She settles naturally into my arms, one arm going around my neck, the other hand resting on my chest. I hold her tight, and warmth radiates from her and into me.

Frannie stares at us, until I give her a nudge with my hip. "Bath? I got her."

She blinks like she was lost in a daze, and then nods.

"Oh...right." A faint blush tints her cheeks, and now I want to know what she was thinking about. But before I can ask her, she's rushing off into the bathroom across the hall from Dove's new nursery.

While we wait, I walk around the room with Dove the way her mom did, pulling a purple elephant out of the crib and holding it up to her so she can see it. "See this little guy? He's frowning because he has to be purple. So we're gonna name him Gray, because it's the color he wishes he was. Sound good?"

Dove coos, and I take that as an agreement. Stopping my pacing, I stare down at the baby girl in my arms. "Not sure what life is gonna throw at us, Dove, but I promise you one thing: I'm gonna make you and your mama happy. Starting today. Okay?"

She lays her head against my chest, nothing but peace and calm radiating from her, and I'm filled with a surge of protectiveness the likes of which I've never felt before. There's a sense of purpose that comes with it, and energy, and drive. To do more. To be more.

For them.

"She usually naps in the morning and the afternoon, so this should be a long one. She probably won't be awake until five." Frannie yawns as she enters the living room in a T-shirt and sweats, fresh from a shower.

We bathed Dove and fed her, and we both ate a couple of sandwiches from the fridge and took showers ourselves. I've been sitting on the couch waiting for Frannie to get out of hers, which was way longer than the one I took in the guest bathroom.

I pat the cushion beside me, and she sits, pulling her legs up to sit cross-legged and placing a pillow against her chest. I grip her chin in my fingers, holding her cheek up to the light. The skin is bruising in earnest now, turning an angry shade of magenta, and the anger bubbles up inside me all over again.

He tried to take what's mine. Both of them.

Instead of letting go of her, I let my hand slip down to find one of hers. "I could have lost you today."

She glances down at our hands. "But you didn't."

I gesture toward her, and then point at my own chest. "Nine years ago, when I lost Echo? The whole trajectory of my life changed. It just fueled my drive to join the military. To protect and serve. When I lost her, I felt like it was such a waste of potential. Of a good life. And I felt like I could have prevented it, if she had just trusted me to help keep her safe."

Frannie's head jerks up, her eyes meeting mine. "It's not the same thing, Thorn."

My chest constricts, because she used my first name and because I don't think she's getting it. "It's not the same situation, but it's the same concept. Don't you get that? You walked out of here last night. Because you didn't *trust me to keep you safe.*"

Frannie shakes her head, her hair falling out of its bun in chunks. "It's not that I didn't trust you! It's that I knew you didn't have the whole picture. I had to protect Dove; it wasn't just about me."

I sit back, studying her. As quickly as they drained away earlier with the relief of feeling her in my arms again, the hurt and the anger wash back inside my heart like the ocean rushing back to the shore. "Why didn't you tell me about her? The most important part of you...and I didn't even know."

She shrugs, a helpless expression on her face. "I was going to...you know I told you there was something I needed to talk to you about. At first, it was because I didn't trust anyone, *anyone* with the secret of her existence. I knew that Eli finding out that I'd had her meant he would never stop until he had her. I couldn't let that happen. Not to her. So I swore to keep her a secret from everyone. But when I did finally trust you, when you earned that from me, it all happened so fast. And then it was too late."

Can I fault her? I still haven't told her about Nevaeh.

Releasing her hand, I slide mine to the back of her neck and pull her close until my forehead is pressed against hers. "Do you trust me enough now? For anything?"

"Yes," she whispers. "And everything. I want it all with you, Thorn Ryder."

I'm kissing her before she finishes the last word, my lips pressing against hers like I need her. Her hands go to my hair, pulling at the short strands like she wants me closer, until she finally pulls herself into my lap and straddles my waist. Her legs press against the outsides of my thighs, and I probe her lips until she finally moans and opens to me. I plunge inside, tasting her, and she rocks her hips into me.

It's all I can take, and even though this wasn't in the plan for this afternoon, I need to be inside her as much as I need air right now.

Groaning, I pull my mouth from hers and pick her up, moving us into the bedroom. Setting her down on her feet beside the bed, I pull her shirt off over her head. She's not wearing anything underneath, and I murmur my approval as my hands splay out over her bare shoulders, just grazing her full breasts as I slide them down to her flat belly. Inching the band of her sweatpants down, I drop to my knees in front of her.

Her hands rest on my head as I work to remove her pants and underwear together, waiting while she steps out of them one leg at a time. When I have her standing naked in front of me, I glance up at her and take in a breath.

"You're so fucking beautiful. And brave. You know that?" My hands slide around to the backs of her thighs as I plant a kiss on her hip bone.

She shivers under my touch, and my dick swells to painful proportions in my own sweats. "I could say the same about you."

My lips land on her other hip bone before sliding down to kiss where a thin strip of dark blond hair leads to her pussy. "I'm gonna taste you…gonna make you feel so good, sweetheart."

She moans, and I haven't even touched her yet. I smile just before licking her right at her center, feeling how dripping wet she is. "Fuck, baby. So damn sweet. Always."

"Oh God, Ryder. I can't take it when you talk. Please…just…"

Swirling my tongue around her swollen little clit, I slide two fingers inside her and curl them upward. Her knees buckle, and I grip her tighter to hold her upright.

"Just what, baby? Just make you come? That what you need?"

I pull her clit inside my mouth and suck, and she cries out. Her walls clench around my finger, and she chants: "Ohmygod, ohmygod, ohmygod…"

She quivers and quakes around me, and I keep letting my tongue swipe and lick and my mouth continues to suck at her until I know she can't take any more. Then I let her fall back on the bed, and I strip down until I'm bare. She watches me, the daylight allowing her to see every inch of my hard cock, ready for her in every single way. Reaching into the nightstand, I grab a condom and rip it open. Sliding it over me with one hand, I brace myself above her with the other.

Looking down at her, I know that after everything we've been through in the last twenty-four hours, I don't want to fuck her right now.

I want to worship her.

Leaning down, I whisper in her ear. "Turn on your side."

She does what I ask without question, turning toward the window. I lie down behind her and pull her in close, pressing my body against hers until a sheet of paper couldn't fit between us. I drop one leg over hers and slide into her from behind.

We both groan at the same time at the depth of the angle, at the feel of our bodies pressed this closely together. I'm not looking at her, but somehow this feels more intimate than it's ever felt before.

"I love you," I whisper in her ear as I start to slide in and out of her, slowly. "So fucking much, baby."

One of my hands rests on her hip, and I slide it up to cup her breast as my lips press against the back of her neck. She moans, arching back against me and pushing her ass into my hips in a way that has my balls drawing up tight way too soon.

"Jesus, Ryder. . . . I love you too. I'm going to . . . again . . ."

I drop my hand, letting my finger draw lazy circles over her clit, and she ignites, catching fire in my arms as she shakes and shudders and calls out my name.

It's the best feeling I've ever had, and I'm not going to get tired of it. I'm going to want to make love to this woman over and over again, every day for the rest of my life.

That's a damn fact.

She reaches up above us and grips the headboard, using the leverage to push her hips back against mine in a faster rhythm.

"Fucking hell, Frannie . . . you're gonna kill me." I grind the words through my teeth as I meet her thrust for thrust, driving until I can't hold back anymore.

Our skin slick with sweat, our bodies collide together, hands slipping to find purchase, and I growl in her ear, "Come with me, baby. One more time."

She's already rising again, her walls clenching and squeezing me tight, and I bite down on her shoulder to keep from roaring with the release that rocks me harder than I've ever been rocked before.

We lie there panting afterward, coming down from the high of sex and love and everything in between, and then Frannie rolls over to face me. She tucks her hands under her chin, sleepy eyes blinking up at me.

"I'm going to keep pinching myself," she murmurs, her voice throaty with sex and exhaustion, "because I'm never going to understand how my life has changed this much, this fast, for the better."

Dropping a kiss on her forehead, I get up and take care of the condom in the bathroom. Then I climb back in bed and wrap her up in my arms, prepared to sleep exactly as long as Dove does.

"Let's not question it," I advise her, as we both fall toward oblivion. "Let's just enjoy it."

28

FRANNIE

The next morning I wake up to one of my favorite smells in the entire world—bacon frying. And when I pad barefoot down the hallway and into the living room, I hear what's about to become my very favorite sound in the whole entire world—the sound of Thorn Ryder talking to my baby.

"That's right, angel, you sit right there and be a good girl. They tell me you can be quite the troublemaker. Wild parties, late nights, loud music…we aren't having any of that this morning. You know why?"

There's no response from Dove, but I hear a banging noise that sounds like a hand on plastic. I cover my mouth with a hand to hide my giggle.

Ryder continues, and I can hear him moving around the kitchen from my position at the mouth of the hallway. "Because we're letting Mama sleep in. She had a hard day yesterday and deserves some extra rest, you know?"

Dove finally speaks. "A-duh."

There's a scraping noise that might be a utensil against the frying pan. "That's right, angel. That's your breakfast. Cheerios. You can have those, right? Google said you could."

My other hand is now required to contain my laughter. Leaning my back against the wall, I roll my eyes toward the ceiling and wonder, again, how this happened to me. I could be halfway through the day in Switzerland right now, with Eli. My own personal version of hell. Instead, I'm here in a penthouse with Ryder, and he's talking to my baby while he cooks me breakfast.

My own personal version of heaven.

My stomach rumbles, and I can't stand in the hallway anymore. Gathering myself and setting my face in a neutral expression, I waltz into the kitchen like I haven't just been standing in the hallway listening to Ryder being the sexiest man alive. Because watching him with my baby has turned out to be the biggest turn-on imaginable, and we can't have sex this morning while Dove is awake.

I have to get my shit together here.

"Morning," I greet him as I enter.

He looks over at me, flipping bacon, and grins. He's shirtless, with those sexy black sweatpants I love, and bare feet. My favorite version of him.

In the kitchen. Talking to my baby.

"Hey. Sleep okay?" He leans over and kisses my mouth, and I can't help it when my hands roam over his broad, hard back for a few seconds while he's close.

Then I go over to Dove, who smiles at me when I walk toward her. She holds up a Cheerio, and I lean over and let her pop it into my mouth.

"Thank you, Dove-girl. Good morning, sweetie." I kiss the top of her head, and her little palm lands a slap on her high chair tray. I scan her, sitting in her brand-new chair.

"I still can't believe they did all this for us. I was thinking, and I'd like to have everyone who helped with this over in a few days over for a barbecue to thank them. It's all I can think of. Cooking is something I can do. And they can meet Dove?"

My voice rises on the last part, because introducing Ryder's friends from work, the men he calls his brothers, and the women they're married to or in relationships with to Dove is like introducing them to us as Ryder's family.

And is that what he wants?

When I look over at him, he's taken the bacon off the burner and set down the fork. He's staring at me with an intensity I'm not prepared for, and my heart skips. "What? What's wrong?"

His blue eyes, as deep as the ocean, hold a note of trepidation as he asks me a question mirroring mine from yesterday. "Can I ask you something, Frannie?"

My stomach flip-flops right before it drops to my toes, and I push Dove's high chair around the side of the island so I can see her as I drop down onto a barstool. "I'm sitting. What is it?"

He swipes a hand over his face before taking a deep breath and locking his gaze with mine again. "How would you feel about becoming a mom...again?"

My mind goes completely blank, and I'm sure my face does the same. The room is silent as he waits for my response, and I suddenly remember that I haven't given him one yet. "I'd say...I've never thought about it. But now that I'm with you, I guess the truth is that yes...I want more kids one day. Do you?"

He swallows, watching me. "I have to tell you something. And the only reason I haven't told you this before is because it didn't come to light that it was going to happen until two nights ago, and then you were gone before I got the chance."

She nods slowly, her eyes narrowing. "I'm listening."

Dove sits quietly, eating her Cheerios and watching us.

"A long time ago, I realized that Nevaeh's family was mistreating her at home. I kept an eye on her as much as I could, made sure she had everything she needed when she was at the club. And I gave her my cell number and told her to call me, day or night, if there was anything she ever needed. It's why she called the other night. But that part you knew."

She nods, her eyes going soft. "I felt something for that girl the second I saw her. And I saw the way you two related to each other. She loves you."

I nod. "Yeah. She's special. And I decided a long time ago that if the opportunity ever arose, I'd foster her. The night I went to her house, her dad killed her mom."

Frannie's hand flies to her mouth, covering her gasp. Her eyes wide, she just stares at me, shaking her head as disbelief floods out of her in waves. "No. Ryder, no."

My mouth tight, I nod. "Yeah. I shielded her, but she was right there, sweetheart. She was there. And so I called in a favor with Lawson's sister, Lilliana. She knows a social worker, and my paperwork was fast-tracked. I need to have a place for them to visit and approve ASAP, but other than that I'm good to go. Until then, Lilliana is keeping Nevaeh with her."

I nod, understanding everything he's telling me. He's had this in the back of his mind the entire time, knowing that he'd have to tell me that he's already made a promise to a little girl who was born into a family who didn't deserve her. Nevaeh deserves so much more than she's been given. She deserves Ryder.

Ryder pushes off the island and moves forward until he reaches me, dropping to a crouch in front of me and placing his hands on my thighs. He looks up at me, the expression in his eyes earnest and somber.

"What I need to know," he says, his voice low, "is whether or not you want to do this with me. I'm already committed to Nevaeh...I won't turn my back on her. But, Frannie, I love you. And I love your baby girl. Will you give me a chance to show you that we can make this work? That we can be a family? All four of us?"

There's a slice of fear in the clear blue of his gaze, and I'm struck with the realization that he thinks there's a chance that I'm going to say no. But I jumped into this with both feet with him a while ago, and there's no turning back now. Not after everything we've been through. Life can just keep throwing us curveballs, and Ryder and I will keep hitting them right out of the damn park.

Instead of giving him an answer, I ask a question. "When can we call Lilliana? I think Dove needs to meet her new big sister."

Because full steam ahead.

A huge grin transforms Ryder's face from seriously handsome to gloriously gorgeous, and he's back on his feet and kissing me, crushing his mouth to mine. Dove shrieks behind us, and he shakes with laughter as he pulls away.

"Did you hear that, angel?" he asks, unstrapping her and lifting her out of her chair.

My chest caves in when he pulls her to his chest like it's the most natural thing in the world. Like he didn't just meet her yesterday. Like she was born to be his.

"You, me, your mama, and big sister Nevaeh are gonna be a family. And we're all gonna be okay."

More than okay. We're going to be amazing.

The rest of that week flies by in a flurry of busy activity. I meet with an attorney to get my marriage to Eli Ward annulled. The attorney lets me know that I have grounds for an annulment and that my paperwork will be filed the same day. It won't take more than a month for it to be complete, which means that in a month I'll be completely free of him forever. I never added his name to Dove's birth certificate, so even though he's her father by birth, it'll never be recognized by law unless he files paperwork to fight for it. And from where he sits in prison, he doesn't have a leg to stand on. The district attorney who briefed us on his case is confident that Eli will receive the maximum sentence prescribed by law for his crimes.

Ryder lists his loft on the real estate market, priced to sell quickly. Within four days, he has three offers, and he accepts the highest one. We start searching for houses, and prioritize the list of needs based on the kids first: a good school for Nevaeh, close to the same excellent daycare where Dove will go on the two days a week that I'm at the hospital, now that I've cut my schedule down by one day. We want a neighborhood that was between the NES office in Wrightsville Beach and my hospital downtown. The commute between the beach and downtown isn't long, because Wilmington isn't a big city, and we decide to put an offer in on a house in an area called Pine Valley, which is smack in the middle of the two. It's like a small town within a small town, and it's full of green, tree-lined streets and golf courses, walking trails, restaurants, and little shops. It's adorable, and only a five-minute drive to the beach.

Ryder and I agree that it's going to be the perfect place for our small family to start a life together. I still have two months left on my lease, but Ryder says we'll get through it.

We decide to put the barbecue on hold for when we close on the house, which gives us about a month to plan and prepare.

It's Nevaeh's first visit to the penthouse that really cements it all for me, letting me know that everything we're doing here is for a reason, and that we're going to be all right.

Ryder went to pick her up from Lilliana's, and when they walk out of the elevator into the foyer, Dove and I are standing in the entryway waiting for them. I'm holding a gift bag for Nevaeh, because even though she isn't allowed to stay with us yet, I want her to know that she is very much a part of our family and that we want her.

That *I* want her.

"You remember Frannie, right, Vay?" Ryder places a gentle hand on her shoulder to guide her into the penthouse.

Nevaeh glances around, her eyes widening as she takes in the grand space. Ryder already explained to her that we're just staying here temporarily, that this won't be our house together. He told her that we'd all be living together as a family, and gave her the choice of whether or not she wanted to be a part of it.

She agreed, telling him that she wanted to be a part of his family no matter where that was.

Shy green eyes meet mine, framed by thick, dark lashes. I realize, with some surprise, how gorgeous this little girl is. She's not as skinny as she was the first time I met her, much better nourished and with a flush in her cheeks. Her bronze complexion has a glow it didn't carry before, and her clothes are clean and new. Her long, dark hair is still curly, but it's brushed and not matted and tangled.

"I remember you," she says quietly. "Hi."

"Hey." I give her a big smile. "This is for you. I'm glad you're hanging out with us today. We've been missing you."

Her gaze lands on the bag. "For me?" She glances up at Ryder. "A present?"

He smiles at her, nudging her forward. "Go get it."

She moves forward, approaching me like a scared rabbit. My heart is sliced in two, and I make a mental note to spend as much quality time with her as possible in the coming months, just loving on her. Showing her what it looks and feels like to be accepted and loved unconditionally. I hold out the bag for her. "Here you go."

We move into the living room and sit on the couch, me beside Nevaeh with Dove on my lap. Dove watches the girl with rapturous eyes, and I can see her little fists curling, itching to pull on those long curls. I hope she'll at least wait until she's introduced.

Nevaeh pulls out a wooden picture frame with hand-painted white letters. It reads:

OUR FAMILY
THORN, FRANNIE, NEVAEH, DOVE

"There's no picture in it yet," I inform her, "because we'll take one together. And I thought you could put it in your room at the new house when we move in, in a couple of weeks."

Nevaeh stares and stares at the photo frame, her fingers rubbing the letters over and over again.

"It says 'family,'" she finally whispers. "No one has ever called me that. Not even my parents."

Ryder crouches down in front of her, the same way he did when he asked me if I could accept Nevaeh into my heart. "Well, we're calling you that. And one important thing about family? We never give up on each other. Got that?"

Nevaeh looks at him with bright, shining eyes. She throws her arms around his neck, and I swallow around the orange-sized lump forming in my throat.

Dove shrieks, a noise she doesn't make very often. But she's clearly tired of being ignored by her new sister. Ryder chuckles and glances at Dove with love in his eyes. "Nevaeh, meet your little sister, Dove."

Nevaeh turns her full attention on the baby girl in my lap, and she smiles. "Hi, Dove."

Dove reaches for her immediately, and Nevaeh looks at me with uncertainty in her eyes.

I lift one shoulder and smile. "You can hold her if you want to. But don't feel like you have to. There's plenty of time for that."

Nevaeh pulls Dove onto her lap, and Dove's expression turns to one of pure joy when she finally wraps a fist around a thick, dark brown curl and pulls. Nevaeh giggles.

"Girls." Ryder slides toward me on the floor, looking at Nevaeh and Dove. "Pay attention and take notes. Let me know how I do."

Nevaeh is still trying to extract her hair from Dove's fist, and I'm leaning over to help.

"On what?" she asks.

"On my proposal."

His answer freezes the blood in my veins, causing my mouth to stop working, my limbs to stop moving. My eyes snap to his, my fingers frozen on Nevaeh's hair.

Ryder's blue eyes are shining, joyful, with a hint of intense triumph that he can't hide as he pulls something out of his pocket. He grabs hold of my left hand and speaks, each word full of meaning and honesty and love.

"The moment I met you, I knew I wanted you. The moment I agreed to protect you, I wanted to strangle you."

A choked laugh escapes my throat as I stare at him, tears stinging my eyes. Disbelief still forces my throat closed, and I'm having trouble catching my breath. Beside me, Nevaeh grabs my other hand.

"The moment I knew your heart, I knew I loved you. And the moment I met your daughter and you accepted mine, I knew I'd spend the rest of my life with you. Tell me you'll marry me." He glances down, a sparkling engagement ring poised at the end of my finger. I stare down at it, the huge round diamond set in a diamond-studded platinum band winking up at me.

My breaths coming too fast, I move my gaze back to Ryder. He's watching me, and before that slice of apprehension can appear in his eyes, I gasp out my answer.

"Yes. Yes! Please put that ring on my finger, Ryder."

Nevaeh takes Dove's little hands and claps them as Ryder slides the ring onto my finger, and then I slide down onto the floor beside him, wrapping my arms around his neck.

29

RYDER

When Frannie and that fucker Ward's annulment is finalized the day after we move into our new house, I drop my head back against my shoulders and send up a whoop of pure fucking joy to the man upstairs. Because there's no way things could have worked out this perfectly for us without a little help.

It's a Saturday afternoon, and we're both in the kitchen, unpacking boxes. Dove is down for a nap in her room, and Nevaeh is in the bonus room upstairs, which we've set up as a space for her with a TV and comfortable seating for when she wants to hang out without us or has friends over.

The house isn't even close to being done, but tomorrow for the barbecue we're planning on having people in the kitchen, family room, and backyard mostly.

"So we're getting married tomorrow." The excitement leaks from Frannie's voice, her eyes sparkling with it.

I place the box in my hands on the huge, granite-covered island in the center of our kitchen and pull her into my arms. My chin rests on top of her messy bun, and I swallow hard as I think about what all this really means.

"Yeah, sweetheart. We're getting married tomorrow."

She pulls back, moving her fingers from my neck into my hair. Knowing what that does to me, I give her a warning look. "You don't want to start with me right now, woman. Not when we can't finish it."

A smirk touches her lips, and I bend to take her mouth with a groan. Killing me slowly, that's what she's doing. And she knows it. Every night she's in my bed, I end up inside her. And every morning I wake up feeling so damn lucky she loves me the way she does, without conditions or limits.

With complete trust. She's let me into her life with no qualms, and given me the privilege of helping her raise Dove. Which is an opportunity I don't take lightly. I cherish the time I get to spend with both of them, and having Nevaeh join our family is just an added bonus.

A family I never thought I'd get the chance to have.

We started Nevaeh in counseling right away, and she's been doing really well. Her adjustment has been pretty damn amazing considering everything she saw and heard the night her mother died, and the counselor told us that part of the reason she's attached to both Frannie and I so quickly is because she never really formed any sort of bond with her own parents. It broke my heart for my new daughter, but at the same time it cemented the fact that she was always meant to be ours.

We just took the scenic route when it came to finding her.

Frannie pulls back and grins at me. "Later, almost-husband. Later, we can finish it." Reaching down, she plasters an innocent expression on her face as she strokes the bulge inside my shorts.

My teeth clenching, I narrow my eyes at her. "You're evil."

She grins, taking a step back. "The best part about tomorrow is that we're inviting all our friends, and none of them even know that they're not just coming here for a housewarming barbecue to see our new house and meet our new family. They're also coming to our wedding."

I take a couple of deep breaths, still trying to pull myself back from the tension-filled ledge she just pushed me toward. "It's gonna be a huge surprise."

"Man, this is nice."

Bain and I stand at the sliders in the kitchen, surveying the big backyard. There are people everywhere, seated around the two long tables set up under the tent in the center of the yard, on the deck on the wooden chairs or the loungers, or around the fire pit that's lit down on the south end by the fence.

My eyes are immediately drawn to Frannie where she's standing in a group of NES wives, including Berkeley Conners, Greta Abbott, Rayne Teague, and Olive Shaw. Their husbands all work on the Rescue Ops team, and they're all gushing over Dove, taking turns holding her and talking to her. Frannie has spent time thanking each woman personally for everything she did when it came to outfitting us with supplies when we returned to the penthouse, and they all brushed her off with the mantra *NES family sticks together*.

Lobelia has been a huge part of our lives, and she rushes past us now, bumping my shoulder and giving me a *sorry, not sorry* grin as she heads down to stand beside Frannie with a tray of drinks in her hands for the ladies. She visits at least once a week to see Dove and hang out with Frannie, and has been essential in helping Frannie get all the preparations set up for the wedding/barbecue.

I find Lawson, Ben, Jacob, and his wife, Grace, sitting with Lilliana, Frannie's friend Denver from the hospital, and his date. Grace is also a nurse, and she and Denver have been talking about the differences between working in a hospital emergency room and working in a doctor's office.

At the other end of the yard, Nevaeh's occupied with Jeremy and Rayne Teague's son, Decker. He's just a couple of years younger than her, and they've been hanging out since the Teagues arrived. I'm glad she has someone her age in our group to hang out with, and Jeremy promised that raising a preteen was going to be exactly as hard as I thought it was going to be. I guess the look on my face when he said that was comical, because he laughed and Rayne punched him. Jeremy isn't known for being the most serious guy around the office, so I'm gonna take his advice with a grain of salt and hope for the best when it comes to the future with Nevaeh.

The rest of the guys from the Rescue Ops team are on the deck with my friend Drew from the Boys and Girls Club, bottles of beer in their hands, and it's the kind of day that makes you want to chill out and relax.

Which I'm going to do, just as soon as I marry the woman of my dreams.

"Let me ask you something," I murmur, pulling my eyes from Frannie.

I take note of the fact that Bain's not looking at me; when I follow his gaze, it's leveled on Lilliana Snyder. I snap my fingers in front of his face, and he slowly slides his eyes to my face.

"What?"

"What are you looking at?" There's amusement in my tone, because I caught him staring and he knows it.

"Shut up." He turns to face me. "What are you asking?"

"When I marry Frannie today, be my best man?"

He blinks. Once. Twice. Then one side of his mouth curves up in a smile. "You serious?"

I nod, grinning. "Yeah. In about five minutes."

"Was wondering why you hired live music for a barbecue."

We both glance into the yard, where a local cover band that came highly recommended is setting up. In just a few minutes, they're going to play the song that Frannie and the girls will walk down the aisle to.

"It's informal. No chairs set up or anything, and the ceremony will only take a few minutes. Jacob's ordained, so he's going to do it for us. No one else knows. Frannie's having Nevaeh and Lo stand up beside her. But I needed you up there."

He nods, holding out his hand. "I'm honored."

Five minutes later, I'm standing in the backyard on the deck. Jacob comes to stand beside me, smiling. I nod to the lead singer of the band, and he speaks into the microphone.

"Can I have everyone turn their attention to the deck, please? Our hosts would like to welcome you to their backyard barbecue. And also to their wedding."

Gasps and whoops are scattered throughout the small crowd in our backyard as every single face turns to me. Jacob opens the sliders, and the band starts to play "Wonderwall" by Oasis.

I should be nervous. I always thought, in the back of my mind where I pictured my wedding day, that I'd be nervous. But maybe that's just because I didn't know what to expect, or what was going to happen. Today, I know exactly what's going to happen. And when it comes to the woman walking through those doors right now in a white sundress hanging off her shoulders, her creamy skin glowing in the late-afternoon sunshine, blond-and-pink hair flowing around her like a goddamn halo, I know exactly what to expect.

So I'm not nervous, but I'm keyed up with anxious excitement, because I'm ready for Frannie Phillips to become Frannie Ryder. I never believed in miracles until I met her, but when they started to happen one right after another, I became a believer.

I believe in us. All the winding roads we've had to walk to get to this point have been a trial, but we walked them. And they've led us right here.

She's holding Dove, and our little girl looks perfectly at peace in her mama's arms, smiling over at me as Frannie takes her place beside me on the deck. She passes Dove to Lo, and we join hands, Nevaeh taking Frannie's hand on the other side, and listen as Jacob asks us to recite the vows that will unite us for the rest of our lives.

It takes me ten minutes to marry her, but it'll take me a lifetime to love her.

I'll savor every single second.

Epilogue

RYDER

I look at my life now, and it's hard for me to picture what it was like a year ago. Now I'm sitting at the kitchen table with my girls on a summer Tuesday night, hanging out with them while I watch Frannie hobble around cooking.

Frannie's been planning a huge family dinner all day, buying all these fancy ingredients for a brand-new recipe. She insists that she wants one last meal with just the four of us before we become five, and when I ask her why she thinks this needs to happen today, she says she just *knows*.

"The doctor says you're not even dilated yet," I reminded her this afternoon following her weekly appointment. "And you're only thirty-seven weeks."

She gave me her stubborn stare. "I'm cooking this dinner tonight, Ryder. Don't argue with me."

So I stopped arguing. But she keeps stopping and taking breaks, and I'm not used to seeing her so…miserable. She looks like she needed to go lie down two hours ago, but she has this determined expression on her face to finish this dinner and I just don't get it.

"Please let me do something, sweetheart." There's a note of pleading in my voice now, because it's just getting painful to watch.

"You can come grab the plates." Frannie's voice is breathy as she responds, finally agreeing to let me help. "It's ready."

She sits down at the table, and I grab the plates of food off the counter. I'm watching Frannie so closely while we eat that I'm not even sure what it is she cooked.

Dove eats exactly four bites of her dinner, which was an abbreviated version of the rest of ours. She looks at me from her high chair and points at the floor. "Down, Dad-dee."

My heart lifts, the way it does every single time she calls me Daddy, and I smile. "Eat, angel."

Her eyes fill with the same resolve I always see in her mother's. Her tone doesn't change, because Dove is nothing if not a pacifist. But she knows what she wants, and right now, she's done eating. "Down, Dad-dee."

She points to the floor again.

I sigh, and unhook her from her seat.

Muttering, I place her on the floor. "Daddy can bring in wanted criminals from all over the world, but he can't say no to his twenty-month-old."

Frannie looks at me, her expression playfully stern. "Or his twelve-year-old."

I look at Nevaeh with a *What's she talking about?* expression and offer her my fist. "Principal's list—straight A's—all four quarters in sixth grade? That deserved some extra gifting, I think."

She smiles at me, her gorgeous little face melting my heart.

Nevaeh worked harder this year than any of us to overcome her own obstacles. She had nightmares for a long time, ones that didn't surface until we'd been living together for a couple of weeks. Terrible, wake-the-whole-house-in-the-middle-of-the-night terrors that took grueling hours of therapy to overcome. And through it all, she loved us and let us love her. She became the best big sister in the world to Dove, helping Frannie whenever needed and being patient and loving when Dove got into her stuff. And she killed it in school every day, earning top grades in every single class.

I couldn't be prouder. Frannie and I knew it would be okay to start trying for another baby when the nightmares stopped.

Frannie suddenly gets up from the table, her belly leading the way, hands supporting her back, and I swear she's more beautiful now than she was the day she held a gun on me in the penthouse kitchen.

And I thought she was the most gorgeous woman in the world then.

Irritatingly gorgeous, but stunning nonetheless.

As she walks upstairs, she calls out to me. "Ryder? Call Lo, okay? She should come stay with the girls while we run up to the hospital. It's time to go have this baby."

My chair scrapes against the wood floor as I shoot up out of it. "Shit."

Nevaeh bounces out of her chair and frowns at me. She runs to close the baby gate so Dove won't toddle up after her mama, and then turns to face me. "Language, Dad. I'll call Aunt Lo. You go check on Mom."

My heart jackhammering in my chest, I nod and take the stairs two at a time.

I find Frannie doubled over in our room, breathing heavily. Fear curls in a black cloud around my heart as I eat up the distance between us in two strides and cradle her bent body in my arms.

"How long?" I growl. "How long have you been having contractions?"

She doesn't answer until the pain subsides, finally looking at me through pain-filled eyes. "Four hours."

My mouth drops open as I stare at her. "Four. Hours? You didn't say anything and you've been feeling pain for four hours, Frannie? For fuck's sake!"

I race around the room, grabbing her hospital bag. Then I rush downstairs and throw it in the Suburban we got when we traded in Frannie's car. The BMW sits beside it in our driveway.

When I go back into the house, Frannie is trying to walk down the stairs, and a string of curse words leave my mouth.

"I swear to Jesus, woman. You're gonna kill me before you have this baby, and then what will you do? Stop trying to do everything on your own, dammit!"

I scoop her into my arms and carry her out to the SUV just as Lo's car screeches to a stop at the curb. It doesn't take her more than five minutes to get to our house since she moved into the neighborhood beside ours six months ago, and right now I couldn't be more thankful.

"Go," she shouts, pausing to kiss Frannie's cheek before she lets herself into the house. "I've got these girls."

I buckle Frannie in and jog around to the driver's side, starting the ignition and gunning it.

"You don't have to drive like a maniac, Ryder. We'll make it. Labor takes hours and hours. I didn't want to sit in a hospital bed for most of it. I wanted to be at home with my girls." She gasps and curls up on the seat, her face contorted in pain.

I watch the road, feeling my own pain as I wish I could take it for her. God, it's fucking torture watching this. How do other men do it?

Thirty minutes later, we're settled in a room at the hospital. I'm waiting outside the door because Frannie's chosen to have an epidural, which I'm fucking thrilled about. I'm also thrilled about being able to stand out in the hallway instead of watching the doctor jam a needle into her spine.

When I return, she gives me a bright smile. "See? All better. You looked so worried, Ryder."

Sitting in the chair beside the bed, I reach for her hand. "I am. And I can't stand seeing you in pain. I just want all of this to go smoothly, and I want it to be over so we can meet our son."

Our son. The words send a jolt of excitement shooting through my system, and from the way Frannie's eyes light up; she feels the same way when she hears them. "Me too. They said I'm seven centimeters. So not long to go."

Not long to go until we meet our son. "You know this will be the first kid who actually starts out with my last name."

She frowns. "All your kids have your last name."

I nod. "Yeah, now. I adopted Dove and we both adopted Nevaeh. This is just different. It doesn't change a damn thing. I'll love him exactly the same as I love my girls. But it's different. Being here from the beginning, you know?"

She grins, and then glances at the monitor. "I'm having a contraction and I don't even feel it! How crazy is that?"

I look at the way the lines on the machine are jumping up and down. "Crazy."

She squeezes my hand. "You know what being there from the be-ginning means? It means you have to do middle-of-the-night feed-ings and change dirty diaper blowouts. Are you ready for all that?"

Now it's my turn to frown. "What's a blowout?"

She lets her head drop back on the pillow and laughs softly. "Oh, just you wait, Ryder. This is going to be fun."

It only takes an hour. An hour, and I'm holding my son close to my chest. Frannie lies on the bed, her body spent, but her face relaxed and full of nothing but joy. Right now, it's just the two of us, but we know it's only a matter of time before we're bombarded by visitors.

We're okay with that. As long as our girls are the first ones to meet their brother.

He stares up at me, his eyes a dark blue, his mouth working re-peatedly, his little nose scrunching. A full head of dark hair covers his head.

"His hair will lighten, you know," Frannie whispers from the bed. "I had dark hair when I was born too."

"Me too," I admit. "He's…God, Frannie. He's so fucking amaz-ing, you know?"

"I know. He's perfect. I love him so much already."

I look over at her, tearing my eyes from the baby in my arms. "I love you so much, baby. You did so good." If I thought I couldn't love her any more, I was wrong. Watching the woman you love have your baby…that shit changes you.

Frannie and I have already been through some life-altering expe-riences together. And there's no going back from this. She's mine forever, and I'm hers.

Little Jett Echo Ryder is the icing on the cake that is my family.

ABOUT THE AUTHOR

Diana Gardin is a wife of one and a mom of two. Writing is her second full-time job, after that, and she loves it! Diana writes contemporary romance in the young adult and new adult categories. She's also a former elementary school teacher. She loves steak, sugar cookies, and Coke and hates working out.

Learn more at:

DianaGardin.com
Twitter: @DianalynnGardin
Facebook.com/AuthorDianaGardin